TRUTH IS A FLIGHTLESS BIRD

TRUTH IS A FLIGHTLESS BIRD

a novel

AKBAR HUSSAIN

ISKANCHI
PRESS AND MAG

ISBN: 978-1-957810-03-4

This edition published in 2022 by Iskanchi Press
info@iskanchi.com
https://iskanchi.com/
+13852078509

First published in Nigeria in 2021 by Narrative Landscape Press

Cover Design and Text Layout by Ayebabeledaipre Sokari

For Anno: for having believed.
For Sofia: for having shared.

I

NICE TRAVELLED LIGHT. No carry-on, other than her wig of chestnut ringlets and her battered purse.

And the quarter kilo of bespoke narcotics.

This short flight to Nairobi had left her dry-mouthed. Biting her lower lip, she thought about the dozen drug packets, each as big as a thumbnail and painstakingly coated in red candle wax, in her belly. She could still taste the acidic tinge of the orange juice she had washed them down with. She stifled a gag.

Her scalp tingled under the wig as the humid air poured into the aircraft cabin. It had been a spontaneous thing, the wig, but now she was glad for it—it made her feel jaunty, in control. And it was one more layer of camouflage.

The seatbelt signs pinged off and passengers began opening the overhead compartments. With the sound, Nice felt she had met another milestone in her trip, and she lapsed into an expressionless good humor, even allowing herself a languorous rub of her tummy, without self-consciousness or hurry. As pregnant women are wont to do.

A bearded man in the aisle seat on her left stood up, knocking Nice's reading glasses with his elbow. "Sorry."

Nice straightened the glasses and gave her neighbor a

half-smile. She was getting useful insights from her debilitating morning sickness—for one, it focused the mind on important things, which, for her now, was to not vomit into this man's lap, and to get off the plane into the cool Nairobi evening.

Nice stood to look down the aisle to the exit. She took a pained breath, watching the harried parents, the mewling infant, the cowled and bird-boned Somali women, and the pinstriped businessmen exhaling self-importance in the cloistered cabin.

The bearded man gestured shyly at Nice with his hands, cupping what seemed to be an invisible offering.

This perplexed Nice, until she thought to fumble at her nose. Her nostril bled onto her upper lip, unseen and unfelt. Ruffled, Nice turned away to her shuttered window. She fumbled for a sharp-smelling moist towelette in the front pouch of her seat. The skin around her nostril burned as she dabbed at it. Nice opened the shutter of her window and watched the bearded man in the plastic reflection, only turning to exit the plane when his wavy ghost had entered the aisle, turning to look at her one last time.

Under the harsh lighting of the arrivals hall, Nice caught sight of herself in a mirrored wall. A wispy yet feminine frame, under a fashionable head of hair.

Aid worker. Smuggler. Time bomb.

The gaunt face tightened, and she leaned forward, resting her hands on denimed knees. She seemed, to herself, unworthy of terms such as 'Mother' or even 'pregnant'. Those were for other people, pushing strollers in sun-dappled suburbs.

The dizziness passed. Nice turned to enter the immigration line, bumping as she did so into an unseen person behind her. "Sorry."

The tall policeman looked bemused and smiled, but only

with his mouth. His teeth were small and gleamed under the fluorescence. "Hakuna shida. Are you okay?" He seemed to be studying her face closely, as if trying to recall her, or match her to a profile.

Nice took in his neat potbelly, his shiny belt buckle bearing a trident and the unreadable eyes. She nodded and apologized again, longing to meld into the queue. She turned to leave.

"Excuse me," came the policeman's firm voice. More insistent now, as Nice risked another step away from him.

"Excuse me. Madam."

Nice stopped and turned back, with what she hoped were also unreadable eyes. She forced herself to walk several steps in the policeman's direction and look directly into his eyes.

The policeman withdrew from under his arm a hide- bound cane and gestured with its bulbous brass top at Nice's face.

They stood under the humming tube lights.

"Heeya. Heeya." He stabbed at the air with the cane, towards her face.

Nice, feeling stupid and alarmed, dabbed at the nosebleed with the back of her hand. "Sorry, I'm OK. Where is the washroom, please?"

The brass head levitated over and beyond Nice's left shoulder, hovering at her earlobe. Nice nodded in thanks and turned to walk not-too-quickly towards the sign for the toilets. "Madam. Heeya."

The policeman handed Nice a handkerchief of white linen, still sharply creased. The handkerchief smelled damp, yet Nice wanted desperately to press it to her bleeding nose for the dignity it would afford her.

The policeman nodded his assent to the unspoken question.

Prior to her pregnancy and the astonishing morning

sickness which had ensued, Nice would never have soiled a stranger's handkerchief with her bodily fluids. But now she inhaled the dank scent of the cotton cloth, feeling it absorb her stubborn blood. "I'm sorry for the mess."

Nice walked with brisk steps to the washroom. She was not frightened yet.

Once inside, she placed her purse on the wet countertop and her glasses into the purse. Her scalp itched. She laved cold water onto her face and felt a measure of relief—from the nausea, the dizziness and the anxiety. More water, each ablution giving her more assurance. She placed a hand on the wig, readjusted it.

"Are you sure you're okay?"

The policeman's voice was conversational yet deafening in the sanctity of the empty washrooms. A chilling brazenness to his posture, standing as he was inside the ladies' washroom, studying her. He smiled, as though some difficult equation had unclicked within him.

The door shut behind him, and they were alone. Nice's mouth grew dry once more. "Yes. Yes, thanks."

Anxious to fill the void, she added, "Sorry about your handkerchief."

"I like the wig. Very realistic." He seemed to relax in the knowledge that he had found what he was seeking. "You come to Kenya often?" He seemed utterly unconcerned about his trespassing into the women's washroom—that someone could walk in at any moment. It was as if he had claimed the entire airport as his private office.

"Yes, for work." Nice consciously checked herself from volunteering any information. "Beautiful country."

"For some. But you seem unwell. Should we go to the medical evaluation tent?"

"Oh, no." Nice ran a finger under her nose to ensure the bleeding had stopped, then stopped herself. "Really, nothing serious. Need some fresh air. I've just arrived from Mogadishu."

The policeman took a few mincing steps across the black and white tiled floor and stood shoulder to shoulder with Nice, speaking at her reflection in the mirror. "Mogadishu? Lovely place." He said this with the same void between the smiling mouth and the sleepy cunning in his eyes.

Nice felt immediate regret at having disclosed her port of departure. But then, she reasoned, there were only two flights that had recently arrived, so it would have been easy for the policeman to figure this out, had he been so inclined.

He seemed not to be so inclined. "I find airports disconcerting. Too many people, so easy to miss the one you seek."

Nice blinked over the tap.

He continued. "I feel I could know you better, given time." He tore a tissue from the plastic dispenser, and absent- mindedly polished the belt buckle with it, never breaking eye- contact with Nice's reflection in the mirror.

Tube-lit seconds passed.

The policeman turned his face to Nice, came in close, seemed about to say something. She felt his warm, even breath and saw the small incisors gleaming.

Before either could speak, the door to the washroom clanged open, and through it crashed a large woman in a flower-patterned garment, swinging plastic duty-free bags.

Without words, utterly unperturbed, the policeman turned towards the newly arrived woman. He walked towards her, leaned in and took one of the bags from her doughy hand. He peered into the yellow plastic bag and withdrew a bottle of whiskey, still in its cylindrical case. Removing the bottle and breaking its seal, the policeman inhaled deeply of the caramel-colored liquid.

He handed the open bottle to the woman in the flowery dress. "Police business." With a barely perceptible nod, the man exited the ladies' washroom.

At the sink, and under the gaping look of the duty-free woman, Nice tore some tissues from the dispenser and then withdrew to a stall to gather herself.

She fished about in her purse and withdrew the small brown envelope containing emetic pills, which would induce a quick and painful vomiting. But losing those precious red bullets now would mean the end of the smuggling mission, which would in turn bring consequences to herself and her unborn baby, Pendo.

She thought of Duncan, who was no doubt waiting for her in the arrivals parking lot. Had she made a mistake asking him to come, involving him unwittingly in this scheme? Nice considered the handwritten note of confession hidden in her bra and took it out. Another route of escape, however catastrophic for her. Sitting on the toilet seat, Nice saw a tear land on a black tile. She had not felt her own tear roll down her cheek, and this gave her some resolve. To go forward was, if she played her cards right, to be free from all that haunted her, and the best way to save her baby. Her child would not pay for her mother's life choices. Nice ran her palms over her face. She was wasting time in this bathroom. She stuffed the pills back into the purse.

She waited until the washroom was empty again, washed her face once more and walked out into the terminal. Inhaled the air-conditioned air, feeling it pass over her still-dry nasal passage.

The policeman was nowhere to be seen. Nice filled out the

arrival card and stepped into the immigration queue, preparing all the while to resume, if necessary, the stilted interaction with more aplomb.

Having gotten her passport stamped, Nice saw the cop. He was standing with his back to her now, near the baggage reclaim. Screwing up her courage, Nice walked up to him, touched the epaulet on his shoulder and handed him back the handkerchief – spotted now with her scarlet blood. "Thank you again."

The policeman took the handkerchief unsqueamishly, tucking it into his trouser pocket. They walked together towards the exit, the clamoring taxi drivers.

The automatic sliding doors hissed open. In the cool damp air, the policeman stopped. Nice looked up into his face, tried to get past those eyes and then awkwardly stuck out her hand.

The policeman shook it, maintaining the eye contact.

The handshake seemed to last a long time.

With his free hand, the cop brought forth the handkerchief from his trouser pocket and held the rubied stain to his mouth.

Between the startling sharp teeth, Nice saw the dart of a vivid pink tongue.

"See you again. Soon, perhaps?" the man lisped behind the fabric. "Safari njema."

Nice stumbled away from him into the waiting throng. She scanned the crowds, standing on tiptoes. Duncan had to be here. He was never late. She was conscious that the policeman could still be watching her, seeing who had come to pick her up. A white man in a collarino. That would only draw more attention. She shouldered her way deeper into the bodies, tobacco and body odor mixing with the damp air.

There, beyond the drop off lane, in a pool of yellowed sodium lights, Duncan was jogging towards the terminal, checking his wristwatch. She allowed herself a sigh of relief and, in the same instant, turned to see if the policeman still watched her.

He stood where they had parted, at the exit of the terminal. Arms crossed over his chest. Eyeing the crowd in a professional manner. Could he see her? Was he looking for her? Either way, she had to be sure, to get out of his line of sight. There, behind some scaffolding, was a series of concrete blocks, effectively hidden from the terminal's exit. A billboard of President Obama grinning stood above, like a beacon of hope.

Straightening her wig, she made her way behind the terminal.

Rain fell from the gunmetal sky.

2

DUNCAN NEEDED TO END THE MEETING so he
would not be late to pick up Nice from the airport. Across his
battered desk, Mr. and Mrs. Legishon sat, red-eyed, their backs
not touching the mauve velvet backrests of the chairs. The late
afternoon sun streamed in through the dusty window and caught
Mr. Legishon's ear lobes, which dangled at his cheekbone. Into
the hole of the left earlobe, he had tucked a mobile phone, by
way of a hands-free kit. Duncan willed himself to look away from
the swaying phone at the yellow pencil he pincered between pale
fingers.

Mr. Legishon cleared his throat and placed one calloused
hand on his wife's stockinged knee. "So, our boy has been
recalled by the Lord."

Duncan had read the police report: thirteen-year-old
Isaiah, playing with friends on a nearby construction site when
an overzealous night watchman spotted them and gave chase.
Isaiah, along with his friends, scrambled down from the bamboo
scaffolding and fled across the construction yard. The police
report stated that Isaiah clipped his toe on a pile of rubble and
fell headlong into an uncovered construction shaft leading to

the sewage works. Removing the boy's body had required a two-day wait for the right digging equipment to be sourced. The company that owned and operated the construction site declined to pay any compensation, citing criminal trespass. The CEO had even tried to claim damages for the work stoppage and retrieval efforts.

Duncan's lower jaw clicked and locked. An old sparring injury. The very first time he had fought in a ring without any protective gear. The doctor at the emergency had shrugged, rolled up his sleeves, and manipulated the jaw back into place with a bone-crunching explosion of pain. No charge, the doctor had said with a smile.

It was something Duncan had gotten used to, gotten good at, even relied upon, as an indicator of when he was not managing his stress levels well. His jaw would click and remain stuck in an open-mouthed position. But he knew what to do without drawing attention to himself. Duncan nodded and ran a hand, as if in thoughtful reflection, across his chin. Then, when Mr. Legishon began to speak, Duncan firmly tugged his jaw back into alignment.

Mrs. Legishon cocked her head, a question in her eyes.

Swallowing the pain, Duncan half-inclined his head with an encouraging smile.

The funeral service had been a closed-casket ceremony; Isaiah no longer looking the way he did in his class photos. Duncan was conscious that it was his job as the pastor of the Westlands Church of the Earth to render some solace to his parishioners, the bereaved parents. The dignified Mr. and Mrs. Legishon now leaned forward to accept from Duncan these crumbs of comfort. Grief had changed something in Mrs. Legishon's face, like a lifelong myope without their glasses.

The pencil bent slightly between Duncan's thumbs.

How to make sense of this sort of thing? How to summon the audacity for a childless, mid-thirties white man to advise two grown-ups on how to navigate the terrifying waters ahead. The reverence with which the Legishons awaited his words made Duncan feel like a phony, just as he had felt when he had first arrived in Kenya four years ago. Thirty-three years old at the time, a newly minted pastor, Duncan was conscious that white male privilege constituted the bulk of his value proposition to the Church. To the parishioners.

Now, he had grown into the role somewhat, but still felt it as a role—as though he was play-acting at being a pastor. Duncan tugged at his collarino, subconsciously reminding himself of the meaning of his uniform, as though it were protective gear. The pencil snapped between his thumbs and the Legishons shot back into their chairs.

Duncan bit his lower lip. "I'm sorry." He exhaled, then added, "So very sorry." It felt sanctimonious to say anything else. Flashes of scripture flashed before his eyes, but it was all so callow, so maudlin, so disrespectful to spout those recycled notions at a mother who had just lost a son. It was not so much a loss of faith as it was a grim realization that the spiritual product lines in which he trafficked could not help. Not really. Not in the face of something like this.

Mrs. Legishon lowered her head. Her shoulders shuddered and there came from her throat low, quick guttural sounds. She was crying and trying to stop crying. Mr. Legishon's eyes flashed at Duncan, asking the unspoken question of what Duncan was going to do to make this better.

Duncan dropped the pencil halves onto his desk, rubbed his damp palms together. He had a trick—a dirty trick in his mind—for moments like these. To look past the stage-dressing and props of religion, past all that to what lay beneath, love and empathy for a parent broken by the death of her child. Engendering true love within himself for this woman who sat sobbing at his desk would mean something. But it would, in turn, make the rituals and wine-filled chalices a mere branding exercise. If love was the only law, in the end, then why bother with the rest? He was a mere salesman, a fraud.

Clenching his jaw, like an actor forced to perform a catchphrase from a blockbuster film he hated being in, Duncan recited, "I have told you these things so that in Me you may have peace. You will have suffering in this world. Be courageous! I have conquered the world." Mrs. Legishon looked up, her tear-streaked face alight with hope. Mr. Legishon nodded slowly at Duncan, pleased to see his wife's recovery and reassured that they had in fact come to the right place for succor. This was the bill of goods they had agreed upon.

Pressing his advantage, Duncan added, "Book of John, chapter 16, verse 33." He was lanced with shame at his salesmanship and the fact that it had worked.

The Legishons held hands. Thin, determined smiles formed on their tired faces. This was the medicine they had wished to be prescribed, the drug they craved. They stood together, thoroughly satisfied with the meeting.

Mr. Legishon held out his hand, veined and rough. It swallowed Duncan's soft, pink one. Duncan promised himself he would not speak another word.

When the Legishons had gone, he sat heavily in his chair staring at the splintered pencil halves. He was exhausted at the performance, by the demands of reaching out to his parishioners, of knowing his sheep, of pretending to know what he was talking about. The whole thing seemed some sort of spiritual ponzi scheme.

An urgent trilling snapped him from these gloomy thoughts.

His phone was flashing the reminder to go to the airport to pick up Nice, who was arriving on the evening flight from Mogadishu. A woman he had loved. Loved still, if he was honest with himself. Another hypocritical man of the cloth.

Duncan took one last look at the broken pencil on his desk, then stood to leave. He exited the decaying structure of the Mission of the Church of the Earth and, in the deepening dusk, walked towards his car.

"Good evening, Pastor." A boy nodded clutching a tattered football.

Duncan nodded back, not slowing his gait.

He crossed the parking lot's broken asphalt, buckled by the invisible roots of an old jacaranda tree. It towered above the compound, shedding lavender flowers like lavish tears. When Duncan had first arrived in the country, he had tried to avoid treading on them.

A coveralled gardener made little piles of the dead flowers while wearing bright orange noise control headphones. Over his shoulder was the jet-pack-like leaf blower that Duncan had ordered from an American catalog. Duncan had tried to explain to the Chairman of the Board, Mr. Leighman back in Virginia, that a leaf blowing machine was a poor use of the Mission's resources. That good men were paid good wages to sweep the grounds. But Mr. Leighman had insisted that all Missions, regardless of location, must have the same resources. More troublingly, Mr. Leighman seemed also to suggest that Duncan was against leaf blowing devices because of some racial motivation, namely that the machines were too sophisticated for Kenyan landscapers. Duncan had taken a deep breath on his end of the phone, prepared to correct this misconception—to explain how, in Kenya, labor was cheap and machines expensive.

But Duncan let it go.

"You're right Mr. Leighman. I'll go ahead and order one." And there it was, on the gardener's back. He was gathering the flowers into a dustpan with his hands. The leaf blower was not even switched on; the man had worn it simply because he had been asked to. Preparing the compound for the arrival of Mr. Leighman and the rest of the Board, who were expected imminently. Duncan nodded at the gardener, who did not seem to notice him or the greeting.

Duncan walked on, his car key pinched between thumb and forefinger, and came upon the jumbled parade of red and white trucks emblazoned "Church of the Earth: Community Outreach." The vehicles carpeted by the sweet-smelling jacaranda flowers.

He zigzagged between the trucks, some of which were parked so close together that he had to turn sideways to squeeze between them. He plucked a jacaranda flower from a windshield as he did so. When he had first arrived in Nairobi, it had been difficult for him to understand the contrast between the beauty of natural things and the sheer ugliness of man-made efforts. Yet he had learned not to be disconcerted by ugly things. Back in New England, he had been socialized to assume ugly things were a result of apathy, or worse, the choicelessness of poverty. In Kenya, even ugly things could cost a lot of money. Nevertheless, those moments, of belly and chest against the hard guardrails of the Outreach trucks, made him dimly claustrophobic.

This aspect of his job also made him feel constricted, out

of his depth. The management of a fleet of twenty or so trucks, everyday wending across some of the most neglected parts of this ill-tended city. It was not something for which the Mission training had even prepared him. Just like the training manual did not have a chapter titled, 'What to say when you don't know,' it was implied that he was to know. Why, for instance, were the trucks parked like this, nose to nose, making it impossible to cross the parking lot without getting dusty?

"All right, Pastor?" The big voice boomed from above Duncan. He started and banged his head on a side mirror.

Ugly laughter came down from the cab of the truck. Effing Olaniyi.

Referring to the Deputy Pastor as "Effing Niyi" made Duncan feel guilty. But the name had stuck. Niyi was a raw-boned Nigerian, lean but broad of build. People often referred to Niyi as "that tall chap," even though he was no taller than Duncan. This irritated him unreasonably.

After he had arrived, he had come to learn that Niyi (who was a good ten years older than him and had been with the Mission for a number of years already) had imagined himself as having the inside track to the Nairobi job. And Duncan's youth and inexperience only convinced Niyi that the deck was stacked in favor of the white man from the get-go. Niyi used the term "Pastor" with an almost palpable irony.

Duncan rubbed the back of his head, looking up at Niyi's heavy-featured face; he was tapping a pen against the wooden clipboard. His black Malcolm X glasses gave him a bookish air. "Checking the supply chain. These clothes aren't going to deliver themselves o."

"Yes. Thanks, Niyi. Carry on."

Duncan sidled between the trucks, still rubbing his head

where a goose egg was emerging.

"Watch your head, Pastor," Niyi said, by way of a parting shot.

Effing Niyi, who was, in fairness, capable and scrupulously honest.

Truth was Duncan felt relieved that Niyi managed the supply chain and the fleet. Most importantly, he managed the truck drivers, with their countless ways to outmaneuver whatever checks and balances put in place to oversee their use of diesel, man-hours and inventory. Duncan saw himself as a big-picture person, not quite admitting to himself that, but for Niyi, this hugely important part of the Mission's operations would be impossible to manage.

Duncan got into his green Subaru station wagon, relieved to be away from the business of the trucks, which vaguely depressed him—bringing him, as they did, face-to- face with his masculine failings. The turn of the key, the polite cough of the engine, the catch and turn of the motor and then, a woman's firm and pleasing electronic voice emerging from the stereo, announcing heaven-knows-what in Japanese.

Duncan pulled onto Mombasa Road, heading towards the airport to collect Nice. The Chinese-funded half-built overpass lay pinned like a broken butterfly against the evening sky. The fractured overpass glided silently by and the red taillights grew denser near the airport. On the median were freshly dug trench-es, beside which lay unplanted saplings, gagging silently. Duncan shook his head at these preparations for the arrival of President Obama, in whose honor these Potemkin Village adornments had been organized. Not so different, perhaps, than his own preparations for the visit of Mr. Leighman and the board.

The drizzle brought forth the smell of damp earth and the

frustration of slowing traffic. The digital clock on the dashboard read 17:33, which only gave Duncan just over a quarter of an hour to be in time to pick up Nice. Frowning through the windshield at the rain and the cops, Duncan got to work weaving through the cars to get through the security checkpoint.

A policewoman waved him over. She wore a neon yellow and black checkered knee-length raincoat and, bizarrely, a cowboy hat. Holding her torch overhand like a dagger, she flashed the light in Duncan's face. "Unaenda wapi?"

Duncan gestured with his chin at the nearest terminal, glowing wetly. He tracked the policewoman with one eye in the rear-view as he pulled away, watched her click her radio and replace it in the pocket of her slicker.

In true Nairobi fashion, ten minutes of rain turned the parking lot entry into a frenzied warzone—no way would he be able to be outside arrivals on time. With one eye on the dashboard clock, Duncan swung the station wagon into a quasi-legal spot. He spotted Nice through his rain-spattered windshield before he got out of the car. She was slouched on a cinder block outside the arrivals terminal under a billboard depicting an insouciant President Obama; the city making ready for the big man's visit.

He jogged across the parking lot.

Nice seemed to have lost weight, her face gaunt and her shoulders bony under her kurta. Her hairstyle looked expensive yet oddly off-kilter. She was one of those self-possessed persons, who managed to look patient while waiting. Her sharp-featured face beautiful in its self-forgetting.

Duncan knew a pang of longing upon catching sight of her. A familiar longing that filled his throat. As he watched, she pulled an orange plastic cylinder from her massive purse and tilted its contents back into her mouth, swallowing them dry.

Duncan got out of the car, jogged across the intersection. He knew better than to be earnest with Nice, and instead went with a jauntiness he did not feel. "Headache?" he grinned.

Nice, looking wan, jumped up and threw her arms around him. He felt her ribcage distinctly when he returned the embrace and then was surprised to feel her shaking softly in his arms, crying.

Nice surprised herself, the sheer relief of seeing him there— steady, slow, loyal Duncan—upon whose feelings she could be playing, knowing that he still had feelings for her since university. She saw him as he must have been as a boy: gullible, earnest and seeking validation. His steadiness, his reliability, the very qualities that had been so repellent, now coming into sharp focus as a lifeline. She felt an urge to tell him everything. But that would only place him in peril. Still, once Pendo was safe, she would come clean to Duncan. It could not be helped. "Come on. Nice." Duncan took her by the hand and led her, under the sodium lights to the car. Nice glanced back at the terminal building, but the policeman was not visible, and she allowed herself to be led.

She had met Duncan at university in Montreal. He had transferred in his third year, telling all who asked that he had been seeking a more cosmopolitan experience than his New England seminary could provide. The same seminary his father had attended, and with whose blessing he had dragged his family across the country preaching.

Duncan told no one, not even her initially, that he had been expelled for his involvement in a marijuana growing and retailing enterprise, in the basement of his dormitory. He would tell Nice that his role had been marginal; that he had been the only one careless enough to use his personal credit card to buy heating equipment on the still-nascent internet, and hence the only person expelled. In Duncan's telling, the boy who had led the operation had been his friend and sparring partner. Three times a week, for two years, they had touched gloves, circled each other warily, then tried to kill each other in three-minute doses. It was this same boy who delivered the pure straight left hook that gave Duncan a dislocated jaw. And it had been in the same gym, peeling steaming hand wraps from raw knuckles, that he had asked if Duncan would lend the money. And might it not be easier if he just used his own credit card to make the purchase, which would then be repaid.

The seminary's letter of expulsion urged Duncan to "avail himself of the sacraments" and specified with more pedestrian emphasis that the seminary would not reimburse any tuition. Duncan's parents asked him to leave their lives with as little fuss as possible. And thus he arrived in Montreal, stripped of his past, blinking at the sights of the big city.

Nice was the youngest of seven siblings—all of whom had been born in India before the family moved to Canada. In this role, she had grown up straddling the cultural divide, often serving as precocious guide and translator to baffled family members. She and Duncan had fallen into an unlikely but easy friendship. One which was beneficial to Duncan because Nice, sometimes unwittingly, decoded the mores of secular Western society, in and around which Duncan had grown older, but without quite adopting or even comprehending them.

Nice had earned her nickname one snowy February afternoon when the two had decided to not attend any classes, but instead to retreat to Duncan's flat to drink tea and smoke pot. They were discussing Duncan's tendency to be perplexed by social situations, sitting on the broad wooden windowsill with only a half inch of double-paned glass between them and the falling snow.

"Your religious training has made you too literal," Nice said, joint dangling from her lip. "But life is poetry, not scripture. You have to read between lines."

"Mm, maybe."

Undeterred, Nice continued, "For Canadians, as a general matter, let me tell you, we want to come across as 'nice'. That is the load-bearing pillar of our national self-image."

Duncan felt like he had x-ray vision the next time he went to a social gathering, which happened to be a poker game at a friend of Nice's. Duncan didn't know how to play any card games, but the friend insisted Duncan come just to have a drink. After having observed a few hands, Duncan noted aloud how civil the interactions of the game were and how he hadn't had that impression from movies and books.

The girl sitting next to him remarked flatly, never looking up from her cards, "It's because we're Canadians."

It must have seemed a little self-congratulatory to Duncan. And delusional, given these same people had stolen an entire continent not so very long ago, essentially by exterminating the original inhabitants. But, as an American, a guest in this land, he only told Nice when he bestowed upon her the nickname. Nice basically agreed, both with Duncan's observation and her nickname without making a fuss. She liked its inside-joke level of irony.

Nice did add that Duncan could not go on identifying as an outsider, but would have to develop and commit to some self-defined version of belonging. This was commonly referred to as "being a grown up." Duncan had responded that he wanted no part of this business of "growing up."

It was one of those conversations memorable for no particular reason yet Nice often replayed in her head. It was unclear just how much growing up Duncan had done. Or perhaps she had done altogether too much growing up. Immeasurable distance lay between that ancient February afternoon and this sodden Nairobi evening, in Duncan's green station wagon. Her cynicism had not protected her from this sorry pass—she would be lucky if she survived long enough to be a single mother. Nice thought of the policeman's steady eyes in the bathroom mirror, sizing her up. She shook her head to clear the image.

Nice lowered herself into the passenger seat. Duncan fastened his seatbelt and put the car into reverse. "You okay?"

"Sure. Yes. Why does everyone keep asking me that?"

She ran the back of her hand across her nose, checked to see that the bleeding hadn't started again without her noticing.

"Everyone?"

They pulled into traffic, nudging their way along the feeder road. Nice stared out of the passenger window, the last of the daylight falling upon emerald wedges of the national park between the drab warehouses which lined the highway.

Nice ran the back of her hand against her nose, sniffed. "A man in the Arrivals terminal followed me into the toilets."

Duncan rubbed the side of his jaw. "I haven't known you to be intimidated by a garden variety pervert."

"He wasn't just a pervert though. It was a cop. I was scared. Got a strange feeling from him."

"A feeling?" Nice did not hear Duncan's question. She was preoccupied again with the policeman and that odd encounter.

Silent, the car wound its tortured way onto the Chinese-built bypass. At the onramp, the traffic choked and slowed to a crawl. The night was blurry billboards and rain-streaked taillights. Under the misting rain, the cowled form of a boy zigzagged between rear-view mirrors. He paused uncertainly outside Nice's window, and held out a tiny hand. His eyes were clear, his smile still boyish. He must be newly recruited into this line of work. As Nice made to roll down the window, the car pulled forward, into the traffic. The boy's face receded, the river of cars closing over him.

Duncan said, "I was worried we would be stuck there for an hour."

She thought of the boy, the short life and narrow choices which had led him to be making a living on the shoulder of a national highway. "Please pull over, Duncan," Nice said. She had made a decision. She would tell him. Why she was here, why she had asked him to pick her up. That she was sorry, but she needed his help.

Duncan clenched the steering wheel, then pulled over.

Nice removed her wig, turned to face him. She saw in his eyes what Duncan now saw, what she had seen in the over-lit airport bathroom mirror—her cheekbones prominent under the congealing glare of the sodium lights, childlike and aged.

Duncan said, "Why were you wearing a wig? I thought it looked—And your nose, it's bleeding."

A lorry screamed past, raising a mist in its wake.

Nice dabbed at the nosebleed, lurched out of whatever intimacy she was on the verge of sharing. "Oh, will this thing ever stop?"

Duncan reached over to the glove compartment and withdrew a pack of tissues. "You were about to say something?" Nice dabbed at her nose with the tissue. She shook her head, gestured at the steering wheel, managing a weak smile.

"Sorry Dee, so dramatic. Let's go, please."

Duncan checked the streaky rear-view, then pulled into the glistening road. "What did that cop want with you?"

Nice punched buttons on the radio, not sure how much to share, how much was too much? "Don't know. Maybe a handout?" Best to say nothing, what was the point of freaking Duncan out? She knew that he was still in love with her, on some level. It seemed irresponsible to abuse that. To admit to herself that she was abusing his trust by calling him to the airport. She imagined, for an idle instant, raising her baby with him, shook her head. So much of life unsaid, unsayable, marooned beyond words. "It's funny that."

Duncan asked, "What?"

Nice understood she had spoken aloud. "You grow up with people, your siblings, your friends. You share everything. And then, one day, you're a grown-up, an uncle, an aunty, and you can't share anything. Not really. We each sleep alone, ultimately."

Duncan took a breath, as if unsure of himself. "I know a reliable Ethiopian restaurant."

Nice smiled at the non-sequitur. With the intimacy of an old friendship, Nice handed Duncan a pack of mint chewing gum. Only one piece remained. Duncan tucked the gum into his breast pocket.

Out of the wet void behind them howled a Toyota Hilux pickup, its naked cab laden with miraa leaves. The pickup drew level, then overtook Duncan's car with a growl.

Duncan said, "Maniac. Usually, they're speeding towards the airport to fly the freshly harvested miraa out to Yemen or Somalia."

Nice felt she was just getting over the shock at the airport, so did not know what to make of Duncan's response. He had always been a bit overcautious, a plodder. Still, she placed a hand over her belly, to give whatever comfort she could to Pendo that everything was okay.

Everything was going to be okay.

Up ahead, the pickup's taillights glowed, and it slowed to keep pace alongside Duncan's car. The ghostly outline of the pickup's driver, masked behind a keffiyeh, leaned its forehead against its window. The ghost reached at something in the passenger seat and returned to its window holding up a yellow metal license plate where its mouth should have been.

Duncan read aloud. "KAJ 769B." A second passed, then Duncan said, "That's my license plate," as much to Nice as himself. Nice leaned forward to get a look.

"He wants you to pull over," Nice said, pointing at the pickup.

Duncan described several concentric circles in the air with his forefinger, miming the action for roll down your window.

The wraith in the pickup showed no sign of having received this message, tossing the license plate over his shoulder into the passenger seat, not breaking eye contact with them—the slick tarmac whipping underneath.

The pickup slowed, almost to a halt in the middle of the two-lane highway. Nice leaned forward to catch the reflection in the side-view mirror. She watched the pickup recede from sight.

"The hell?" Duncan strained into the rear-view at the now empty highway.

Nice gave a nervous giggle. "Should we turn around?" But she did not want to turn around. To go back to that policeman, to Mogadishu, to her life choices, to the violence which stalked her. She had to keep going, to deliver the drugs, to save Pendo.

She glanced at Duncan, and admitted, to save herself.

Duncan chewed his lip as if thinking the suggestion over. As she watched him, Nice knew she could influence him, simply by being decisive. She bit her cheek, then said, "Dee, it's maybe better to drive on and report the license plate stolen tomorrow. Probably a carjacker anyway."

Nice watched the veins in Duncan's hands, which lay along the steering wheel. The car lurched forward. She leaned back, checking that her seatbelt was clicked in. Interlacing her fingers across her belly, without being aware of having done so. Ancient instincts zeroing in.

At the crest of a hill, the pickup came roaring back.

It was flashing its headlights, the whine of the truck's diesel engine filling Duncan's car. Duncan accelerated once more, but the truck leveled in the adjoining lane. The driver was gesturing at Duncan to pull over.

It seemed to Nice that the entire cabin of the car was vibrating from the velocity. She had never been in a car going this fast. Duncan looked away from the truck and gave a nervous laugh. "Karibu Nairobi, Nice—"

The truck pulled dead in front of their car, brake lights blindingly close. Duncan jammed the brakes, steering evasively. Nice knew the kaleidoscoping of light and space as the car fishtailed. The headlights careened, illumining, for one crazy instant, a pregnant raincloud, and then the car was crashing through the brand-new steel guard railings. Beyond the tarmac, the green Subaru sailed headlong into an electrical pole, the impact crumpling the engine block.

Sparks showered onto the bonnet. The windshield shot white in an instant.

The highway fell silent, save for the reggae music still spilling from the broken green car. Falling rain silhouetted in the ephemeral veil of the sodium lights.

Halfway down the hill, the pickup's taillights glowed red against the wet tarmac. It reversed back up the hill, crossways in the middle of the highway, its headlights drew even with the jagged guard railing. The driver-side window descended.

With camouflage-hued binoculars, the keffiyah'ed driver glassed the crash. Shaking his head, the phantom spoke rapidly into his radio.

3

THE MAN PINCHED HIS SCROTUM through his khaki trousers, rolling it between his thumb and forefinger. Profiled in the slatted sunlight, absent-minded as a pregnant woman rubbing her belly. He looked out into the grassy yard and the gravel path which led away from the house, up a hill, behind which the afternoon sun sank. "Now what am I supposed to do with this man here? I never told my guys to run them off the road."

He bared small teeth, looking at the priest's unconscious form on the dusty floor.

The man continued his tirade. "Get me the girl, I said. The girl." He threw up his hands, "Now I have to clean up the car crash and deal with this joker. He's been asleep the whole day. These things cost money you know."

A woman spoke in even tones, as if to calm him, "Every mistake shrinks the margin." She was shrouded in shadow in the unlit corner of the room.

"Yes, you have a way with words, Ciru. The margin is shrinking. And this man is still asleep." He placed a boot over Duncan's limp hand as if deciding whether to kill a spider.

The woman interjected. "There's no need—"

The man in khaki brought his boot down hard on the pale fingers.

Duncan gave a bleat, his eyelids flickering at the stimulation. With his fingers still trapped under the boot, he tried to peel himself upright.

The man bent, hands on knees, to examine Duncan's stirrings. "He awakes."

Duncan, unequal to the task of responding, or even lifting his head, grunted.

"Come on. Come on," the khaki man said, a tetchiness surfacing through this last syllable.

Duncan's face was level with the creased khaki turn-ups and shined black parade boots. Duncan's eyes, the only part of his body that seemed not to be in pain, trapped inside his immobile skull, could see no further than the man's brass belt buckle, which rested under a compact beer belly. The belt buckle bore the image of a trident. A police uniform of some sort.

Duncan's terror eased a little. A policeman, this could be a good thing. This whole thing could be a misunderstanding. If only Duncan could clear the fog in his head.

Sighing, the standing man bent still further to make eye contact with Duncan, taking care not to dirty any part of his uniform by pressing the tip of his right forefinger against the floor for balance. The khaki man took a mobile phone from his pocket, and pressed buttons until it played tinny music. He then placed the device on the floor beside Duncan's head. Duncan could feel the vibrations of the phone in his skull.

"You know this song?" The khaki man shook his head sadly. "It is a sad song, about a mother whose son is lost, tending his sheep. The mother searches. The mother searches." He waved a hand, indicating the vastness of this enterprise. "The son cannot be found. So, she turns to God and begs for his help. But there is only silence on the moors, the silence of an absentee landlord. That is the chorus, in fact."

Duncan struggled to follow the story and what it might mean for his own short-term future. He tried to gather himself by observing his various pains. The pain in his skull seemed to emerge from its base and Duncan willed his hand to reach the back of his head, brushing against the open lips of a gash. "Are you even listening to me, Father?" the man asked, over the music.

Duncan continued to observe himself. Under the electrical storm of the pain, lay a throbbing core of anxiety and he could sense something important had been taken from him. The need to focus on understanding what the policeman wanted.

His face still drooling against the dust, Duncan tried to ask, "Where is my friend?"

"Similarly," continued the squatting khaki man, not recognizing Duncan's moan as human speech, "you too must seek divine intervention, Father. Because you are just an inconvenience to me. An expensive inconvenience."

The khaki man stood, a viciousness in his motion. "And where is your lord now?" he hissed, prodding Duncan's rib cage with the tip of his boot.

This sensation brought a measure of clarity, even relief, from Duncan's headache. Duncan shuffled his torso about and was eventually able to sit up, his back to the wall, the palms of his hands resting flat against the floor. His field of vision wobbled, and he closed his eyes to steady himself.

This seemed to enrage the khaki man. "I have been waiting some time for you to wake up. And now you must speak."

Duncan, with the intention of clearing his mouth and

throat to speak, spat a bloody wad of phlegm.

The khaki man, face contorted with rage, yanked Duncan's head by the hair.

The chorus of the song warbled on.

The woman's voice came, deep and clear, from the unseen corner of the room. "Hinga, stop that. Be professional." She seemed, from her tone, to be weary of dealing with the man's impulsiveness. As if this was a recurring theme in their relationship, her steadiness countering his jumpy anxiety.

The khaki man—she had called him Hinga—loosened his fist, as though electrocuted by the woman's voice. Duncan's head slumped onto his chest.

The unseen woman spoke again, this time to Duncan. "Can you speak?"

Stars wobbled behind Duncan's eyes as he tried to shake his head.

From the gloom beyond the slatted window emerged a small, walnut-faced woman towards the end of middle age, wearing a red and green kikoy dress that gathered at her waist, upon which she wore a sash of braided grass. The woman stood barefoot on the cool clay floor. She glided through the bars of sunlight upon the floor, brushing past the khaki statue, and sent the mobile phone skittering across the floor against the wall near Duncan. The song ceased.

In her right hand, she bore a glass of water.

Duncan took it with soundless gratitude, noting that the knuckles on his right hand were scraped raw. Hinga retrieved his silenced phone from the corner of the room, eyes hooded in his sullen face. Keeping one eye on Hinga, Duncan drank the glass in one smooth swallow. He cleared his throat, spat once more. "Where is my friend?"

The woman had a clear-eyed vigor. "We have rescued you from the scene of a car accident. Do you recall this?" She took the empty glass from Duncan. "You ran your car off the highway, and you seem to have broken your head. You have been unconscious for some time."

Duncan nodded, green stars rising unbidden. "But where is my friend? She was in the passenger seat. I need to find her." Buoyed by this declaration and his ability to formulate it, Duncan took in a deep breath and began to stagger to his feet. He needed to make sure that Nice was all right.

Hinga shoved Duncan, who fell in a heap, looking up in impotent rage. "Your friend, she is in very serious trouble. How much has she told you, huh? About her friend in Mogadishu, about her muling—"

The woman stood between them, holding the cop by the forearm. They spoke to each other, rapid-fire, in a language Duncan could not follow. The tone was that of a quick and dirty negotiation, in which neither party could truly be satisfied. They went back and forth in this manner, above Duncan's crumpled form, until the woman turned again to Duncan, with a discordant smile.

"Your friend is in a safe place. This man is a friend. He is police. He will take you to her." This was, it seemed to Duncan, a lukewarm endorsement, but at least they had acknowledged that Nice did exist. That the accident had, in fact, occurred.

The policeman gave a self-effacing nod. "I am Hinga." He extended a fine-boned hand. Duncan, held out his own hand, wincing at the pain of this exertion.

Hinga issued a laugh of manly empathy.

Duncan swayed, noticing for the first time Hinga's green and gold epaulets. His small sharp teeth.

Hinga held Duncan's shoulders, steadying him. "Will your white God not help?"

Duncan's body shrank in irritation and pain from his touch, and this only made Hinga give out another full-bellied guffaw.

Grimacing, Duncan asked, "Where is she?"

"This way," Hinga gestured at a wooden door which leaked sunlight. Shuffling against the wall of the shack, Duncan made his slow way. The woman stood aside, watching.

As the wooden door swung open, Duncan was blinded by the setting sun. Goosebumps came up on his arms in the chill air. The shack gave onto a grassy yard, in which wandered feral chickens, examining puddles of last night's rains. Up a small hill, behind the chickens, was a baby-blue Peugeot 504, framed against the bruised sky.

Hinga gave an elaborate bow towards the car. Duncan followed, inch by painful inch. From atop the hill, the sun sank between the skyscrapers of Upper Hill, glistening like a fever dream. Duncan blinked at them, imagining office workers humming as they shut down their computers. Preparing for happy hour.

Hinga popped open the boot. Was Nice in there?

The open boot lid obscured Hinga from Duncan's view. Rounding the rear of the car, Duncan saw that the boot was empty, save for a spare tire and loose tennis balls. Working up the steam to demand an explanation from the cop, Duncan turned to face Hinga, anger unfurling now beneath his fear.

Smiling all the while, Hinga tipped Duncan into the boot and slammed it shut.

Duncan heard receding footfalls, the fruitless labors of the nearby chickens.

Then silence, like a cloth-sack over his head.

4

DUNCAN LAY IN THE STIFLING DARK, his legs accordioned against the lid of the car boot. In each hand he held a tennis ball. Unbelievable. So, he was being kidnapped. By a policeman. But what did they want? And how did Nice play into this?

He was conscious of the pain in the base of his skull and a disorienting fear. As Duncan closed his eyes, his jaw locked once more with a click. The last time, with the Legishons, seemed a very long time ago. He took a few slow open- mouthed breaths, brought his hand to his chin and yanked hard. The pain was good. The pain was a beacon in a fog of fear.

Duncan felt about his pockets. His phone was gone, as was his wallet. So, the cop and the woman knew his name, his work, his address. The keys to the Ministry were bunched with the car keys, which he did not recall ever removing from the ignition after the crash. Indeed, Duncan could produce not one recollection between the showering sparks on the green bonnet and awaking at the polished parade boots of the cop.

While mulling this mental void over, Duncan found the packet of chewing gum in his breast pocket—the one given him by Nice—like a message in a bottle, bobbing in an open sea.

He fumbled at the pack, removing the outer foil to extract the gum. His clumsy fingertips let slip the unwrapped piece, which fell into the inky abyss beside his head. The sunken gum gave forth its synthetic minty odor, engulfing Duncan in a sense of disproportionate loss.

He felt the fear suffuse him once more. He was a fool to have thought the policeman would help. He was once more adrift in a sea of other people's intentions. Their unknowable motivations. He punched the boot lid.

He turned his head to better feel for the gum, setting off a firestorm of pain. Locating it near his ear, against the hairy felt bed of the boot, he put it into his mouth. Taking care not to bite or bend the gum, and still with closed eyes, he herded the tiny errant strands of felt from the boot floor to the tip of his tongue. Then he wiped his tongue against his invisible shirtsleeve.

Only then did he allow himself to chew the gum. His mouth filled with its evanescent sweetness.

And only then did he permit himself to think of Nice. Nice—fierce, beautiful, impetuous Nice, with her slow-burning instinct for self-destruction. What had the cop meant by serious trouble? Was that what Nice had tried to raise in the car, when leaving the airport? Would she really be so stupid as to get involved with a smuggling operation?

In his metallic coffin, Duncan sought for a specific memory of Nice, something to humanize her, to focus his own efforts on managing the terror. With the gum already losing its flavor, he recalled a boozy dinner in a shack on a Caribbean beach. A trip he and Nice had taken while still at university.

The night he had admitted to himself that he loved her but lacked the stones to pursue her.

They had swum in the briny sea and drunk the sweet local

beers, the slender bottle necks corked with lime wedges. As they ate at a shabby seaside restaurant, a bedraggled boy of about eight or ten brushed up to their table, begging only with his eyes. Neither the barman, his face pillowed in his forearms resting on the bar, nor the other patrons, took any notice of the ragged boy. Duncan had recoiled from the boy's clear-eyed gaze, which seemed at the time, and under the influence of sun and beer, unanswerable. Nice, on the other hand, wordlessly handed her plate, still heaped with beans, rice and a chalky-tasting white queso, to the boy. The fork still standing in a mound of rice. Then, and over Duncan's muttered remonstrations, Nice had also handed the boy the three-quarters full beer. The boy nodded in noble fashion, then vanished with the goods.

Later, having paid the sleepy barman, Duncan and Nice emerged onto the beach outside the shack, sated and disoriented under a full moon. Outlined in the moonlight, they saw the boy feeding a much smaller child, spoon by careful spoon of rice and beans. Feeling observed, the boy had looked up at the two and slyly raised Nice's beer in silent salute. Nice had, in turn, given Duncan a quizzical look—a twisting of her mouth, a tilting of her head, and a slight arch of the eyebrows. She had worn that same inscrutable look, later, when they kissed over a shared nightcap, the emerald water of the pool lapping softly. Duncan ran his fingertips over her marmoreal forearm. Nice closing her eyes tight, as though to shut out the world which made one beggar child feed another. It was a memory he often revisited.

Duncan felt his breath catch in his chest, shallow with the fear. What had the cop done with her?

He tried to silence his mind with action, by focusing on his breath. He began squeezing the tennis balls in alternate fists, inhaling when his left hand contracted, then counted to three, and exhaled as his right hand squeezed. He had done this, by his hazy count, a thousand or so times before he heard the crackle of a radio.

The crackling grew louder. Hinga's booming voice came through the lid in staccato bursts. "Ova. Ova."

Keys clunked at the boot lid. Hinga stood framed by the boot and the sky, head tilted, regarding Duncan. The cop said, "Get out."

Duncan released the tennis balls and clambered stiff-limbed out of the trunk. His head swam, but the chill air was fresh. He focused on chewing the stale gum to center himself. But his legs buckled, and he fell, sitting propped up against the bumper.

Hinga was still as a stork. At his side appeared the woman from the shack. The only change in her appearance was a shawl protecting her against the night air. 'Where did you get the chewing gum from?'

Duncan looked up, patted his breast pocket twice, slowly. The woman gave Hinga an expert side-eye and spoke again. "Listen Duncan. We don't wish to harm you, or your friend. We are professionals."

Duncan nodded. "What is it that you want?"

The woman's lips disappeared. "What she bears within her. Come. Let's take you to your friend."

The cop extended his hand. Duncan ignored it, hoisting himself up from the bumper instead. He followed Hinga and the woman down the hillock, past the blinking silhouettes of the office towers. At their feet, the still-busy chickens clucked. Beyond the darkened shack stood a sort of mechanic's workshop, lined with carcasses of saloon cars resting on cinder blocks. Then the slum began in earnest, and they entered a warren of indistinguishable alleyways, lined with bubbling sewers. The cries of unseen children playing in neighboring alleys reached them. An elderly man carrying firewood, bent under the weight of a canvas bag, its strap cleaving his

forehead, shuffled by. He avoided eye contact.

The trio walked on, the cop speaking sharp-sounding words in Swahili, looking past Duncan at the woman. The woman responded in the tone of a grown-up soothing a petulant child, but Hinga was not having it.

Unable to bear the cop's stubborn insistence, the woman shouldered Duncan aside and faced the cop. They stood under a concrete wall, spangled with bougainvillea. The woman seemed to be biting her tongue, choosing words intended to uncoil the cop's ropey forearms. But Hinga was unmoved, and, in his torrent of remonstration, Duncan heard the words "Somali" and "pesa" repeatedly.

The woman took a step closer to Hinga and placed her hands on her hips. Duncan, temporarily invisible to the arguing couple, took in his surroundings. A narrow gulley led off to the left. Duncan gave a side-long glance at the back of the woman's head, sizing up the bitterness of her disagreement with the cop.

Surprising himself, Duncan decided to make a dash for it.

Duncan ran towards the narrower alleyway, in a blur of concrete and sewage. Pausing to catch his breath, Duncan took in the silence in his wake, knowing the argument between the cop and the woman had been adjourned for the more pressing matter of chasing him. Duncan pressed on, lurching more than running, his hands scraping raw over the rough walls on either side for support. The side streets grew so tapered that even a loaded bicycle would need to be walked. A few more dizzying turns in the smelly labyrinth.

His pursuers seemed utterly silent—only the shrieking children.

The side street spat Duncan out in front of a half-open doorway through which he could see a courtyard in which young men were laughing and drinking. The scent of nyama choma rose sharply in the chill air. The young man at the grill was bald, a gold dollar sign hanging on a chain between his collarbones. He looked up with bloodshot eyes, took in the sight of the bloodied white man. He gave a smile as though pleased with this surprise, set down the tongs. "We-we! White man."

Duncan panted. "Please. Please help me, I'm—"

The man came around the grill, extended his hand. "Get up. We will get you a Tusker, nah? Make you better quick-quick."

Duncan paused, then took the man's hand. Was this a trick? His breath was ragged, and his head ebbed and flowed with a liquid pain. If he could just get inside the courtyard, shut that door.

Then, he heard Ciru's cry. Breath boiling in his chest, Duncan caught sight of the chasing couple—the woman trailing the policeman, who ran with a silent efficiency, head- down, arms pumping, like a man used to chasing others.

Duncan made to enter the courtyard, shut the door behind them. But the policeman had spotted him, called out, and come to a halt at the head of the alleyway, dark sweat staining the khaki front of his shirt.

The man from the grill drew back, in horror, his body language transformed at the sight of Hinga. He pushed Duncan out of the doorway, towards Hinga. "Sir, I didn't know—He never said—I'm sorry. So—"

But Hinga merely held up a palm. Then, not stopping to

catch his own breath, the policeman balled a fist and crashed it into Duncan's solar plexus. Duncan crumpled backwards onto the broken concrete of the alleyway and splayed out his hands to catch himself. He fell hard, his right arm elbow-deep in the uncovered sewer running along the roadside. The door slammed shut.

In the bilge, a condom lay half-submerged, pale as a newt. Duncan's cheeks made an involuntary quivering.

Hinga leaned both palms against the wall over Duncan's body, sucking in deep breaths. "Mjinga. Never run from police. Or don't they teach white people that?"

5

HINGA'S SALIVA SPRAYED over Duncan's closed eyelids. Duncan lay still, the welt of the wound at the base of his skull against the concrete wall, while the cop swore at him. In sheer exasperation, Hinga slapped Duncan, backhanded. It was an act calculated to cow, and Duncan felt a rage, and an instinct for self-preservation, stir within him. Now Hinga was kicking Duncan, in the ribs, in the hips, in the arms. It was a sloppy, anger-driven flurry, and Duncan blocked a tibia with his forearm and grabbed Hinga's heel. Still gripping the heel, Duncan rolled away from the cop, yanking on the cop's leg. Hinga crashed into the gutter beside Duncan with a yelp of surprise and pain.

Lying side by side in the stinking alleyway, both men took ragged breaths.

Duncan turned his head to find Hinga on all fours. The cop's khaki uniform front was blackened, slick with sewage, and his forearm bore a pink gash from wrist to elbow. The cop wore a crazy grin. It was the first time Duncan had seen his eyes uncaged.

Hinga got up, so that he was on his knees. Still grinning, Hinga reached to his honey-leathered holster, itself a ruin from the sewage, and drew a cartoonishly large revolver. "Made in

Israel," Duncan mouthed, reading along the circular lip of the barrel.

"Just look at this," the cop said, looking at his shirtfront.

Duncan made no response, unable to remove his gaze from the hypnotic bore of the cannon levelled at him.

"If you make another sound, if you call for help, then I will end your pretty friend." Hinga spat, pink and rich, into the soupy gutter.

Duncan felt the roof of his mouth with his tongue, tasting coppery blood. He had never had a gun pointed at him. The melodrama of the gesture, the sheer size of the weapon, the cop's pinched face above the ruined uniform— these things made Duncan giggle. He knew he had to stop and this knowledge made him giggle all the more.

Hinga stood, still pointing the gun. "Now, you find this funny? This is serious."

The blank look on Duncan's face prompted Hinga to go on.

"Very serious. You think your God will save you?" Hinga's hand made small circular motions at his hips, as though to churn Duncan's thoughts. The revolver too, described, a dangerous-looking oval.

Duncan stopped giggling. It hadn't even occurred to him to consider that his God might see fit to intervene. He hadn't thought to recite a prayer, even in the face of imminent harm, possibly death. Unenvisageable. What did this say about his faith, his work—the way he had conducted himself with the Legishons, their boy's broken body irretrievably jammed into a crevasse, like a cork in a bottle—the magic words he had stupidly spouted with the sole intention of making them leave his office? Was he himself just another juju man? It seemed a lifetime ago.

Had Kenya made him so cynical? Or he was just realistic about the indifferent churnings of the world. Duncan bit his lip, then conceded to himself, "No. I don't think God will. I think we may be alone here."

"Your fairytales are for the weak. You do well not to take your own drugs." The gun continued its maniacal looping.

Duncan knew something distinct was expected of him here but could summon no suitable conversational gambit.

The cop spoke on with a deadpan earnestness. "You don't even know how alone you are, how far from home. How you will be buried in the foundation of a luxury condo building in Westlands."

Hinga's fine fingers spidered on the chrome and leathered handle of the gun, which had ceased its meanderings.

Still on his back, Duncan looked at the gun, its heft in the slender hand, the gashed forearm, the ruined shirtfront of the uniform, the ludicrous epaulets, and finally the triangular face, the neat moustache above the sharp teeth, and the granite of the unblinking eyes.

The smell of nyama choma from the adjoining courtyard mingled with sewage in the cool night air.

Duncan raised one arm behind his head. "Please, I just need to find my friend."

"You don't need to worry about all that now. Just close your eyes and make one last prayer if you have it in you." The cop paused, parting his small white teeth. "And hope God gets your message on the hotline." The cop's vivid pink tongue, like the reptilian pilot of this human body-ship, darted out and seemed to taste the air, investigate briefly the moustache and then, satisfied, return to its lair behind the sharp teeth. The imminence of the violence seemed to be causing the cop a deep pleasure.

Hinga hummed the refrain of the folk song which had played on his phone back in the hut.

Then you will know,

The silence of an absentee landlord. Oh, then, only then, will you know loss.

"Because the witch and I have no use for you. We only need your friend's parcel." Hinga looked over his shoulder, distaste in his eyes, back at the woman, who was striding towards them, purpose in her steps.

Hinga continued. "It's just not worth the trouble to have a mzungu loose end like you about."

He spoke these words with a quiet satisfaction, as though he won a long and complicated debate with Ciru. That the solution which the violence proposed would put paid to any further discussion on a difficult subject.

The gun was exquisitely tooled. It took up the entirety of Duncan's field of vision, his very consciousness. Duncan, confused and defeated, closed his eyes. In his skull, red spouts of pain. No thoughts of God. He couldn't even summon a prayer for Nice.

After what seemed a long time, the air was rent with a crackling. Duncan dared to squint at his tormentor.

Where the gun had been hovering, there stood only shimmering air. Cautious not to make too sudden a movement, Duncan retrieved his arm from the cloudy sewer water. He sat upright, his hand dripping grey liquid. From where Hinga had been kneeling, as if a product of the gloom, appeared Ciru.

She was neither panting nor sweating and had pulled her dun-colored cloak about her shoulders against the chill of the night. In her left hand, she held a long metallic rod from which unspooled a wisp of blue smoke. The sweet smell of charred flesh, denser than that of the barbecue, gathered between the woman and Duncan in the alleyway.

The policeman lay at the woman's feet, slouched over in an unnatural pose. His body looked as though it had been pitched forward by the impact of an invisible truck, buttocks off the ground, legs splayed. On the cop's upper back, Duncan could make out the khaki of the uniform had been burned through and two semi-circles of livid brand marks stood on the caramel-colored flesh of the shoulder blade. Duncan willed himself to be motionless, under the absurd impression he could somehow remain unnoticed.

Ciru bit her lower lip, as though calculating a difficult sum in her head. "Now look what you made me do." She bent, and wiped the tip of the metal rod on the back of Hinga's shirt. Looking up at Duncan, she added, "Confused?"

Duncan wiped the back of his hand against his bloody mouth.

"In pain?" She stood, stepped over Hinga's body towards Duncan.

Duncan could see that the metallic rod in the woman's hand was not, as he had started to believe, a wand of some sort. It was an electrical cattle prodder. Duncan could not take his eyes off the prodder. The woman's plastic shod feet shuffled as she approached him.

"But this is your birthright. Confusion, suffering. Our collective birthright. You know this, Father. It is the product you peddle, is it not?" Her voice took on an enquiring, concerned tone. "It is also the product I peddle. I, like you, am initiated, although I work in less clinical conditions."

Duncan felt an acute desire not to be rude, as though he were in a conversation at a church coffeehouse, and so gave a blank nod by way of acknowledgment and encouragement. He willed himself to look away from the smoking prodder, at the woman's face.

Her grey-flecked eyes suggested a smile. Her greying hair was pulled back high and tight, a few errant strands falling over her cheekbones. A lean face on a wiry, boyish body. "But don't think for a moment that I am not as dangerous as Hinga." She glanced at Hinga's figure. "I am more so, because I now have nothing left to lose. People like him, like you Westerners, you Christians, have taken everything from me."

Duncan blinked, unsure if his situation had gotten better or worse.

She squatted near Duncan. "I come from a long line of healers, medicine women. And people like you, your missionaries, and your soldiers outlawed us, smashed our links to our own community, changed us from healers to conmen. Which is how I find myself here.' She gestured about her, the silent bylane, the unconscious policeman, these were exhibits to her argument.

She stood and cocked her head to one side, taking Duncan in. "On your feet please."

Duncan felt strangely compelled to obey. He began to stand. As he did so, Duncan had to consciously remind himself he was under no obligation to be sociable or polite to this woman beyond the extent to which politeness or sociability would up the odds of a non-violent outcome. Or help him get to Nice. Having had that revolver in his face had triggered something in Duncan, an internalization of the principle that time was short. And unpredictable. That love was the only form of courage that mattered.

He came to his feet, wobbling.

"Lean against the wall." The woman gestured generously at

the concrete and bougainvillea. "You will relax your diaphragm if you are leaning against it, and the return of normal breathing will relieve the shock."

Again, Duncan could not but succumb to the vaguely medical advice. He leaned over, resting his forearms against a bare patch of concrete beneath a cloudburst of mauve flowers, and pillowed his forehead on his forearms. The position felt comfortable, but there remained an underlying sensation of ambient menace.

"There, isn't that better?" asked Ciru.

Duncan repressed his eager urge to nod boyishly and said nothing. He felt her small hand, hard and skillful, cupping his shoulder blade and rotating in slow circles. He closed his eyes.

"Just close your eyes so you can shut out any further stimulation." Again, a pinprick of annoyance at the base of Duncan's mind at being so nakedly manipulated. But that flicker stood no chance against the circles on his back, now expanding. He allowed himself to be soothed.

She continued in her reasonable voice. "I don't agree with Hinga's philosophies. A dead white man is, simply, bad for business."

The back rubbing stopped, and Duncan took this as a cue to lean away from the wall, as though a transaction had been concluded between them. They faced each other, like opponents touching gloves in the middle of a ring. Standing no more than a meter apart, Duncan could see fine creases in the smooth sides of the woman's face, the creases seeming almost to merge with her greying hair.

"You think I look old and tired." The woman cocked her head to the side and crinkled her eyes. "Well, you're a little worse for wear yourself."

Duncan felt he had to speak. He had to stop pretending Nice wasn't out there, and there was simply nothing he could do to find her. To try and snap himself out of the delusion that this woman was a social acquaintance and that nothing much was at stake. But his head was still in torment.

All that came from his white-spittled mouth was, "Thank you."

"Do you remember my name? I introduced myself at the house before we began walking."

Duncan shook his head no. He was terrible with names, and, he thought somewhat defensively, he had been through a lot in the recent past.

The woman put out her hand, with some diffidence, as though trying on a foreign custom for size. The effect was disarming.

She said, "I am Ciru."

He had to push her, find out about Nice.

Steeling himself, Duncan said, "Ciru. Please. My friend, Nice. I must find her." Duncan felt a bone-deep exhaustion and leaned one hand against the wall for support.

Ciru's manner stiffened, but her nut-brown face remained unclouded. "You are now a tourist in a dangerous land. I can guide you, but your friend—" Here Ciru paused and looked briefly at Hinga splayed at her feet. She hitched her shawl over her left shoulder with an unseen hand and seemed in doubt as to how to continue. She looked at Duncan. "I shall take you to see your friend. But you must, what is that curious expression of yours, 'manage your expectations'."

"What does that mean?" Duncan tried to keep his voice even-keeled.

"We must hurry," Ciru replied. She turned to the unconscious cop, who now lay on his back, unseeing of the starred Nairobi night sky. She spoke over her shoulder at Duncan. "Here, help me tie him up."

"Wait. Just wait a second here. What are we — What are you doing to him?"

"It is already done. There is no turning back now with a man like this." A sadness tinged her voice, as she looked at the cop. "I've come very close to doing this before. Hurry, so we can go to your friend."

Ciru bent over the prone man, and cupped the policeman's left shoulder in her right hand, in what seemed to be an incongruous gesture of solidarity. Their faces were no more than ten centimeters apart. Then, in one motion of fantastical strength, Ciru pulled back her arm and flipped Hinga's body prone such that his face lay against the concrete street.

Duncan stayed perfectly still, impressed at her physicality, appalled by her determination.

Ciru produced from beneath her shawl a length of rough sisal-twine rope. She had begun to tie the policeman's hands behind his back when he seemed to stir. Wordlessly, instantly, Ciru dropped the rope and unsheathed the prodder from the small of her back. She then administered—that seemed the right word to Duncan as he watched—one tremendously powerful shock. Duncan noted, again with the same silent mix of horror and awe, that Ciru had chosen the exact spot of broken skin. The cop jerked back into his shock-induced slumber, spittle pooling by his broken lips.

The wound on his back was now fist-sized, the torn flesh ringed with weeping skin, itself encircled by the torn khaki. The smell was appalling.

Ciru picked up the rope and continued as though there

had been no interruption. "Some cats only see the light after they bleed a few pints," she hummed, then looked up at Duncan from the task. "Do you like Mobb Deep? My son says the 90s were the golden age of hip-hop lyrics. I like the beats mainly."

In his confusion, Duncan noted that Ciru had also managed to re-sheath the prodder. Once the cop was expertly hogtied, Ciru withdrew an orange box-cutter from her person. She held it underhand. It made clicking sounds. The tip of the box-cutter's exposed blade hovered over the base of the cop's skull.

Duncan's eyes widened.

Ciru spoke at him darkly, "And now, our offering to the goddess Kyiruri, mother of the darkness, wearer of a thousand shapes, drinker of blood and seawater."

Duncan blinked.

Ciru knelt beside the left shoulder of the man on the floor. She made a vertical incision through the khaki collar. Then, pinching the halved collar taut with her right hand, she followed the longitude of her initial incision with her blade, along the knots of the spinal column until the shirt was rent in half.

Duncan winced and regarded the warren from whence they had come for a second evasive maneuver. Considered shouldering open the door to the courtyard. When he heard a low hissing.

Ciru was laughing.

Laughing so hard she had dropped the box-cutter at her knees and was resting her forearms on the shoulder blades of the unconscious man, rocking back and forth in muted mirth. The prodder's mark on the policeman's back peered like a punctured eye, from between Ciru's forearms. Her shoulders shaking. Ciru's laugh issued from the gap between where she held her tongue against the roof of her mouth.

When this thunderclap of merriment had passed, Ciru wiped her eyes with the heel of her hands. Duncan watching her the while like a mute child.

"Oh, white people are as credulous as children, aren't you? I just wish you could have seen your face."

Duncan felt his ears grow hot.

"Now, Duncan, don't worry, I'm a healer not a witch doctor. There's no sacrifice. There's no mother of darkness or seawater drinking. Kyiruri is a neighbor of mine. This is not the heart of darkness. Just business. We need to get his shirt off."

Duncan touched his own wound at the back of his head.

Ciru continued. "We don't want everyone to know we are carrying a policeman. Do we?"

So they walked on through the dark alleyway, with the shirtless cop, now just a shirtless man, crucified upon their shoulders and swaying between them. They saw no one, heard nothing, as they paraded down the sullen byways of the slum. Only empty doorways, lurid signs shilling soft drinks, and meandering plastic bags.

The shirtless man gave off a sour sweaty smell. The tips of his parade boots scuffled against the concrete. Duncan was repelled by the fact that his own arm sometimes brushed against the angry wound on the man's back.

"But your face was priceless though." Ciru allowed herself to reflect on her joke, low hisses of laughter punctuating the huffing work of the carrying.

Duncan, bothered from exertion and pain, petulant from shame, asked, "Where are we going? When can I see my friend?"

"Don't worry, Theresa is probably fine," Ciru used Nice's passport name, so for a moment Duncan was confused as to whom she was referring. Ciru raised her eyebrows and pointed with her nose at the bare-torsoed man dangling between them. "We must take care of this first."

Ciru steered them towards a low unfinished building, which hung, like a broken marionette, from the profile of the crane standing above it.

6

SWAYING UNDER THE DEAD WEIGHT of the body, they made their way up the darkened gravel path to the construction site. Their progress was marked by the crunch of the coarse grit underfoot, the huffing of their exertions and the steady dragging of Hinga's boot-toes.

A hundred meters ahead, a light clicked on in a small askari shed. Ciru stopped them and called out, "Ni mimi." The light clicked off.

Turning to Duncan, Ciru said, "Wise men do not burden themselves with matters unrelated to them."

They reached a set of shallow concrete steps leading up to the incomplete structure. Without warning, Ciru stepped out from under the weight of the body. Hinga's body collapsed to the gravel with a crunch, almost dragging Duncan with it. Duncan, repulsed and exhausted, stepped back from the body, which lay cheek-down against the gravel. Ciru fumbled for something under her cloak and her hand emerged with a clink of keys. Her thin slippers swatting the stairs, she reached for the padlock threaded, like a pendant, onto a coarse chain through the rough circular holes of the tall wooden doors. When she had swung open the doors, Ciru turned back to Duncan with a half-smile. Duncan noted her hands were empty, although he had not seen her replace the keys. There was an efficiency to her movement, her words, her very being. A practicality bordering on ruthlessness.

"Almost there," Ciru spoke with encouragement, as if to a child on a field trip.

A damp smell wafted from the open doors.

Duncan and Ciru stooped to the gravel to take up the unconscious man again.

"After this you will take me to get Nice, yes?" Duncan asked, to reassure himself as to the terms of the bargain.

"Yes," panted Ciru as they trundled up the stairs, the cop's boots clipping the top of each step as they climbed. Duncan tried to satisfy himself with this.

Once inside the doorway, Ciru again let drop the cop. "Could you warn me before you do that?" asked Duncan sharply.

Ciru busied herself with threading the links of chain through the doors and locking them, the pendant this time facing the inside. In the few seconds before Ciru locked the doors, the smell had grown more insistent.

Leaving Duncan behind with Hinga, Ciru stepped forward into the gloom, the silhouettes of walls looming, giving no sense of space or layout. Duncan, uncertain, stayed with Hinga's body, with the reassuring certitude of the exit, locked as it was, a few paces behind him.

Ciru's voice, petulant, carried back from the dim corridor. "Hurry up."

Duncan felt an automatic stir of having disappointed Ciru, and he said, "Sorry, I wasn't sure whether—Should I leave the policeman here?"

"He's not going to drag himself. Keep up."

Duncan considered the unconscious man, his infant-like vulnerability. Hearing Ciru's footsteps receding into the dark, Duncan flipped Hinga over onto his back. Then, gripping the cop's right hand where it met the fine wrist, Duncan dragged the cop along the corridor, following Ciru's whispered footsteps over the sawdust-strewn floors.

"Careful here," came Ciru's voice. Duncan made out a ledge, a drop of about two feet in the concrete floor. As he crossed it, Duncan winced at the thudding of Hinga's body as it landed behind him.

They were now in a large open room, some sort of lobby area. At the rear, Ciru beckoned, as she parted a set of plastic curtains like a diver entering the water and disappeared from sight. Duncan followed, dragging Hinga as best as he could.

Through the hanging curtains, the gloom merged with the smell of clay and smoke. Duncan stood to ease the ache in his arms and lower back, and to allow his eyes to adjust. Sucking at the dank air of the chamber, Duncan could discern the outlines of a concrete mixer, its egg shape squat in the dark.

Ciru hissed. Duncan followed the sound with his eyes.

Ciru, sitting on a shadow, waved him to the far wall.

Obeying, Duncan took up his charge, this time by the boot heels, and made his lumbering way towards Ciru.

She was standing over a wooden trapdoor, on which rested an industrial-sized freezer. The trapdoor bore a ring of iron. Ciru gestured to Duncan with her chin and eyebrows, in the direction of the freezer. The gesture was subtle as a lizard's motion in the dimness.

"Please move the freezer." Ciru's voice carried from atop her shadowed perch, each word distinct, each tinged with impatience.

Duncan dropped the legs of the cop and shouldered the freezer. The appliance shuffled along the dusty floor.

Then Ciru bent to the trapdoor and tugged it open. The maw revealed nothing.

Duncan, resting his elbows on the freezer, said, "Do you have a lighter or some—"

But he was interrupted by what sounded like a tussle and stood peering transfixed over the expanse of the freezer. He heard Ciru exhale and then a thud, more of a sensation than sound, under his feet.

Ciru clicked on her phone, its white light irresistible and blinding. With his eyes screwed shut against it, Duncan walked to Ciru's side at the open trapdoor. He felt the hard contour of her shoulder blade and opened his eyes. The trapdoor gave onto ten or so deep wooden steps and a clay floor.

Upon which lay the sprawled cop. "You threw him down the stairs?"

Ciru shrugged and began descending. "He needs to wake up anyway," she said over her shoulder.

In the basement, Ciru knelt to prop her phone, its torch still blazing, against the last stair, the hard alien light projecting onto the room the air of an ancient crime scene being revisited with modern forensic techniques.

She did not speak. Taking Hinga by the neck and the belt, she swung him across the clay floor and, in one arcing motion, sat him doll-like with his back against the rough stone wall. Hinga's hands, still tied together lay limp on his lap beneath his tight-as-a-drum belly. His head hung over his bare and glistening chest.

Duncan, sitting on the stair above the phone, like the musing director of this montage, noted with regret the man's ruined boots and the gash in his forearm, now more scarlet than pink.

Ciru withdrew handcuffs from the cop's belt, which glinted in the fierce light. Taking up the bird-like hands, she clapped one handcuff over his right wrist, and clicked the other handcuff into an iron ring which lay embedded in the wall about six inches over Hinga's head. The fluidity of her motions, the familiarity with which she sought and found the iron ring in the wall—these suggested that this was not the first time this space had been used.

Ciru sat next to Duncan. "This is his office. Where I am usually his assistant in these matters. But not today." She reached for the phone and turned off the torch, plunging their world once more into the undisputed dark in which it seemed to belong. She jabbed at the keys of the phone with a bony forefinger.

"I need some motivation music for this next bit," Ciru muttered under her breath, perhaps not even realizing she had said it out loud.

The tinny phone speakers began to play a song which seemed familiar, even to Duncan, whose taste in music had ceased evolving at least a decade ago. A tinkling piano riff over a Fisher Price percussive arrangement.

Ciru was smiling, the phosphorescent outlines of her teeth, hanging in the dank dark. Ciru clicked the volume buttons up. The bassline strained the speakers.

She did not exactly dance. It was an almost imperceptible shake of a shoulder, a sinuous flowing from hip to neck, something that Duncan, sitting transfixed, knew his body could never do. Not to rhythm, not to rhyme. He watched her, a ghostly presence shimmering in the glow of the phone's light.

There came another sound from the darkness.

"Here? You brought me here?" came the growl of Hinga's voice from the gloom behind Ciru's performance.

Ciru, without turning or stopping, gave a ululation, which reverberated through the dark chamber.

"Release me. And turn that rubbish off," said the cop, his voice growing in composure and confidence.

Abruptly, Ciru took up the phone from Duncan's feet. She swung, and, in a low crouch, holding the phone outstretched, bathed the cop in the glacial flatness of the torchlight. He sat there, just as they had left him, naked to the waist and his arms cuffed above his head. But his eyes glowed fiercely, and his chin jutted forward as he spoke above the music.

"Ciru! Untie me before I lose my temper." Hinga's tone suggested a man holding a beast on a taut chain.

Ciru made no response, only holding her oddly martial stance and the unwavering light pouring forth from her hand. The music played on.

"Ciru," he shouted.

Still, she ignored him, as though using the moment to work herself up to a moment, to generate momentum for some violent ritual which was to come. Ciru turned and danced some more, the orbits of the torchlight touching off the room into kaleidoscopes of shattered light.

"Ciruuuu!"

Ciru gave Duncan a little curtsey.

She turned off the music, placing the phone, its torch still blazing, between Hinga's feet. Hinga grimaced against the proximity of the light and turned his face up, his eyes screwed shut.

The silence hung between them.

Ciru said, "Temper? Ah, Hinga, it is good to raise this. You are an angry man. Sloppy and arrogant. The whole slum wants your head." Ciru arrested her sentiment, which threatened to avalanche into tirade.

Duncan saw the outline of her back and shoulders rise, then slowly fall, before she spoke again.

"I have asked you many times before to calm down, to not beat the boys, to not double cross gangsters."

"Ciru, what are you talking about? Get me out of these handcuffs."

Ciru stepped nearer the circle of light, her feet almost touching the phone on the floor. "But you've got heart, Hinga. I'll give you that. You know, I know, we can never go back to working together."

She paused, shoved back his forehead. "You have no value to me, except for one piece of information. You know what I need to know."

Hinga kept his face upwards but unscrewed his eyes for a reptilian second, as if to examine the line of questioning more closely. He did not speak. Then he squinted shut his eyes again.

Ciru exhaled through her nose, then resumed the prosecution. "Were you involved in what happened to my boy and me in New York?"

Silence.

"I never wanted to go there, to raise my boy overseas. But he did, and I promised him we could start a new life there. So how did you get us deported, brought back to this place?" She spat. "How did you reach the American authorities?" hissed Ciru. She squatted over the torch, as if over firelight.

Undone by Hinga's intransigence, Ciru withdrew her prodder from her cloak. Holding it in her right hand, she stepped into the circle of light. Pressing the prodder against Hinga's knee, she forked the forefinger and second finger of her left hand.

These she pressed into Hinga's closed eyelids, crowbarring the unseen eyeballs. "Open your eyes. Just look at this mess."

Hinga's eyelids fluttered against Ciru's fingertips, like butterflies receiving ether.

Ciru said, "Pain is inevitable. Suffering is not." She squeezed the base of the prodder against the kneecap, unleashing the snap and fury of a localized electrical storm. The explosion of light faded into an echo which replayed against Duncan's retinas. The air grew cloying.

Ciru reached into Hinga's breast pocket and withdrew a black police beret. Then she picked up her phone and clicked off the torch. She strode, night vision apparently unperturbed, past Duncan up the stairs.

Duncan followed, unbidden and disoriented. Once upstairs, Ciru waved him over to the egg-shaped cement mixer. She brandished Hinga's enormous revolver at him. Duncan stupidly raised his hands over his head.

Ciru said, "Take his cap." Duncan so did. It was wet. "Put it on."

Duncan again obeyed. Ciru turned and walked towards the entrance.

"Are you going to leave him there?" called Duncan after her.

Ciru's voice floated back across the gloom. "Don't worry, he'll wake up soon enough. Rats love cartilage."

7

CIRU SNAPPED SHUT THE PADLOCK on the tall doors. Behind them, the flashlight in the askari hut clicked on, then off. They set off along the gravel path, Ciru setting a keen pace without ever breaking into a trot.

Duncan, though a full head taller, pulled the cap low and struggled to keep up. "We're going to get my friend, right?"

"We have to collect something from my place first." Seeing Duncan's face begin to sour, Ciru added with finality, "I need to get the key."

They walked with their backs to the broken building which held Hinga, through the indistinguishable alleyways. A gibbous moon showed high. Duncan's tongue was dry and swollen; he tried to recall the last time he had eaten.

Unlike on the way in, the slum seemed now to be rousing itself. A thumping music scudded over the squat huts. As they walked, shouts of unseen revelers threaded through the distant baseline.

The alleyway emerged onto a plaza in which the partygoers had draped brightly colored crepe over concrete and corrugated tin. Vertical flags emblazoned with golfing brands hung sullenly in one corner of the courtyard, as though they resented being at this party instead of a windswept fairway. The crowd of young men and women stood about, less dancing to the music than bathing in it. The gathering was in its dawning. The music was unfamiliar to Duncan, but he saw Ciru's buttocks squirm involuntarily from its proximity and sensuality.

The youth mostly ignored Ciru and Duncan, but one young man, bandoliered with bands of white plastic sachets from each shoulder to each hip bone, bounded up to them.

"Dyno-mite?" his voice straining over the music.

The sachets reminded Duncan of ketchup packets from McDonalds. Ciru shook her head on their behalf and replied, "Congratulations!"

The young punter gave a suit-yourself smile and danced backwards into the crowd to a rude wooden stall from which he dispensed the sachets in exchange for fistfuls of coins.

"Is that some sort of drug?" asked Duncan, as they proceeded across the square.

Ciru hitched up her shawl and smiled. "Homebrew, meets the taste and budget of our young people. Very potent. A local boy just got a recording contract. It's one of the only ways out of this place. Alive." She spat and wiped her mouth with the back of her wrist. "Come on, hurry."

The renewed sense of urgency buoyed Duncan's spirits. Nice would have enjoyed this party. She would have insisted on tasting the Dyno-mite. She might even have known the music. Once he got her back, he would talk to her about everything, about the possibility of rekindling what they had experienced that long-ago weekend. Why had it taken a kidnapping to make him realize these things?

Ciru tugged at his sleeve and they moved on—the gathering

taking notice neither of their arrival, nor their departure.

They came to another in a series of filth-strewn streets, and Ciru slowed outside a one-story wood-framed structure. A faded sign, lying along the dusty gravel, read: "Dr. Mikende Problem Solver. BY APPOINTMENT ONLY".

While Ciru unlocked the front door, Duncan looked up to the structure's roof, to the origin of the sound of weight being shifted on the tin. The grotesque outline of a marabou stork stood, erect and motionless. It stared into the middle distance in the direction from where Ciru and Duncan had come. The bird's grave posture, its tuxedoed appearance, and its immense size gave it the impression of an undertaker with hands clasped at its back, beset with financial woes. The creature gave off an odor of decay. It did not look at Duncan, who stood at the lintel of the entrance, not a meter below.

"You know why their heads have no feathers?" said Ciru. Duncan looked away from the creature and blinked at Ciru.

"So they can put their entire head inside dead animals."

Ciru smiled in admiration. "They are adapted to their lifestyle. I admire this very much. Come in, come in."

Dr. Mikende's visiting room was dominated by a rough-hewn table and a couple of plastic stackable chairs. The surface of the table was bare save for a yellow legal pad and an empty coffee tin in which lay ballpoint pens. A naked bulb hung from a wire, casting a warm yellow light.

Duncan entered and looked about uncertainly. Ciru asked "Tea?"

Duncan closed the wooden door against the chill.

In one corner of the room stood a small solar-powered jiko on which Ciru now placed an oversized battered kettle. Duncan took off the police beret, nodding, and fell into a plastic chair. The chair was too low for the table, and Duncan found himself looking up at Ciru as she prepared the tea. Without asking Duncan, she heaped three tablespoons of sugar into each cup and poured boiling water on the leaves. The smell of freshly brewed tea filled the space, and Duncan leaned back into the chair, anticipating the sweet milkiness of his tea.

Ciru stood over him, her outstretched hand holding the steaming cup. Her face was blank, the gesture one of efficient empathy.

"That's how it goes," said Ciru slowly, "first you wait for the water to get hot, then you wait for it to cool."

Duncan thought he understood but did not venture to reply. Silently, he took the cup and turned it, so he held the handle. Huddling his other hand around the hot cup, Duncan said, "Thank you, Dr. Mikende."

Ciru sat opposite. "Long night."

Duncan nodded into the steam of his cup.

"Look. Just drink your tea. I'll get the key to where your friend is staying, and we'll be off."

Duncan sipped his tea, vague dread rising within him.

Dread at what was yet to come.

"Now, I think you should know if you don't already. Your friend Theresa, the one you call Nice—she is mixed up in something bigger than just me." Ciru shook her head with distaste, "According to Hinga, she is spoken for."

Duncan put the cup on the table, the tea spilling over. "What does that mean? Why can't you just tell me how to get her out?"

Ciru gave a bitter laugh. "Oh, the Anglo-Saxon love of the bottom line. Very well. Hinga told me Theresa was working for Somalis. Somalis who paid Hinga to keep an eye on her, make sure she made it through immigration with the package she is carrying. He told me he saw her at the airport, let her through, sent his boys to pick her up."

Duncan's eyes widened. Nice had mentioned the creepy cop at the airport. It must have been Hinga.

Ciru allowed this to sink in. "Have you had any run-ins with any Somalis recently?"

Duncan watched the steam swirl above the tea, recalling the miraa-laden truck which had caused the accident, the face of the driver veiled by his keffiyeh. Nice removing her wig, the blood flowing over her lip from her nose, a black rivulet under the sodium lights of the highway. What had made Nice so desperate that she would be muling drugs from Somalia? What was it that she had been trying to tell him in the car? *You couldn't share anything. Not really.* She must have known she was putting him in danger as well by having him come to the airport and not telling him anything.

Ciru shrugged. "But who knows how much of what Hinga says is true. Anyway, I don't like to work with Somalis—too unpredictable, too violent. Bad business. And I certainly wouldn't betray them in a deal." She exhaled slowly and looked into her teacup, cupped between her small hands. "Hinga would, though. That's why he has to go. Anyway, the point is that while I can show you your friend tonight, we need to understand what Hinga has done. You understand?" Duncan thought, then said, "But why not? I can pay you."

This perked Ciru up. "And pay you shall, Father. But something like this needs to be carefully arranged. If the Somalis connect me to this, or to Hinga's disappearance…" Ciru broke off, contemplating the dark enormity of that scenario.

Duncan took a swallow of tea. "Well, what are your terms?

What do you want for the life of an innocent?"

Ciru stood. "Her innocence is debatable, and you need to start thinking about that. Let's walk and talk."

Three raps shook the front door.

For the first time, Duncan saw Ciru flustered. She pushed back her chair, crouched over the table. She put a forefinger to her mouth for Duncan's benefit and looked about the room with huge eyes. Another thwack at the door, rattling the faux crystal doorknob. Ciru, finger still affixed to her lips, motioned Duncan up and towards the rear of the room.

She gestured to another door, which Duncan hadn't noticed. Ciru opened it, standing at the jamb with her arm outstretched. Duncan went in, turned around to face Ciru, who proceeded to inch the door silently shut against him. He ventured to poke his fingers through the closing crack, only to have Ciru's furrowed brow appear briefly, and then the door hinged closed as he withdrew his fingers out of self- preservation.

A key turned in the door, and yet again that night, Duncan found himself trapped in darkness.

He still held his teacup. As his eyes adjusted, Duncan could make out a low, flat whitish surface. He backed away from it and stood against the door, then slid along its length until he was sitting on the floor with his back to the wall. Duncan set down the teacup and placed his hands palm-wise against the floor. Tiles, matchbox-sized. Duncan closed his eyes. His senses heightened.

He was in a bathroom and the white outline was a bathtub. He listened, eyes screwed shut for focus, at the voices behind the locked door. No obvious violence had so far broken out, which could be counted as a good thing.

The newly arrived person was possessed of a piercing female

voice. Clearly American, mid-western to Duncan's ear. "Sa-ree aah ayum a liddle layte." Upon hearing the accent, Duncan got to his knees and held his ear to the door. He knocked over his empty teacup, which clattered on the tile floor. Duncan knelt, his forehead flush against the door, holding his breath.

As if for his benefit, Duncan heard Ciru say, overloud, "Hakuna shida, I'm just having a cup of tea." Ciru seemed to play up the East African accent for her visitor's benefit, as if the exoticism was part of the service. This Ciru was a curious mix of charm and ruthlessness.

"Did you forget I was coming?" asked the American woman. Her voice inflected upwards at the end of each statement, as though she was conversing with a puppy.

Ciru belly laughed. "Honestly, I had. Even for me, an appointment this late is unusual. Did you come alone?"

"Oh yes. I left the driver and the car over at Bradley's Arcade and came the rest of the way on foot. I wore the shawl over my head like you said."

Duncan allowed himself to uncoil his body. His mind flooded with an edgeless solidarity with, and contempt for, this unseen compatriot. He imagined a freckled face veiled by impenetrable incuriosity, visualized her thick calves rising above pink running shoes and ankle socks.

"How is your daughter?" asked Ciru.

"No news from the doctors and their fancy scanners, we still don't know if she will ever talk again. It's just test after test, going back and forth to the States, thousands of dollars, and for nothing—there is just no clear diagnosis." The American woman sounded tired. "It's taking a toll on my marriage."

"And you followed my instructions?"

"Yes, oh yes," said the American woman. A pause, and

then she came clean. "Well, the hair of an albino? That was hard to get ahold of."

The conversation seemed to stall or else became inaudible.

Ciru spoke in a strident tone. "You must follow my instructions very carefully if you want your daughter to get better." She seemed to check herself, to weigh her tone with more care. "You came to see me. I'm a traditional healer, and I know that sounds strange to you. I also know that you must be desperate that your five-year-old daughter has suddenly stopped speaking." Another long pause. Ciru seemed to be measuring her tone. "I can try to arrange for the albino's hair." "Thank you, Dr. Mikende. We really want to help

Madison, or at least know what is wrong with her."

"We also need python fat, at least a cup of it. Don't look at me like that. Python fat. Or if you don't know how to render it, just bring me the python. Bring me the snake or its fat, so we can perform the ritual together. Are you clear on this?"

"Yes, oh yes. Where can I get the snake?"

Ciru gave her a throaty laugh. "Last I heard, the US embassy in Nairobi had a dedicated snake wrangler. Now, this is Nairobi, too much is for sale." The mirth wilted from Ciru's voice. "And have you got anything for me?"

"Oh well, I brought—"

The sound of a scuffle came through the bathroom door.

A thud, and then silence.

Ciru's voice was hard. "I don't want your money." Another thudding. "I told you before, you insult me by offering it to me over and over. What I want is information— why was I deported from New York? How can I get my boy back to the States?"

Duncan pursed his lips in the darkened bathroom. This was the same thing Ciru had asked Hinga. Duncan shuddered, thinking of the cop's plight.

"I'm so sorry I—"

Ciru interrupted, "Pick up your purse. Please. Did you get the information I asked of you?"

"Some of it. I mean, Tom asked around with his colleagues at the State Department, and they say the same as we already know—that you and your son were deported from New York because of some national security arrangement with Kenyan authorities. Very hush hush. INS received a tip from Kenyan national police that you and your boy were—"

Ciru interrupted icily. "Did you get the file? The actual documentation?"

"No, no I couldn't, we can't get our hands on that." "My boy was two months away from graduating. We did nothing wrong. Edmund blames me for what happened, for him not having a degree, for us living here. Like this. For everything—" Ciru's voice deflated.

"I'm sorry, look I'll dig some more, try and get a name or something."

Ciru's tone became conciliatory, thinking perhaps of the medium-term prospects of this relationship. "I'm sorry I get so upset, it's just, you should have seen my boy's face in that jail cell. He blamed me, said I had brought this upon us. He turned his back on me that night. Forever."

"Ah understand. Okay, I should go. I'll keep you posted." "Thanks." The front door creaked.

Ciru called, her tone maternal, "Remember—python fat."

8

DUNCAN KNELT, EAR TO THE DOOR, holding his breath. When the door opened without warning, he fell forward, his head landing at Ciru's feet.

She regarded him. "Didn't your mother teach you eavesdropping is bad manners?"

He picked himself up, said nothing.

Duncan noted a black plastic bag on the table, alongside Ciru's empty teacup with its bright red lettering, "The man (arrow pointing up) The legend (arrow pointing down)". French fries dusted with chili powder spilled from the bag onto the table. Duncan's stomach growled, and he looked at Ciru, uncertain of protocol.

She nodded at him. "Your fellow American left them here."

The fries were cold and greasy, but Duncan was grateful for them. Ciru also took a few, her jaw working sinuously.

Duncan wiped his hands on his trousers. "Listen, can we go now? Please. I've helped you kidnap a policeman and now swindle some mid-western lady. We've got to get Nice."

Still chewing, Ciru held up a forefinger and leaned against a plastic chair. She reached for the teacup and tipped it back, draining the sugary dregs. Through the remnants of her mouthful of chips, Ciru said, "Actually, I'm trying to help that lady. Sometimes you have to force the world to make sense. Isn't that what you do for a living also, Father?"

Duncan thought immediately of the Legishons and their unnecessarily dead son. He couldn't allow that to take up space right now. "Look, I don't care about any of that. Take me to see Nice right now."

Ciru examined her teacup, trying to decide whether what remained warranted further effort.

Duncan continued. "And what has your deportation from New York got to do with all this?"

Ciru looked at him over the chair, turning only her eyes. "Yes, we lived there, my boy and I." She returned her gaze to the teacup. She set it on the table, upside down. "Of course, as he likes to remind me, he is a man now. He won't even return my phone calls since we moved back to Kenya. Says people communicate through text messages these days. I need to find out if Hinga is behind this. To make some sort of sense of this. It's the only reason I haven't had him killed, till now."

Ciru hitched up her shawl, motioned Duncan to the front door.

Duncan shivered in the narrow alleyway as he watched Ciru lock her doors. Done, Ciru looked up at the figure of the stork and held her hands cupped upwards at waist height. Duncan thought he saw dim movement, a rippling of the air, fly up from her hands to the bird. The bird reared itself, thrusting forward its chest and outstretching its wings, which spanned the entire rooftop of Dr. Mikende's office.

All without sound.

Ciru turned with a smile and joined Duncan. Duncan struggled to keep pace. He hesitated to ask her to slow down or to himself break out of his speedy walk, as though that would shake some unspoken truce between them. More to distract Ciru than anything, Duncan asked, "Can I have my phone back, please?"

Ciru did not slow, or even appear to have heard the question. The sounds of the neighborhood party, churning steadily, carried in the cool still air.

Duncan, uncomfortable with the silence, insisted, "Do you have a lot of mzungu clients?"

"A few." She turned to face him, walking backwards. "You are perhaps surprised? That such people would come to me for help?"

Duncan hoped this was a rhetorical question, so made no response.

Ciru spoke as though her question had been answered. As though she did not have many friends. "Your colonizing religions had balls, I'll give them that—to actually advise people on how the afterlife would work. But now, you are removing all your taboos, trying to woo the public with your permissiveness." She narrowed her eyes at Duncan. "But what you have forgotten was how you came to power, by catering to people who need taboos. People need structure, they need reassurance when their child is ill."

A vision of Mr. Legishon's stretched earlobes flashed before Duncan. The Nokia phone dangling.

Ciru stopped walking and pointed a finger at Duncan. "I provide action in the face of desperation. It is a necessary service."

Duncan tried to speak but Ciru held up a hand. "But I was unable to provide for my boy in the States, unable to set him on a path different from mine, better than mine. I did not keep my word to him."

She began to walk again, slower now, but still a pace or two ahead of Duncan. Ciru kicked at a plastic bag which floated by in ghostly silence.

"This place," she said, inconclusively.

Duncan felt honor-bound both to try and cheer her so that she would remain on task and to steer the conversation to Nice. "But that woman back at your office, what was the information you needed? Maybe I could try to help in some way, in exchange for getting my friend released."

Ciru waved a hand at him. "I know the game. The likes of you don't have that kind of access. Stick to bringing me money." She turned into a dark bylane.

But in the darkness, Duncan could sense Ciru's desolation. There was also a tinge of shame in the hasty, clipped tones of her voice, at having had such a personal problem outed.

Ciru stopped outside a squat dark building, indistinguishable from the others lining the dingy lane. No sound now, the rapper's celebration party having been left behind. Ciru pulled a key from under her shawl. Duncan noticed it was a single key and not on a ring or bunched with others. It seemed a reckless way to carry a key, especially one that held with it the promise of Nice's safety. There seemed no limit to what Ciru was liable to produce from within the folds of her shawl.

Ciru lifted the key to the padlock on the iron grills of the door, on which was lettered, in yellow-green paint, "Kiki Kinyozi". Then she paused, dropping her hand. She turned to face Duncan.

"What?" said Duncan. "What is it now?" He was unable to prevent his impatience from seeping into his voice. They were so close to Nice.

"This," Ciru's voice was weary but firm, "this place." She stopped. She motioned at the door. "This sort of thing is," again the pause and an arc of her hand, "is new to you. You are from another world, I know because I have tasted your world. This is a serious place. Don't act like a tourist here. Adapt yourself to circumstances—like a marabou."

As though this constituted a comprehensive explanation, she turned once more to the padlock. To Duncan, it seemed a baffling, indeed irritating, digression, yet more theatre to be added to Ciru's eccentricities. He said nothing and was even vaguely relieved to just be getting on with it.

The iron grill swung open towards them, and, with her fingertips, Ciru pushed the wood-paneled door of Kiki Kinyozi in. Ciru disappeared into the darkness, stepping around the door, and then Duncan heard the stutter of tube lights. Instinctively, he closed his eyes.

When he re-opened them, Kiki Kinyozi was bathed in the harsh over-light of tube lights. Duncan stepped over the doorframe. Black and white tiles checkered the floor. The walls were mirrored, from floor to ceiling.

Ciru walked to the last of a row of black leatherette barber chairs. She beckoned Duncan over.

He joined her.

Ciru knelt. Duncan saw this chair was several inches higher than the rest. Its aluminum base was affixed to a thick rectangular piece of wood. This wooden sub-base was painted to match the black and white checkering of the floor tiles.

Ciru bent and unthreaded the heavy screws at the corner of the wood base. When she had done this to her satisfaction to three of the screws, she rotated the chair, wooden base and all, in Duncan's direction.

Duncan stepped closer. He looked into the hole the barber chair had been obscuring. A column of iron handles descended into the dark. Duncan looked at Ciru, who faux curtsied in extravagant invitation.

"After you," she said.

He began to ask for Ciru's phone so he could use its torch—or better yet, his own damn phone back. But he just sighed and started to descend. Ciru's plastic-shod feet slapped against the handles above him, so he forced himself downward, focusing on a step at a time. Dank air rose to meet them.

Duncan was so focused on keeping his fear contained, that he lost his balance as the ground arrived without warning underfoot. He fell away from the umbilici of the metal handles, into the darkness.

Ciru, still perched several feet above in the vertical tunnel, gave a hard laugh, which echoed in the cavern. Her mirthless voice was tinged with concern. "I wouldn't lie there if I were you."

Beyond the pain and stench, Duncan grew aware of a lowing from the dark.

9

"YOU'D BETTER STAND UP," said Ciru, voice low and urgent. Her silhouette hovered above Duncan.

Duncan didn't want his back turned to the lowing, and so stood quickly, wincing from a new pain in his ankle. The back of his shirt and trousers were wet from where he had fallen. As Duncan's eyes adjusted to the twitchy light of Ciru's phone's torch, he could see her small features twitch in concentration as she read the shifting contours of the mustiness.

"Come on," said Ciru, clicking off the torch, without looking at Duncan. With her eyes still fixed on the far end of the room, now curtained in gloom, Ciru reached out and took Duncan's hand, their fingers interlocking. There was something maternal about her, something out of line with where they were, where she had led them. Duncan was conscious of the clamminess of his own hand, against Ciru's dry, clean one. Duncan allowed himself the luxury of squeezing it in the dark, and the fear in his belly shrank a little.

Ciru led him forward. Duncan began to ask a question, but she quieted him with a look. He tried to consciously slow his breathing and took in the smells. A vivid slashing of stale urine, invisibly pooled on the dark floor, caused him to clench his hand in Ciru's and she gave an efficient squeeze of acknowledgment back. They were almost upon the source of the lowing, Duncan's consciousness trained on it, as though it was the final flourish of some unseen ritual.

Duncan did not see what seemed to be a log underfoot and caught his toe on it. The lowing stopped. Duncan stumbled and might have fallen had Ciru not steadied him. She let go of his hand and reached for her phone under her shawl, clicked on the torch. The LED gave a radius of illumination of a couple of paces. Ciru handed the phone to Duncan, who stood behind her holding it with his arm outstretched.

In the contourless LED light, Ciru bent to the thing upon which Duncan had stumbled and pulled it backwards, as though to flip it over. Duncan's discomfort made him jerk the torchlight.

"Steady," Ciru's low voice was a slim tether of reason, and Duncan clung to it.

The shapeless thing flipped over. On its underside, it bore the pale features of a young woman, cheekbones and eyebrows dramatically shadowed by the torchlight. Duncan dropped the torch. The vision vanished as the phone clattered to the floor.

"For God's sake, man," said Ciru.

Duncan was too stunned to apologize, to even move. What was this place? He must have driven past this building a hundred times. What horrors lay just beneath his feet?

Ciru retrieved the phone, knelt and shone its clinical light into the young woman's face. Light-skinned, though the bleaching effect of the torchlight made it hard to be sure. She seemed a wax statue, perfect to the smallest detail, down to the blackheads on her nose. Ciru brought her left hand to the woman's nose and placed the fingers under the nostril. Then she gave a sudden flick at the tip of the nose, just a blurred movement in the torchlight. The woman's eyelids flickered under the cold light, as though her dreams had been rippled.

Ciru looked back at Duncan, "Is this your friend?" No, Duncan shook his head. No, this was not Nice.

"Shame," said Ciru, standing and smoothing her shawl, "at least this one is alive." She took back the phone, clicked off the torch.

They moved on, Duncan following as though he were being towed through the dimness. His mind unable to process his surroundings. He wanted to scream, to run. But where? To whom? From whom?

Ciru stopped and Duncan almost walked into her. They had reached a far wall of rough concrete. Duncan looked over his shoulder at the dark from whence they had come. Impossible to gauge distance.

Ciru said, "Step back." Her voice bore a restrained urgency to it. Duncan felt something brush against his shoes. He looked down. Two caramel-hued hands, affixed to nobody, were resting in silent supplication on the tongue and laces of his trainers. The nails on the hands were painted scarlet, and on the nails of the forefinger and index finger of the right hand, the paint was chipped away to the cuticle. Duncan clenched his face. But did not move. Could not move. Where the hell was Nice?

He looked at Ciru.

She turned upwards her palms and arched her eyebrows. He slowly pulled back his right shoe, scraping its forefoot against the grainy clay floor. The hand fell limply away, but its partner still rested on the left shoe. Duncan heard Ciru's nasal exhalation of frustration. He pulled away his other shoe, again without protest from the phantom hand.

Duncan watched Ciru make her way along the wall to the far corner of the room. She lit the torch once more and walked with her right hand outstretched, fingertips skimming the wall. The lowing began anew and, this time, Duncan felt annoyance leavening his fear.

Could the poor woman not just shut up? It was astonishing, how quickly he was adjusting to this place.

"Over here," Ciru called.

Duncan could make her out. He walked away from the edge of the wall, each step a calculation. With breath held, he tiptoed past prone outlines on the floor, as though trying not to disturb passengers asleep on a plane.

Ciru was kneeling over a figure. It was that of a woman.

In the torchlight, her skin gleamed.

"Your friend, she's Indian, no?" Ciru looked up at Duncan from her squat.

Duncan hurried towards what appeared to be a voodoo doll version of a woman, head and body shrunken, leaving her eyes and teeth outsized. Her skull lay vulnerable as an egg against the floor, the arctic light making great pools of darkness under her eyelids. A scarlet gash above her left eyebrow had swollen her eye shut.

Duncan clenched his jaw, knelt, oblivious of everything else.

"Well, is it her?" The impatience in Ciru's voice snapped Duncan back.

"No," he whispered. The blood thudding in his ears carried fear and self-preservation.

Ciru snatched the phone from Duncan's hand. She pointed it at the room, as if to ascertain who else might be hiding in its corners.

"I will walk around and search for your friend. You stay here." Ciru enunciated carefully, as though this information could upset Duncan.

"I don't want to—"Duncan looked up at Ciru, willing himself to stand, to walk with her, to be able to hold her hand.

But she was already away, the gloom swallowing the torchlight, the slap-slap of her slippers receding.

Duncan tasted the bile in the back of his throat. His head fuzzy. He sighed, then lay next to the sleeping woman on the crusty floor. The woman who was not Nice. As their shoulders brushed, she gave a low moan, the only indication that she was still alive. Duncan recoiled from the contact, but then was still. He closed his eyes because the darkness was just as complete.

Time became, in the dark, an uncertain, jittery thing.

When Ciru returned, she spoke in a low voice. "She is not here. Your friend, Nice."

Each word delivered in a minimalist monotone, as though calculated to conserve the limited bandwidth of Duncan's cognition.

Duncan nodded dumbly. Then where was she? His eyes muddled with anxiety.

Ciru lowered her face, as if in disappointment. "There are several such safe houses in this slum. I will search the others." Panic rose in Duncan's throat. "I will come with you, we will—"

But Ciru turned and strode into the gloom from whence she and Duncan had entered.

Duncan shuffled after her, desperately following the torchlight. "Wait, Ciru, I can—"

She clicked off the torchlight.

Duncan suddenly aware of the vastness of the cavern. Its location a blank, shorn of any frame of reference. That Ciru could simply leave him in here as well, that no one would know where to even look for him. "Please, Ciru."

Silence.

"You begin to understand, Duncan, how vulnerable you are here."

"Yes. Yes, I do."

She turned the torch back on, began up the metal stairwell. "Come up. Let's talk in the fresh air."

Outside, the alley seemed to Duncan to be an alpine meadow, each lungful of cool air bringing a measure of clarity, of calm. He placed his hands on his knees and could see his breath.

Ciru turned to face him and rubbed her thumb back and forth over her forefinger.

Duncan took in the gesture for cash. The timber and corrugated iron sheeting creaked overhead. Korogo. Duncan looked up to see a marabou stork, hulking and motionless, on the roof of the building. The scrofula pocking its face looked contagious. This stork also had white-spattered pipe-cleaner legs, knotted black knees.

Had the same bird followed them from Ciru's office?

Its talons hooked over the edge of the corrugated iron roofing of Kiki Kinyozi. From within its mottled red face, behind the razor-sharp gray-bone of its beak, the bird's black eyes regarded Duncan evenly.

Duncan took a step back, away from the bird and the building.

Ciru, her arms akimbo under her shawl, raised her eyebrows and lifted her chin to the stork, which in response opened its long beak. From six feet away, Duncan received the odor of sun-warmed garbage.

She turned to Duncan and spoke with bullet-pointed efficiency. "Now, here is what we will do. You will go and get $30,000 from your office—"

"What about Nice? Just hang on—" He held his palms up to his chest. "I'm a servant of the Ministry. I don't have that kind of money. You're going to have to—"

"No. You are going to have to. Adjust to this new reality. I know this is hard for you. Being a grown-up. Having people rely on you. Not being able to use magic words to get out of situations." She gestured at the air around her head and continued. "Your friend's life is in your hands. I will get the word out to Toogood the Somali, but only after the cop situation is fixed. You will do your part if you want her to live, to see her again."

Duncan, unable to grasp the demand made by Ciru, thought back to Nice, and said softly, "I will try."

Ciru's lip curled. "You have become a Kenyan, with your 'trying'. Don't try. Just get the money. Thirty K US, tomorrow."

As if to emphasize the finality of this, the stork, stocky as a dwarf, yawned again.

With the sweet rot of the marabou's breath wafting over him, Duncan tried to think through the various options for getting this money. It was, to Duncan, a staggering sum, almost exactly the same as his student debt. A debt which he was projected to fully repay in his fifty-second year.

"That's why we have children. We all need something to live for." There was a sadness in Ciru's voice. She looked at her feet. "That's why we need to help her. That's why we need to ask the cop where he has hidden her."

"The cop, your partner—will he tell us?"

Ciru pursed her lips. "Ah yes, Hinga. But we must be very

persuasive. Come, let us get him. Then you must go and get my money."

The bird took improbable and silent flight, leaving a wake of foul air in the alleyway where they stood.

Ciru tracked its silhouette against the starlit night.

10

HINGA'S HOWLS COULD BE HEARD from outside the empty building.

Ciru gave a satisfied smile. "Such a drama queen."

Although Duncan had no loyalty to the cop, the sheer abandon of the screams evoked something close to empathy. These were the sobs of a man who, just this morning, had dressed, polished his boots, and drunk his tea, with the calm sense that dinner time would see him back in his creased pajamas.

The screams reverberated through the empty building. Duncan could discern no pattern to their frequency or intensity. His nerves grew jangled.

Torch in hand, Ciru tugged open the trapdoor. Duncan followed her down, steadying himself against the bare brick wall. He was prepared to go to great lengths to make the screaming stop.

When he saw Hinga in the flickering torchlight, Duncan was overcome with pity and disgust. The cop lay bare-torsoed and manacled, his back against the wall. Hinga's eyes stood saucer-like in his head, possessed of manic rage. Spittle bearded his mouth and chin. When he saw Ciru, Hinga struggled with his manacles, which clinked merrily at the effort.

Ciru giggled.

The cop was barely recognizable as the smooth-talking operator with the polished brass belt buckle and the glinting epaulets. In his place lay a broken man. It occurred to Duncan that so much of what was referred to as dignity was just a matter of clothing. He had read somewhere that this was why Zen masters draped themselves in elaborate robes when testing pupils—to dare them to look past the forbidding appearance, to the unscripted reality beyond.

Ciru, with a smile, stepped towards Hinga. "You know, Hinga, that anger is just impotence." Without flinching, she bent and wiped the foam from Hinga's chin. He gave another howl, this one unadulterated hate. Incapable of human speech. Ciru, as if deciphering the cries, responded, "Now, now."

She patted his gleaming head. "Let's have a look at you."

She shone the torch at Hinga's knee. Scorched black cloth circled the knee of the khaki trousers. Beyond this ring, the cloth grew crimson. Hinga yanked his head away from the wound, his face folded and his eyes shut tight.

"You must look. We must see. How else can things improve?" asked Ciru.

Duncan hesitated, then whispered to Ciru, "Ask him. About Nice? Where is—"

She whipped around to face him, her eyes wide with a madness, her body poised for violence. Greater agendas playing out.

Duncan shrank back into the shadows.

Ciru turned back to her prisoner. She sucked air between gritted teeth, her face creasing in an expression of disgust. "What happened? Could you not shake them off? There must have been a dozen fat rats at work here? Here, take a look."

With these words Ciru arched her eyebrows as if inviting a second opinion from Duncan, or Hinga himself. Duncan demurred. Hinga arched his back in exquisite frustration, his manacles clinking.

Ciru's tone soured. She turned on Hinga as though repelled by the spectacle. "Just tell me what I need to know. Why did those police round me and my boy up in New York?" Spit flew from her mouth, droplets crystalline against the torchlight. "I kept my nose clean in America. I was starting fresh, working hard, so I know something followed me from the slum. Just tell me."

She stepped on Hinga's knee, standing clear off the ground. Hinga groaned, his eyes screwed shut. Sweat stood on his face and neck. His chest rose and fell in shallow swells. Her forefoot resting against Hinga's wound, hands against the slimy wall for balance, Ciru twisted her torso. "Tell me you did it."

Hinga moaned. His jaw worked, as though chewing on the pain. Ciru turned her foot against the open wound, this time holding onto the chains which manacled Hinga to the wall. She did not speak. She seemed to be holding her breath in a let's-get-this-over-with way, the way one does in a dirty washroom.

Hinga opened his eyes, sclera flashing against his pinched, glistening face. He jerked back, waving her away. "Mjinga. Fuck. Get off, yes. Yes." He gagged, but nothing would come. "I paid someone in immigration."

Ciru looked puzzled. Then she tilted back her head and gave a belly laugh, the torchlight shivering. Ciru asked with frankness, "Really? I had only my suspicions to go on so far. Oh Hinga—"

She stepped off Hinga's kneecap. Hinga's body slumped as though his spinal column had been liquefied. Duncan cringed.

This woman, would she really take him to Nice?

"You are a master liar, truly one of the best I have ever met. How did you do it?"

Ciru sat cross-legged, in front of Hinga. She placed the torch in Hinga's lap, the underlight giving him a gaunt, ruined look. Ciru sat there girlishly for a moment, as though waiting for Hinga to play his turn at a board game. Hinga's head hung against his chest.

Taking his chin in her hands, she asked, "So, doesn't it feel good? Secrets are such toxic things. Now you are free." Blood dribbled from Hinga's mouth.

Ciru stood and began to speak in rapid-fire Swahili. She took back the phone and began to untie Hinga's manacles. Once both of Hinga's hands were free, Ciru turned to Duncan. "Come over here and help."

Duncan came warily over, unsure of the task at hand. "Did he tell you where Nice is stashed?"

Ciru pointed at Hinga, still as a corpse with his hands in his lap, and said, "Up we go." Duncan lifted the cop with a jerk, careful to avert his gaze from the weeping mess that had been Hinga's knee. Once Duncan had Hinga upright and supported with an arm around the waist, Ciru clicked off the torch.

They started up the stairs.

From the darkness behind Duncan, Ciru said, "Hinga, I just had to know before I killed you." Duncan's shuffling stopped and Ciru bumped into the two men. She cackled. "I'm joking, I'm joking. You are so serious, Father." Her laughter echoed up the stairwell.

Why had she turned off the torch?

By the time they reached the front door outside the security guard's box, Duncan was soaked in sweat. The gash in his head hummed. Hinga was heavy and silent as a carcass. Duncan panted into the night air while Ciru locked the door. She rubbed her hands together to ward off the chill air.

"So, Father, we have a deal, you and I?"

He nodded and shifted Hinga's weight, uncertain whether to drop him. Duncan had no idea how to get the money together but felt certain that if he could only get away from this woman, from this God-forsaken place, he could at least think. Find a way to get Nice out of here.

Ciru set off along the broken path. She whistled tunelessly. It was the song the cop had been playing on his phone, the one about the absentee landlord. Duncan sighed and followed, the unconscious cop getting heavier by the second. "Ciru, do you know where Nice is?"

But Ciru needed more convincing. She turned to face Duncan, walking backwards as she spoke. "And you won't pull any crazy Anglo-Saxon stunts on me?"

Taking in Duncan's blank panting face, she added, "You know, go back on your word. Make me sign a treaty in a language I don't read. Give me a blanket with smallpox. Sell me seeds that don't reproduce. Establish a 'trading post' at the mouth of the river."

She made air quotes with her fingers around "trading post." Again, Duncan nodded. This woman, this crazy witch. Ciru seemed satisfied with his answer and turned back to continue leading their march.

Where were they even going? To Ciru's office?

Duncan was too exhausted to ask, or care. It took all his consciousness to place one foot after another.

Before long, they heard once more the booming bass lines of the ghetto party. Judging by the volume of the music, and the ebb and glow of the lights, the party seemed to have gathered steam. Ciru, seemingly unaffected by all that she had seen and done this night, squirmed and danced as they came onto the square they had seen earlier.

The scene was transformed. Everywhere people ate, drank, danced, fought, kissed, argued, groped, and joked. The makeshift bar was overrun, five, ten, people deep at its rough counter. And the music. The bass reverberated up their forearms and down their spines, sound and sensation merging. The crowd was amped, eyes bulging, jaws grinding, bloodstream pumping Dynamite.

Bright-eyed, Ciru came to help Duncan. "Come, let's do this together." She placed her shoulder under Hinga's arm. Finally, thought Duncan. Loud music had never been Duncan's thing, and now it cleaved the gash in his head. People brushed past him, not seeming to notice him, or otherwise caring that he was a white man carrying an unconscious shirtless man.

Ciru began to grumble under her breath.

But Duncan realized that Ciru was muttering to Hinga, now running her thumb along his skull, leaving a fine white line, like chalk. The words themselves indistinct, but the tone equal parts recitation and low, fierce recrimination.

Then Ciru was shouting into the crowd, her head and throat tilted back. "Bandi! Thief! Help!"

Hinga raised his head from his chest. His lips moved, but the words were swallowed by the noise of the crowd.

Duncan looked around behind Ciru to see who might have tried such behavior on a middle-aged woman walking abreast of two men. He could see no one who had targeted Ciru.

Yet, again she shouted, "Rape! Save me!" The people nearest to them began to stir, to interrupt their conversations, to cease their gyrations. The glazed eyes of partygoers took the trio in, as though seeing them for the first time, like an image hidden in a painting. The veil of their chemical stimulation parting to allow for this vision.

What was this crazy woman on about?

"What are you doing?" Duncan hissed at Ciru from the corner of his mouth.

She ignored him, redoubling her shouts. "Thief! Mgondi!"

The group of partiers closest to Ciru had switched off from the party now. A hatchet-faced man, shirtless and sinewy, except for a big belly taut as a drum, spoke, as though breaking a spell. "What is it, mama?"

Ciru turned from Hinga, leaving him to be supported by Duncan alone. As Duncan was turning towards her, Ciru kicked Hinga in the small of his back.

Hinga spun into the crowd.

Ciru continued to whip the crowd into a frenzy, her arms raised as though she was leading an orchestra. "Help me, brothers. Stop the thief!"

The party burst its skin like an overripe fruit. It was a relief for the partygoers to have something tangible upon which to vent themselves, the uncaring society beyond their walls having sent something for them to feast upon. Hinga was carried aloft onto the shoulders of the mob.

A dreadlocked man swung a whiskey bottle onto Hinga's temple, the amber glass splintering and pinwheeling against the sodium lights. This act stripped Hinga of his status as a human; he was a flesh puppet to be torn apart by the rioting crowd.

Duncan's last glimpse of Hinga was of the cop's wounded leg, which Hinga was holding straight up, trying to protect it.

Then the leg, and its owner, were gone, swallowed by the swarm.

A woman teetering in hot pink platform shoes emerged from the crush, holding aloft Hinga's belt, its buckle twinkling like the booty of war it was. Her T-shirt read "This girl is a genius" under a picture of two hands, their thumbs cocked back in self-referential praise.

The human mass which had swallowed Hinga whole began a bleary chanting, "Tear him up. Tear him up. Tear him up." Music, merriment, mayhem.

Ciru pulled Duncan's head near and stage-whispered into his ear, "Korogocho crowdsourcing." She joined the chant, pumping her fists. "Tear him up!"

Although he had heard her, Duncan asked, "What?"

Ciru just patted his shoulder blade, as if encouraging a floundering child with a sum.

A fat man rushed towards the fray with a red plastic jerry can of petrol.

Ciru, her eyes serene, even sated, tugged at Duncan's arm. "We'd better go now. They're getting post-erection on him."

When Duncan's face indicated he had caught her pun, she laughed on their collective behalf.

11

IT WAS MATERNAL. The way Ciru tucked the money into Duncan's breast pocket. Her other hand was on his shoulder, her thumb lying alongside his clavicle in a manner both protective and proprietary. Streaks of sunrise stretched across the fading night sky. They were surrounded by commuters, men and women dressed in business casual attire. They stood in a ragged queue at a matatu stop near Ciru's office.

Ciru patted the money in Duncan's breast pocket. "Adidas."

Duncan blinked, uncomprehending. A woman with a straw basket on her head gawked, trying to size up the relationship between Duncan and Ciru.

As though to a difficult child, Ciru said, "Three stripes. Three hundred shillings. To get you home." Then, leaning in close, her lips touching his ear, Ciru whispered, "Your friend's life depends on this."

Duncan nodded.

The quick dawn now broke in earnest over the slum, its purpled clouds unsullied by the night's events. Weaverbirds tittered in the lone acacia tree above the bus stop. The second cup of sweet tea Ciru had given Duncan and the basic ablutions he had performed in her washroom, had steadied him.

91

His head still swam though, and he felt as though he were watching the opening scenes of a play, one in which he himself was an invisible observer. To Duncan's left, a man in dusty slacks stood lopsidedly, holding a leather briefcase, shifting his weight and staring into the middle distance. Opposite Duncan, a puffy-faced woman held a newspaper at arms' length as though trying to find a hidden pattern in the words and columns.

A minivan screeched into the stop, sending a ripple of nervous energy through the waiting throng. The matatu's door slid open with a wrenching sound of metal on metal, and a rodent-faced tout stepped down to face the waiting passengers. There followed an eyes-averted jockeying to the open door of the matatu, which the red-eyed tout guarded, thin forearms folded across his shirt. He regarded the assembled crowd with some hauteur. The tout's t-shirt bore on it a red skull and crossbones. Across the windshield of the minivan, emblazoned in white lettering, were the words "Hitler SACCO".

Duncan, who had never ridden a matatu unaccompanied, queued until he was in front of the tout. Duncan sensed that admission required something more than money, but could not make out what. The tout held out a hand. The nail on the man's pinkie was two inches long. The rest of the nails were neatly trimmed, though the cuticles were bloodied ribbons.

"Twende twende," came the tout's reedy voice, harsh with a time-is-money impatience. Duncan fumbled at the money in his pocket, the money Ciru had given him a moment ago. As Duncan began to count it, the tout snatched it as though disgusted by Duncan's sheer incompetence. Duncan's scalp prickled with irritation and exhaustion.

As he shuffled aboard, it brought to Duncan's mind a long-ago breakfast at a rustic-chic bagel place near the New

England seminary, when he had just started getting involved in the marijuana business. Duncan, new to the rigors of daily pot-smoking, was consulting the fold-out paper menu he had taken from a counter, entirely in his own world. Feeling observed, Duncan had looked up from the menu. In the faces around him, patrons and staff alike, a naked irritation at the sheer bad form of a man taking up that much time and space. The middle-aged Latina woman, her apron bearing blood-smeared handprints, had wordlessly snatched the menu from him, gesturing at the board hanging above the counter on which the menu was reproduced in an alarmist font. Just as wordlessly, Duncan had turned and left, eating his breakfast at the window-side table of a nearby McDonald's, his pale fingers trembling with rage as they unwrapped the delicate paper in which his sandwich was served.

Duncan felt even more out of place as he was ushered to the back of the matatu, where he was jammed between the lady with the newspaper and another lady carrying what looked and sounded like a duffel bag full of chickens. She placed the bag on Duncan's lap, its canvas form alive with clucking and wriggling, and gave him a thin smile of apology, as though this was an unavoidable unpleasantness between neighbors.

Duncan looked out of the window.

Ciru still stood there, smiling as though sending her boy off to summer camp. Disarmed, and piloted by his reflexive desire to please, Duncan waved. Self-revulsion and exhaustion flooded him. If he could just get away from her, get some space to think. He closed his eyes and rested his head against the solid shoulder of the chicken lady—surely she owed him this much. She did not seem to notice as the tout slapped the roof of the van with his open hand, calling out for just one more passenger, "Mmoja twende!"

The minivan coughed into life.

Duncan awoke with the chicken lady poking him in the ribs with a yellow pencil. He started, and the woman laughed, an easy open laugh. Her big square teeth flashed in the early sunlight as she tilted her head, enjoying the moment. She pointed with the pencil beyond the streaky window of the matatu. Disoriented, Duncan followed the pencil's worn pink eraser tip, then beyond to the dusty sign for the Somali embassy whizzing by. Duncan exulted in the knowledge that, for the first time in a long time, he knew where he was—not more than half an hour away from the Church of the Earth.

He had to get off this vehicle before he lost his bearings again. The very thought panicked him. He stood, banging his head against the low ceiling, and spilling the duffel bag full of chickens to the crowded floor.

"Ay! Wewe!" exclaimed the woman. She reached for the bag and brought it up to her lap, cradling it and cooing at it in exaggeratedly hurt tones. Her face creasing with joy, she unzipped the duffel bag and thrust in her forearm up to her elbows, caressing the unseen creatures.

She did not look up as Duncan shouldered his way, stooped and harried, towards the tout's seat. The tout looked up at him with insouciance. Swaying in the aisle, Duncan explained that he needed to stop. A Kenyan usage came unbidden to him: "I must alight."

The tout pointed ahead, through the "Hitler SACCO" lettering of the windshield of the matatu.

Duncan bent to follow the tout's instruction and saw beyond the clotting traffic a faded colonial building which he recognized as simply "The Mall". There was a sports shop in the basement of the Mall where Duncan bought single tennis balls, fuzzy and sweet-smelling. Not having the energy to argue with the tout, Duncan squatted in the aisle. Through the dust-streaked window, Duncan saw a Church Outreach van, in its cheerful red and white livery, drive by on the other side of the road. He held his palm against the glass, in silent communion with the passing vehicle and the life it represented. It was also the path to Nice.

When the van shuddered to a halt outside The Mall, Duncan, along with every other paying passenger, alighted. It was chilly. Duncan glanced at the sun and estimated it was just after 6 a.m. Instinctively, he patted his pockets for phone and wallet. Without these, Duncan felt naked and unnerved in the jostling stream of dismounting people. He stood outside the minivan and watched his fellow passengers disperse, each with a place to be, a thing to do. Duncan took a deep breath and began to jog back to the Ministry.

A dusty hour later, his head throbbing, Duncan stood outside the rust-colored gates of the Church compound. Duncan looked at the heavy brass lock fastening the pedestrian entrance cut into the metal gate. He had bought it a couple of years ago in the States on home leave. Again, he patted his front pocket for the key.

Alarmed and annoyed, he rapped the sheet metal of the gate with his knuckles. There was no response, and Duncan felt the embers of a frantic rage. He struck the metal of the gate again, this time with the open palm of his right hand. The clang was satisfying, but still no one came to open the gate. Then, gripping two of the spikes which sprouted from the lip of the gate, he hoisted himself up.

Looking over the gate, Duncan saw Jacob, the askari, fast asleep not ten paces from the gate. Jacob's deck chair sat in a puddle of sun. The askari's limbs were scattered in the slumber of a person who does manual labor for a living. His stretched ear lobes fell to his shoulders.

Duncan shouted, "Ay. Jacob!"

The askari's head stirred, as though a distant sound had reached him. Jacob's glazed eyes focused, and he came on unsteady legs to the gate. At Duncan's head above the gate, Jacob enquired, without obvious hurry in his voice or manner, "Late night, boss?"

Duncan did not say thank you, brushing past the slow-eyed askari through the open gate. When Duncan reached his room, at the very back of the crumbling colonial mansion, he found this door also locked. Duncan did not check for his phantom keys. Instead, he shouldered the door open, the jamb splintering.

Once inside, he sank to the floor and sat cross-legged.

He thought of Nice and blinked away his tears.

12

A SENSATION OF BEING TRAPPED IN HER OWN BODY, staring out of a hatch window, a chimp in a drifting spaceship. Conscious, but unable to command limbs. Drowning. Not like in the films, no sputtering fight against the process, against the water. Just an impotent longing for air.

But Nice was not one for impotence. As she spiraled into near panic, Nice marshaled her fear into a measure of rage, of a deep need to not go down without a fight. The reason for the fight forgotten in the heat of the moment. Her feet fluttered, she raised her eyes to look past the dark water, up towards the light which twinkled above. Her breath came in burning jags, each inhalation demanding conscious effort. Behind the pain, underneath the burning sensation, she grew aware of a soothing voice in her head, asking her only to let go. Just let go, and the fight will end. The pain will stop.

None of this matters.

Except for her unborn baby, Pendo: the beloved. To remind them both of how loved the baby would always be. Regardless of circumstance, love would be their religion, love would be the physics of their universe.

And those laws of physics dictated, in a manner as non-negotiable as gravity, that Pendo must be taken away from this filthy basement, to a safer place. Pendo mattered. Pendo would leave a record in space and time. Nice had already made that promise to herself, curled up on the cool steel floor of her Mogadishu shipping container.

The urgency of that promise shocked her awake.

In the inky darkness, Nice could not at first tell whether her eyes were open. She willed her arm to move, and it rose slowly from the sticky floor. Her hand finally appeared when it was inches before her eyes, an assessment of the density of the gloom.

Relieved that the drowning sensation had retreated, Nice tried to recall her recent past. How had she arrived here?

There had been Toogood's henchman Teesh, his huge open hand containing a dozen or so wax-coated pills, each the size of a marble. Toogood, glass of orange juice in hand, watching with solemn eyes as Nice ingested the drugs, swallowing them with a long pull of the tart, fake orange juice. The sun-stunned airstrip, the soldiers' sunglasses glinting, making her ill, to the point that she fell against Toogood. He righted her by the elbow, careful to avoid any other physical contact, as though the pregnancy had tainted her. Under the thwack-thwack of the propellers, the awkward goodbyes with Toogood, now equal parts awkward ex-boyfriend and micro- managing boss. Then the short flight from Mog, and that strange, frightening cop at the airport. Then Duncan, with his earnest smile, his Subaru somehow still bearing the smell of distant suburbia. The pattering rain on the windshield.

And then, the lurching whip of Duncan's car on the slippery tarmac, crunching through the guardrails. Each spark falling distinctly upon the bonnet, as time and space collapsed onto one another. Her body flooding with adrenaline, scrambling her senses, darkening peripheral vision. Shutting down out of sheer self-preservation.

Nothing more.

Was Pendo all right? Nice jerked upright. The sudden motion sent a shard of agony through her head. She ran a hand over her belly, freshly conscious of its cargo. Her baby came unbidden from the cosmos, a lifeline of something true. Nice rubbed her eyes with the heel of her filthy hands.

Nice had always known she had a high pain threshold. She still remembered the day she had learned it, the way one sometimes learns intimate things about oneself, from strangers. As a little girl, she had been holding an ice cube in her fist until it melted, a performance that had her friends in shrieks. Nice recalled their intense faces, wondered what had become of them, dentists, lawyers, hausfraus. Were they happy? Certainly happier than she was, at the moment.

Nice looked to the pain which emanated mainly from her head. The pain was good to dwell on, the pain imposed its own terrible imperatives upon her scattered priorities. The pain was feedback from the natural order, a reminder of the responsibility placed upon her, if nothing else as a vessel for Pendo.

A clarity struck Nice. Those filthy drug capsules, hand-rolled by Toogood's man, the one with a distinct layer of grime on the cuticle of the nail of his four-inch-long right little finger. That poison was in her body now, nestled next to Pendo's dreaming form. Bile rose in her throat, and she gagged. Nothing would come, nothing but the resurgence of the burning in her head and lungs. Tears in her eyes, she placed a hand upon her belly. Flimsy protection against the indifferent world, against her own self-inflicted violence.

Self-inflicted.

It seemed a pattern in her life. The trickle of poor decisions turning into a stream, enabled by the resources of an adult job. Her leaving her elderly parents to go work in Somalia. The lifestyle on a military base further deepened her alienation, the sense that there was no core of her to protect, that it was all up for grabs, and the show could end at any moment. Everything was designed to be disposable, from the living quarters fashioned out of shipping containers, to the accelerated camaraderie, to the sachets of shampoo she used to wash out the grease from the shared helmets they were all required to wear.

The rest of the world spun on, banging out its meaningless rhythms. The messages from friends, invitations to weddings, then baby showers, these things slowed, then stopped altogether. Became echoes on social media, until Nice carved that from her life as well. No more smiling faces from the other end of the planet, no more well-fed children dressed as witches and goblins, no more reminders of her self-imposed exile from a home that had baffled her.

Her work took her to dark places. But without the satisfaction of being able to actually help anyone there. Not really. Sweating silently under her ill-fitting armored vest, she would watch goatherds-turned-warlords bicker over bounty, unmake generations. Nice had tried to reach out to the Somalis and other East Africans who worked on the base, to fashion some sort of alternative to the default Anglo-Saxon caste system which had imposed itself. Once, she had tried to sit in the lead vehicle of the convoy, but the security officer, a Nepali ex-special forces officer named Ravi had called her back urgently, his eyes wide under the brim of his blue helmet. Taking in the soft eyes of those remaining in the car, she walked back to her assigned car. Later, while sharing a cigarette, Ravi had explained that the lead car was filled with Africans, in the event the convoy were to happen upon an IED on the road.

Their car was to be the sacrificial vehicle.

There was, underpinning it all, a brutal calculus of who mattered more, which death would generate what manner of paperwork, headlines, and consequences. And so, the Africans rode in the first car, sending up prayers, collecting their danger pay, and dispatching it home.

Unmoored, Nice took to sneaking out from the base for walks. She covered her head with a shawl and kept to public places. Enjoying the anonymity, the relative normalcy of the city, of its people who remained concerned with the quotidian, tired of dealing with the existential uncertainties which swarmed, like a gathering storm, beyond their reckoning for the present.

And it was on one of these walks that she had met Toogood. Who had spoken to her as a peer, on the beach. A fellow refugee from childhood, straddling the world from whence he had come and the world to which he would belong. In this, they were alike. But in his clear-eyed ambition, his single-minded vision of what he sought—in this, they were very different.

For under the boyish charm beat a heart preternaturally hardened by the suffering it had known. His old world, its clannish traditions and arcane obligations, jostling with his vision of his own pin-striped future. His resourcefulness his only weapon, the slingshot with which he stared down the world. His own family vanished, never spoken of. Only a sister, whom he had spirited to boarding school in Kenya as soon as he could afford it. Thereby losing her to another world, saving her by alienating her. There was a cold-blooded practicality, almost rapacity, to Toogood, born of the difficult odds he had faced his whole life.

Their relationship was supposed to be a fling, a joyous dalliance without consequence, celebrating life in the midst of war, requiring no exit plan. Two young, beautiful people embracing that they would not be young or beautiful forever. Nice was not one for possessiveness, and she knew that he still saw other women on the base, and she too took no oaths of monogamy. It was a relief against the constant low-grade panic, the boredom, the cloistered living conditions. And so it was that she had been with another man, an irreverent bearded Australian with a mysterious job title, teetering on the edge of alcoholism. It was, she was to find out, a grave misreading of the rules of engagement, one that made such an arrangement unacceptable. For it caused public loss of face to Toogood.

Toogood had come to her shipping container, bearing Cadbury chocolate and heroin, rare treats each. But he was already drunk, or high. Mean and jagged with his words. He paced the container, accused her of sleeping with entire platoons of blue helmets, which Nice declined to deny out of self-respect. Out of a need to be true to herself.

An icy calm came over Toogood. "I understand, you wish to protect your friend. But this is war. The only protection from war is to go away from it." He patted the hard mattress of the single bed. A smile crinkled his eyes. "We will remove him from the war, yes?"

Nice had not known how completely to fear him until that moment. Until that moment, the flickers of fear he caused were, in fact, cause for attraction, arousal. But now, with no mating dance to be performed, the fear towered. In fact, she could not recall such terror before, like being locked in a lion's cage, feeling its eyes flicking over her body. There was an unblinking malevolence there, in the face of which all her rules, her values, her feminism—these were worse than useless. Downright dangerous.

So she had denied seeing the Australian. And this mollified Toogood to a degree, to the point that the chemicals which raged in his bloodstream had subsided. And he turned to her, still gruff, and pulled her close. Took her ponytail in a fist.

She froze, uncertain as to his intention, as to that of which he was capable. Neural alarm. There, in this non- consensual embrace, understanding, for the very first time, that he was a killer. Just how far she had traveled from the suburbs of Montreal. And how, in her delusional state, she had smashed through all the guardrails which stood between her and this manner of incident.

This manner of man.

He held her in this way, silent, as if weighing some decision. For what seemed a long time. Then he cocked his head. A cooing apology, his lips against her ear. The sweat and smoky scent of his cool, smooth skin.

The sizzle of the cooking heroin. He proffered her the needle. Nice shook her head. Not like this, not in this. But the madness welled up in his eyes once more. Out of self-preservation, Nice took up the needle, pressed it to her skin. Dimpling against the pressure. A tear slipped down her cheek, onto the wounded forearm. Toogood took her hand in his, held the syringe steady. His thumb upon her thumb, against the plunger. A pluming of blood.

With his other thumb, he wiped away her tear.

And then, the world shrinking upon itself, the gyroscopic motions of the ceiling, the earth itself. A vague sensation of Toogood's hands on her, of him speaking Somali words she could not follow. Nice clung to the sense that this was all OK, that she was consenting, still in control, a fellow participant. It seemed important somehow, to her sense of self. That this was still part of her adventurous life, that she was not choking on all the adventure, which was rising like seawater in a ruptured boat.

A great, crashing darkness had carried her away.

They had not seen each other for weeks after that.

Toogood had been busy, business was good.

The Australian had explained, with uncharacteristic sheepishness combing his beard with his fingers, to Nice that he was being transferred back to Melbourne for a bit. Toogood had a finger in every pie on the base. No information passed Toogood by. He gathered information like a stockbroker making red pencil circles on a balance sheet.

That night seemed a hideous dream. A lesson learned. A sobered stock-taking. Again, work was the anchor, an all-consuming, never-satisfied pit into which she plunged all her energies, all of herself. It worked to numb her, to slow the spinning of the planet down to a pinpoint which seemed manageable. It was going to be OK, she just needed to stay out of Toogood's way. She needed to get off the base, maybe even find another job in another place, a place not guarded by men in armored vests. Still, the fact that Toogood had not contacted her was to be counted as good news.

And then the sickness came upon Nice. A headache that nailed her limbs to her mattress took control of her body. Dragging herself to the toilet required a steeling of will. Once there, her kurta soaked with sweat, she would place her cheek against the cool porcelain of the toilet bowl, exhausted from arid retching. Nice closed the blinds, begging for sleep, ignoring the buzzing of her phone. Its tidings seemed trivial things, in the face of her sheer exhaustion.

She spent a few days in seclusion, successfully deluding

herself that she had missed her period for another reason. That it had not been several weeks already. That her nausea, her exhaustion, were due to work-related stress, dehydration. The smallest things would double her over, instantly——the smell of the re-used cooking oil from the cafeteria, the glare of the sun against the armored vehicles if she forgot to wear sunglasses.

A colleague came to see her. She could see from the shock on his face that she looked grim. He shouldered her to the medic on the base, past gaggles of staring soldiers. One giggled. Another gave a half-hearted catcall. Nice was past caring, just the next step took all her energy.

And so the news of her pregnancy was never a private matter.

Rather, it was announced in that shambling walk across the sun-stunned courtyard to the olive door with "MEDIC" stenciled on it.

Stunned, but also relieved at having a diagnosis, Nice began to catalog her concerns. For one, she was surprised to admit to herself that she wanted to keep her baby. The words, "Her Baby"—even those seemed borrowed, from some suburban mother on her way to buy booties from the mall. Nice considered, for a brief moment, terminating the pregnancy. But the concept, the very thought of an abortion, made her run to the toilet, gagging the bile with which she had become so familiar. No, the baby was a cold shower, the wakeup call she needed, a hand outstretched from the heavens.

This was not a mistake, but a lesson.

According to the base doctor, she was in fine child- bearing health, with youth on her side. What she needed, if she was serious about having the child, was to be in an environment more emotionally conducive and access to fit- for-purpose health care. She nodded, already making plans about handovers and a letter of resignation.

She sat, in a patch of sunlight, back against her bedframe. Before her, a pile of her things. There were to have been two piles: "keep" versus "give away", but the former had simply not had any candidates yet.

Pendo would always be in the "keep" pile.

Nice looked to the door before she heard the knocking. Silence.

"I know you're in there, Nice."

She could envision the smile on Toogood's mouth. Perhaps he was running a hand through his hair, a gesture she had once found so endearing.

The act of standing brought on a wave of nausea. She had known this moment would come, had rehearsed for it. A simple script: no big deal, an abortion in Nairobi, no recriminations, nice and easy, just back away from the dangerous creature: see, I'm no threat. Once she was away from here, she would just vanish.

Nice wiped her mouth with the back of her hand, stood straight.

She pulled open the door, the mid-day sun streaming in.

Toogood stood silhouetted before her.

"May I come in?" He held his hands aloft. In one, a bouquet of pale roses. The thorns removed.

She ushered him in, conscious of the pile of things on the bare floor, suggesting that she had been caught in the act of something dastardly.

Toogood sat on her bed, unbidden, like its owner. She was in a cage with a lion, she reminded herself. He patted the bed.

She chewed her lower lip. So dry.

He shrugged. "You've been missing. Unwell, I'm told." No surprise that Toogood would have known, it was his business to know. "These are for you." He lifted up the bouquet.

Nice regarded the flowers, which drooped like just-suffocated fish. Her rehearsed comments seemed childish bravado, flimsy before Toogood's audacity, the diesel engine of his raw will.

He smiled, placed the flowers on the bed, shifted his elbows onto his knees. "I understand you are pregnant." Toogood ran his hands along his denimed thighs, then continued. "Is there anything I can do?"

Nice steeled herself. This was the moment, her only chance to set the narrative. She tucked her hair behind her ear. "I am. For now."

Toogood smiled. "Nothing can happen unless you want it to——that was what you said when we first met. Seems a long time ago." He leaned back, lifting one long leg over the other. "So, you will not keep the baby?"

Cursing herself, Nice shook her head. "I want to have the . . . the operation in Nairobi and—"

"Good, this is good. You should go as soon as possible, this week itself. I can arrange it for you."

Nice's heart lifted. He was for the abortion, just as she had suspected, he wanted no part of the mess. She just had to play the damsel in distress a while longer, enlist his help to ensure he trusted her. Once in Kenya, she would never return to this place, to this life, she would take Pendo away. "Thank you, Toogood, yes, there is a flight tomorrow, but I am on the waitlist and can't get on the roster due to—"

He waved his long-fingered hands at her words, dismissing the waitlist. It would be done. But his smile suggested there was more to come. "Please, Nice. Carry something to Nairobi for me." It was not a request. Toogood stood, wiped his palms against his jeans. "Something small."

Not waiting for her response, Toogood walked to the door and opened it. Toogood's henchman, the one they called Teesh, walked in, stolid and unsmiling. In his right hand, he held a carton of military-issue orange juice. In his left, a clear Ziploc bag with what appeared to be red balls of wax.

Teesh held out the drugs, "Your belly will be more packed than a rush-hour matatu." He laughed from his belly.

Now, in this greasy darkness, Nice touched her own belly, recalling the hatred she had felt stir within her, as she sat on that bed, beside the gasping flowers.

13

A DISTINCT CLINKING. Metal on metal. From the gloom above.

Someone was coming.

Nice blinked, trying to assess the pain which still throbbed at her temples. Just how debilitating the injury it hinted at might be. She closed her eyes, steeling herself to roll over onto her abdomen, then quickly onto knees and elbows. At this early stage of the pregnancy, maybe lying on her tummy wouldn't harm Pendo. But she did not know. There was so much she didn't know.

Hot tears welled and, with them, self-pity.

Nice clenched her jaw and rolled. Her head aflame. Sucking in shallow breaths, she brought herself to all fours. Spittle dribbled from her mouth. Still, there was relief in this position.

From above, the shuffling of a person walking across a wooden floor. Furniture being pushed aside. No concerns about stealth.

She had to get to her feet, find a spot to hide in. Nice staggered upright, the density of the darkness disorienting. Her hands were streaked with filth. She ran them over her face, stopping at the hairline above her eyebrow. A crisp line of dried blood. Probing with her filthy fingers, Nice made out distinctly the lips of the wound, the swelling around it. A fresh trickle of blood came over her eyebrow.

An echo of light from above. Someone was coming.

Wiping her brow as best she could, Nice lurched backwards, away from the light, beneath which she could make out the shape of a staircase.

Now steps fell on the wooden stairs. Confident steps.

The wavering light of a torch.

Nice turned, shuffled into the gloom, to find some manner of a hiding spot. There, in the far reach of the chamber, a brief shimmer. What could it be, like a porpoise breaking water? Looking over her shoulder at the shimmying torchlight making its way down the stairs, Nice thought she heard humming. She made for the far corner where she had seen the distant glimmer, there was simply nothing else to orient by.

She paused, senses straining to discern stimulus. The humming grew louder.

Nice shuffled as fast as she dared in the dark, as fast as her broken body would permit. Had she imagined the glimmering, what could it be? Where could it be?

And then it was upon her, a shrouded figure, red-eyed. The creature parted the curtain of gloom in a shock of pale skin, under a fringe of white-gold hair. Icy fingers, clinging to Nice's shoulders with a grip of pure bone. Nice shuddered back, trying to push the creature away. Its red-lipped mouth open in a silent entreaty. But its grip was too fierce, that they fell in this strange embrace. And rolled to break from it, upon the ground which seemed to have a strange covering, like a sodden carpet. The sour smell of human sweat.

Nice cried out, all concerns about silence discarded. Raked her fingers against the creature's ghostly face, into its ruby-red mouth. They rolled across the soggy floor, until the ghost established its dominance, pinning Nice's arms under her bony knees, her skirt hitched up to her knees. The face pale, freckled, eyes wild with pain and fear. Blood trickled from her nose into her mouth, but the albino woman did not notice. She spat at Nice, "You, you have jailed me here." She had the strength of rage, of madness. The vividness of her pale arm reaching out, taking Nice's throat, squeezing the windpipe with her bony fingers.

How long had she been locked down here?

Nice made to speak, but could produce no words. Her consciousness flickered. Just get her off. All she could think was that this, this albino, was sitting on Pendo, crushing her watery nest.

A face appeared in Nice's field of vision, behind the albino, who still focused all her energies on throttling Nice. It occurred to Nice, in some dissonant observation, that it was a kindly face, a face which would not be out of place in a library, or a museum. This must be the person who had been humming on the way down the stairs. A woman in late middle age, her walnut skin smooth, framed by salt and pepper curls tied back in a loose bun. She was smiling, as if she were minding two children playing. The woman smiled, "But there is much magic here."

The albino turned with a snarl and leapt at the woman. But she was ready, had stepped back into the shadows and held out a staff of some sort. The albino woman towered over her new victim and made to close the gap, the two shadows joining to become one with each other, and then with the larger gloom which absorbed them noiselessly.

As Nice massaged her throat, an arc of electricity lanced the darkness, imprinting itself upon her retinas. A flash of pure brilliance, vivid and ephemeral as a clap. The darkness was complete again, and the creature had vanished. In its wake, an echoing blindness. And the distinct waft of smoldering flesh.

Silence.

Nice rolled a few times in a direction she could only guess as being away from the tussling. An exhaustion came over Nice, and she lay back, hands clasped against her scalding throat. Her skull bouncing against the sodden floor.

"Do not cry, pretty one."

Nice opened her eyes, to see the humming woman, phone in one hand and staff in the other. She looked unharmed, but the breast pocket of her blue oxford shirt had been torn half off. "I'm the keeper of this sorry zoo." She gestured at the darkness, into which the torchlight of the phone spidered. "And some of the charges," the woman gestured over her shoulder with her chin, "are slow learners."

Nice sat up, wincing.

The woman knelt, placed the phone face down in a puddle of torchlight. Then she pointed the lance at Nice. It glinted dully. Some sort of branding iron, the tip of which hovered hypnotically in front of Nice's eyes, like a snake's mouth. From the end of the cattle prod, a thin rope of smoke. The smoke looked solid in the torchlight, as though it could be climbed. "But not you, pretty one. You are one of the smart ones. Yes, I know your type. Almost too smart."

Still rubbing her throat, Nice managed to croak, "Please… I shouldn't be here. This place—I must report to a very dangerous man, can't be late—"

A cackle of laughter. "Oh, I know all about your man in

Mogadishu. But you are far from his protection. That cop—"
She stopped to sneer. "That cop he bought to ensure your safety,
that cop is dead. So, no one in all the world knows where you are,
or whether you are dead or alive." She licked her lips. "Except
me. Oh, and that albino woman, if she ever wakes up again."

"But—but, why me—Was it that cop at the airport?

The one with the sharp teeth?"

But Ciru only shrugged, as though disappointed that the
conversation had to take this turn. "I know you are carrying
something for the Mogadishu man?"

It was astonishing to Nice how quickly she reverted to
type, to wanting to stand up to the bully. Even here, in some
fetid Nairobi dungeon, her blood rose. "Nothing. There's been
a misunderst—"

The slap echoed in the dark basement. "Too smart for your
own good."

Nice held a hand to her stinging cheek, her head cleared
by the violence. Her body reacted by sending all resources to
address the possibility of imminent physical harm. This woman
was different from anyone she had ever met before. There was
a curious combination of ruthlessness and yet humanity to
her. Even that slap had been, somehow, maternal rather than
wanton, uncalibrated violence. How best to deal with her? Nice
was surprised, and frightened, that the world could contain a
person such as this, that the world contained more multitudes
than she had imagined, like peering at an amoeba through a
microscope.

"I am Ciru", the woman said with a smile. "I will hurt you,
end you, if necessary. But know that, as of now, I won't." She
shrugged.

Nice was aware that it was her turn to speak, yet her head

was curiously empty. No stratagems, none of the half-truths in which she dealt on a usual basis. This woman Ciru clearly thought that Nice had something of value. Perhaps it was best to level with Ciru, things couldn't exactly go any worse.

Or could they?

Ciru tilted her head to regard Nice sideways. "Don't think too hard, smarty. Looks like you already have a headache." And she laughed at her own joke in the manner of a person who does so often, a sincere cackle ringing out in the dark.

Nice bit her lower lip. "Drugs. I'm carrying drugs for Toogood."

"Toogood?"

Nice stammered, "I mean the man from Mogadishu, Ibrahim."

Ciru gave a low hmm. "And what else?" "Nothing, I promise, I—"

Another slap. This one harder, rattling Nice.

Ciru knelt. "I'm not your mother, but I want the truth. / All of it. It is what I deal in."

Could she be referring to Pendo? Nice looked into Ciru's eyes, which glittered in the torchlight.

Ciru did not break the eye contact.

Questions, doubts, and regrets came flooding into Nice's head. But above the clamor, one single primal urge: to survive, to get Pendo away from this place, this woman who somehow frightened her even more than Toogood.

"I am pregnant." Nice realized she had never said the words aloud. That she would have to say them in a place like this. She willed herself not to cry, expecting ridicule and violence from Ciru.

But Ciru's demeanor seemed transformed by the words.

She nodded, placing her fine-fingered hand upon Nice's knee. "A healer can see, a healer knows."

Nice felt a tear roll down her cheek, making a crystalline trajectory to the ground. And then she began to sob, her shoulder racked, surrendering to the sensation, to its cleansing.

Ciru let it happen, waiting. Then she said, "Your baby is fine, for now. But you need to act right."

Nice wiped snot from her nose, nodding abjectly. More than anything, she wanted to act right, to be given the chance to act right. No more thoughts or doubts now, just follow the urge, obey the ancient chemical signals.

Ciru was silent, engrossed in political long-division. "You seem to have given me the truth." She removed a piece of lined paper from a pocket, held it out, trembling, between forefingers.

The handwriting on the slip of paper seemed familiar to Nice, until she understood that it was her own. This was the confession note she had written in the event of an emergency, which she had hoped never to use. The one she had considered giving to the cop, Hinga, at the toilet in the airport.

Ciru smirked as she watched Nice's comprehension dawn. "In my line of work, information is more precious than gold, than guns." Then she stood, suddenly business-like. "One-time offer: give me the drugs now and leave this place. The cop is dead, and I have no connection to this Mogadishu man with the strange name, this Toogood."

Nice looked up, crying and smiling. In the new-found conviction of her resolve to save Pendo, above all else, and at any cost, this deal required no thought. "Thank you, thank you."

Ciru lifted her shirt, revealing a child's fanny pack tied to her waist. The white and purple swirls vivid against her brown skin. She unzipped it, then paused. Then she turned away from

Nice and rummaged some more.

When she turned back, Ciru bent to Nice, who still sat jack-knifed on the rotten ground. Ciru gave an enigmatic smile and brought up her left palm, in which lay a red powder. Ciru ran the thumb of her other hand across the palm. She gestured at Nice with her red thumb.

Nice understood to incline her head.

Ciru leaned in, ran her thumb along the middle part of Nice's hair. As she did so, she brushed her mouth against Nice's ear. "A solemn vow, you understand. Accept my blessing, or you will accept my curse."

Nice swallowed. Noticing that Ciru had stepped back, Nice raised her head.

Ciru bent and blew at the red powder, into Nice's face, her eyes. Nice started, shimmied back from the witch. Her eyes smarted, then began to stream. Nice's scalp and face began to grow numb. She tried to open her mouth, or raise an eyebrow, but found she could not. The room swam, and her face tingled.

Ciru came in close, tilted her head to better regard Nice. "When did you ingest the drugs?" She took Nice's chin in her hand. "Do you follow me?"

Nice tried to recall the recent past—the memory of Teesh's fist dangling the plastic bag of drugs. His eyes unblinking as he watched her swallow the little red balls, incongruously jolly, like Christmas ornaments for a miniature tree. It seemed so far away. "Yesterday, or the day before. I don't know."

Seemingly satisfied, Ciru stood, wiped her palms against her skirts. Then lifted her shirt to unzip once more the fanny pack. Frowning, she pulled a small plastic bag and withdrew from it a handful of orange pills. Then rummaged some more until she found what she sought: a three-inch scalpel. It glinted in the torchlight. "Like life, so much of your own choosing."

Nice wiped her streaming eyes with the back of her hands, shuffled to her feet reaching for the pills.

But Ciru closed her hand over them. "I'm only doing this because of the baby. And I would—"

Nice blurted out, "Her name is Pendo."

Ciru gave a high, one-syllable laugh. "Well, Pendo has saved you. But, and this is part of our deal, you must raise her right, love her correctly." Ciru's eyes grew misty, as though she was recalling something difficult. "Love her fiercely. Do you understand?"

Nice lowered her head and cried. It seemed something like that would be beyond her.

Ciru gave Nice the pills. "These will bring forth the drugs. I will fetch the water."

Bleary-eyed, Nice regarded the pyramid of pills in her palm. This was a fair price, for a fair bargain. She would live up to the promise.

Ciru whistled through the gloom, utterly insouciant. She returned, with a sloshing plastic water jug. "There may be some discomfort. We will wait."

Nice nodded, wiped the snot from her nose with her sleeve. There was solace in the decision, in the resignation.

She drank deeply from the jug, realizing just how thirsty she was. And it was fitting, that she would take more pills to undo those that she had taken in Mog. She bit her lip, then took the pills and washed them down.

Ciru squatted on her haunches and rubbed her hands, as though before a fire. "Won't be long."

Nice sat, cross-legged. "You said, 'Love her fiercely.' You have children?" She lowered her eyes, conscious of the impudence.

But this witch doctor had her trapped in a dungeon, so normal conversational rules were suspended. "Do you have children?"

Ciru looked up from her reverie, as though noticing Nice for the first time. Eyes crinkling. "You are afraid of silence?"

"I'm sorry, I didn't mean to—"

"I have a boy. A grown boy. Whom I love, whom I loved, as best I could. As a single mother."

Nice's lip trembled; she felt a strange sense of intimacy with this witch doctor. "I'm going to be such a bad mother. People don't change." She thought of her own best-case scenario—that of being a single mother, and then once more of Duncan, his steadiness as a friend, a foreshadowing for the loyalty required of a life partner.

"Motherhood will change you, from within. It will make you ruthless for what you love. You'll see."

A spasm gripped Nice. She groaned and rolled to her side curled up as the sensation tore through her. Her abdomen clenching like a fist.

Ciru stood over Nice. "Now deliver unto Ciru."

Nice began to wave the woman back, to get some space. But the urgency of the chemicals in her body overrode all. The sensation of shame itself becoming a luxury to Nice, all considerations of dignity cast aside in the fire of the pain, the endless voiding of her stomach.

When the worst of the spams had passed, Nice rolled onto her side, utterly spent with the effort.

Ciru unsqueamishly picked through the puddled waste, harvesting the drugs, distinct as rubies in the torchlight. "We must leave."

Nice groaned as Ciru shouldered her through the gloom. They passed the albino, lying face down like a bloodless

118

apparition, expertly hog-tied.

Atop the stairs, they emerged into the tube-lit glare of what appeared to be an auto mechanic's workshop. Tools lined the wooden workbench neatly, as if awaiting orders. A chainsaw of cheerful red lay at her feet. Nice slumped into a tattered wicker chair, while Ciru locked the door which led to the dungeon below. Nice caught shocking sight of her face in the mirror, a red mask, with flesh-colored rivulets flowing from her eyes to her chin. She blinked at her reflection and staggered to a washbasin She turned the tap and washed her face, sweeping her hair back as she did so.

Outside, the dusk was deep, and the air smoky and cool. Nice's clothes steamed slightly. As Ciru pulled down the steel shutters of the garage, if that was what this was, Nice took her bearings. An alley in an urban slum. She turned to look down the sewer-lined street, each ramshackle house indistinguishable from the next.

"Where are we?"

But when Nice turned, the witch doctor was gone. When she had recovered from the sheer panic of this discovery, Nice found herself strangely relieved to be alone. Something had shifted within her, internalizing the notion of belonging to this beautiful, violent place. She looked up, regarded the bejeweled East African sky, spinning like a top above this very spot.

Then Nice shivered, hugged herself, and began to shuffle barefoot down the street.

14

IN THE PALE LIGHT OF HIS ROOM, sitting on his single bed, Duncan was all too aware of his new foreignness from this place. Seeing Nice, then having her taken like that. Those people tearing the policeman apart, that crazy witch. Something had shifted within him.

In the shower, he ran a hand over the bruising on his arms and ribs and could not recall any discrete moment where he might have gotten them. Maybe the cop's kicks? But he did not want to think about the cop, or anyone from last night. Under the lukewarm water, Duncan began once more to cry, this time with abandon, and this time with a discernment of his most palpable emotion—rage. Was it normal to have so much anger, lurking beneath the surface of normalcy? How had he accumulated such a reservoir of rage?

He dressed in jeans and a black t-shirt, what he thought of as his off-duty pastor outfit. In his bare feet, he padded about the room, unsure of what to do. How to get that money? Would Ciru even be true to her word? The way she had dispatched Hinga, it had a professional cold-bloodedness to it.

Duncan made a cup of instant coffee and looked in the

tiny fridge under his desk. His fingers touched the carton of milk. Empty. Effing Olaniyi had doubtless come through here and raided the fridge. With each sip of the battery acid coffee, Duncan nursed his anger. An abstract, expansive anger which encompassed the blackness of his coffee, Nice's situation, Ciru's sense of humor, and everything in-between.

The neat single bed, the spare closet, the desk with its slumbering laptop. Above his desk hung Duncan's wooden broadsword. He saw, with an anthropological eye, his possessions, understanding—truly, for the first time—his own evanescence as hard fact. A PlayStation sat, mute and patient, under the television. This too lanced Duncan with shame—that his room was like a shrine to an unending adolescence.

His sanity took on an intermittent quality, like a light switch being flicked on and off.

There was also a rootless sense of unfaithfulness. To Nice. To the idea of himself. He had to do something to turn the situation in his favor, to make it so that he wasn't relying on the witch, or anyone else.

He flipped open his laptop.

The internet swam with discussions and images of witch doctors. Photos of sepia-toned white men in sola topees and walrus moustaches, standing alongside solemn African chieftains and juju men. The witchdoctors wore an entrepreneurial look, knowing eyes hooded under feathered headgear. Duncan kept searching, plowing through blogs and photo feeds, in the vague hope of seeing Ciru's familiar face peering out from his laptop.

He stumbled upon "East Africa Blues", the blog of a Nairobi-based American expatriate, who identified herself as Susie Q. Duncan liked the layout of the blog, an uncluttered blue and white motif. Susie Q seemed to have stopped updating the blog a while back, so had likely moved away since, but Duncan liked the layout and the sensibilities of the author, enough to keep reading.

He clicked through, eyes unblinking and mouth slightly open. Susie Q was a trailing spouse, her husband (or "partner" as she insisted on calling him) seemed to work for the US government in some capacity. They didn't seem like a military family, or at least Susie Q did not spout the vacuous jingoism which Duncan associated with US military personnel posted abroad. And Susie Q's sense of what was funny encompassed herself. The blog had the usual expatriate musings, the sort Duncan had himself made in the privacy of his diary. Security concerns, or the bemused bafflement of a visit to a local supermarket.

Susie Q noted in one post how a "family-sized" container of yogurt was only 500mls, saying, "This wouldn't last a day in the fridge of an American teenager." In another post, Susie Q remarked how, when she had tried in vain to find skimmed milk, the supermarket attendant had advised her that, due to the recent lack of rain, there was also a paucity of grazing for the cows. Hence no skimmed milk on the shelves. The logic was not inherently flawed because it had been awfully dry and dusty recently, Susie Q noted, but seemed simplistic. Was this a plausible explanation? Susie Q asked.

Then Duncan came upon a post entitled "Office Hours":
So my partner wanted badly for something to happen at ork (best not to get into specifics here), and a Kenyan colleague suggested we go see a local outcome molding specialist (or OMS, OK, so I made that up to avoid using the ridic term "witch doctor"). Now to be clear, I agreed to go along in the spirit of irony and anthropological amusement and not with the expectation that any O's

would be M'd by this S. The partner also had mixed feelings but we went.

The OMS was in the boonies, which is a polite way of saying "a festering slum." She (this was another thing I liked, that the OMS was a woman) said she was holding office hours (her words) from 7 to 11 p.m., and we were welcome to come then. Due to logistical and security concerns, we (partner, myself, and Annabelle, who turned two last month! and whose nanny is out of town) took a taxi over there straight after work.

The OMS was middle-aged, with a kind face. She was wearing a blue men's Oxford shirt, the sleeves rolled up to her elbows, over a Kikoy wrap-dress. Not very black magic, but a pretty cool outfit all the same! Anyway, the moment she sees Annabelle, who is toddling around the room with her stuffed lion, the OMS puts her hands up and says "Oh, an American toddler. Please don't shoot me!"

Partner and I are confused until OMS explains that she understands American toddlers are notorious for finding hidden guns in their parents' closets and purses and using them to shoot people dead. American toddlers, according to OMS, "LOVE" (her word, her emphasis) this sort of thing. Partner thinks this is in poor taste, his face literally darkened—I didn't actually know this was a real thing, just something you put in a novel to be dramatic.

Anyway, I personally think her comment was hilarious. Annabelle was, in point of fact dear reader, unarmed.

This had to be Ciru. Only she would come up with this kind of crazy remark. Susie Q went on to relate how the OMS mentioned that she was planning a move to New York, because it would give her son better education options. OMS bragged that her son had, in fact, already been admitted to Medgar Evers College in Brooklyn.

Her son.

Duncan clicked open another window in his browser. He looked away from the screen for a moment, at the blank wall above the laptop, trying to recall the name on the board in front of Ciru's office.

Then, he typed in the search box: "Medgar Evers Mikende".

The witch did have a son, it seemed. Edmund Gatukui Mikende was, or at least had been, a communications major. He was also active in the international students' association and captain of the table tennis team.

Duncan slid open the drawer of his desk and took from it a red leather notebook. On the last page were written all his online passwords. Duncan's Facebook profile had only the minimum information required to create an account and no photographs. Logging into his account, Duncan searched for Edgar's profile. He found several with the same or similar name as his search terms, but only one was listed as living in Nairobi.

The user handle was *EdGat*.

EdGat's profile was available only to his friends. Fueled by immediacy, Duncan sent EdGat a friend request.

A muted beep informed Duncan that EdGat had accepted the invitation and was available to chat. These millennials, Duncan shook his head, were pretty reckless with their online activities.

Duncan took a sip of his now-cold coffee and stood up. He had already been at this computer for a couple of hours, sipping coffee in clean clothes, all while Nice was imprisoned in a zombie-infested prison. Duncan's meeting with Ciru was not until 7 p.m. He sat back down at the computer. What he needed was to channel his anger, to use it as steam to power his interactions with the world.

He drained his cup and clicked open the chat interface. Duncan wrote to EdGat, "Hey man."

The cursor blinked.

EdGat replied, "Poa poa. Do we know each other?" Duncan stuck to his breezy non-committal tone, guessing that a person who accepted a friend request almost immediately from a perfect stranger wouldn't nitpick.

Duncan typed, "Nah bro. I'm from the States and new to Nairobi. Trying to get used to living out here. I see you lived in Brooklyn."

EdGat: "Yes, but repping the 254 now. Karibu." Duncan: "Thanks. You want to play table tennis or hang

out."

EdGat: "Please please refer to it as Ping Pong. Assuming

you don't totally suck (which, given that you called it table tennis, is a fair inference), happy to play."

The apple doesn't fall far from the tree, thought Duncan. They made a plan to meet at a bar in the Central Business District later that morning. Clearly, EdGat didn't have a great deal going on in his life, eager as he was to play table tennis with a perfect stranger, on short notice. Or maybe he just loved Ping Pong. Or maybe he was mentally ill. With a mother like that, who could imagine his childhood?

Duncan's head raced with these thoughts as he pulled on his sneakers from the pile of discarded clothes. He still had a lot to do before his Ping Pong summit.

Duncan ran his fingers along the splintered door jamb. Despite his martial arts training, he was unused to, and repelled by, violence outside the walls of a dojo. The bloody mouthpiece, the thinly padded leather gloves, these were ritualistic accouterments to be shed before entering the real world.

As he fingered the brass handle of the broken door, it swung outwards, daylight falling onto the polished clay flooring. His room gave onto a north-facing corridor, along which arched windows cast a sloping light. Walking through the dust motes, each descending its own luminous shaft, Duncan felt spiritually large. There remained, his purposeful walk said, a chance at fixing himself, at taking action to save Nice. To breathe life into the life he had imagined for them. This time, he would be more definitive.

The corridor emerged onto a college-style quadrangle, designed no doubt by some homesick and unimaginative Englishman. But the East African climate, and Duncan's persistent micro-management of the gardeners, had transformed it into a lush hothouse. The fine-bladed lawn, shorn close and soft, was carpeted in lavender jacaranda flowers.

As he walked across the green courtyard, Duncan was scarved by red-veined dragonflies. When he had first arrived in Kenya, these creatures had repelled him, four or five inches long, and inured as they were to being around humans. In the first month of his arrival, while holding a staff meeting in the courtyard, Duncan had shrieked when a dragonfly landed on his nape.

Effing Olaniyi, for his part, had been unwilling to give up the mileage of Duncan's public indignity. At the next staff meeting (held indoors), Niyi had presented (on behalf of the entire staff, Niyi had noisily clarified) a beaded dragonfly keychain. This was followed by laughter, mostly good- natured, though underwritten by Niyi's over-hearty braying. That dragonfly, dangling from the ignition of his Subaru yesterday, had borne silent witness to the crash and to Nice's disappearance.

The reception area and public office were on the south- side of the quadrangle. Duncan ducked into the brick-arched portico, briefly blinded by the sudden shade of the structure. He nodded at Faith, the receptionist, marooned behind her burgundy hide-covered desk, by way of a polite but quick greeting.

Faith sprang from her seat, as though she had sat on a pin, and said in her bird-like voice, "Good morning, Pastor Duncan."

Although Duncan resented this conversational ratcheting up, he forced himself to stop. He turned and rested his fingertips on the weathered leather of the desk. "Good morning, Faith."

Faith brandished a green leather appointment book and began to remonstrate. Something about unanswered calls to Duncan's phone. This was too much for Duncan, and he waved the book aside with one hand and signaled the office door with his other, like a referee making an off-side decision.

Faith persisted, her voice rising. "Shouldn't you at least put on a jacket?" Duncan shook his head, determined to not let anything Faith had to say into his head. Nothing could be permitted to steer him off course.

Even as Faith's words continued to sail at him, Duncan opened the faded plywood door of the office, shielded himself behind it and then slipped inside. Duncan's last image of Faith was that of her eyebrows raised in urgency behind the green appointment book, her animated face morphing slightly at Duncan's abruptness. When the door swung pneumatically shut behind him, he locked it.

Duncan exhaled. He had not realized that he had been holding his breath.

The office wore a used-up look. This was a result partly of the passage of time, and partly of the unspoken intention to broadcast an air of serious abstemiousness on behalf of the Mission. The rust-colored carpeting threadbare. The plywood desk bore a yellow-glassed banker's lamp and a desktop computer from the mid-90s. Duncan had never used it, working off his laptop instead.

On the desk, lying broken in half, was the yellow pencil from the meeting with the Legishons. It seemed a lifetime ago. Duncan picked up the pencil halves and threw them in the dustbin. No time to overthink things. He had to act fast, faith or no faith.

Behind the desk stood the sort of chair deployed at weddings or banquets. Armless, uncomfortable for any length of time and upholstered in the obligatory red synthetic velvet. Behind the chair, below the entirely decorative wall- mounted air conditioner, was an in-wall safe. The safe was also something Duncan had inherited, and it baffled and irritated him. Installed as it was at shin-height, accessing it was something which had to be done on hands and knees, face close to the pilling carpeting. It lent to even the most routine task, such as retrieving the corporate checkbook to pay for the Mission's utilities, a frantic and furtive element.

Duncan keyed in the passcode—the last four digits of Nice's social security number. He pawed through the jumble of keys, phones and papers until he found a small Ziploc bag. Inside were four thousand US dollars, all in crisp hundred- dollar bills issued after the year 2000. Benjamin Franklin pursed his lips in fragile patience. There were also about thirty thousand shillings, Mzee Kenyatta sitting, trapped by his jacket and tie, within the clear plastic. The Mission's in-case- of-emergency fund.

Unseen knuckles rattled the plywood door.

Faith's voice came, slow and rising, in the questioning tone used to engage with the imminently violent or the mentally ill. "Duncan?"

On his hands and knees, as if in prayer to the money, Duncan replied, his voice harried, "Yes. Coming. Coming. Just a moment." What could she possibly want that was so urgent?

Duncan picked out his passport, a 2G Nokia phone, and its charger. These, and the money in the Ziploc, he shoved into the pocket of his jeans. Duncan locked the safe and stood. Smoothing his clothes and his hair, Duncan inhaled slowly through his nose, willing his heart to slow. "Juuust a second."

He paced across the shabby room. The lock turned noisily, suggesting that whatever had transpired behind the closed door had been unsavory, necessitating the dark and damp of secrecy. Duncan pushed the door outwards, and the pneumatic door closer hissed slowly.

Outside, beside Faith's desk, were gathered a group of white people, all of them regarding Duncan like a zoo animal. From their collective presence and facial expressions, Duncan registered notes ranging from mild alarm to full-blown shock. Front and center, as though leading the gathering, stood Effing Niyi, wearing a dark suit and an inscrutable look. The palm of his right hand was planted like a flag on Faith's desk. It was as though he was physically standing between Duncan and the people behind him. Which of them was he shielding?

And who were these people? Duncan sensed a gravity to the forces which had called this gathering into being. He realized his hand was in the back pocket of his jeans and withdrew it, unsure what to do with it. His passport fell at his feet.

Duncan stammered, "Sorry." He bent to retrieve the passport. When he looked up, Niyi was performing an exaggerated flourish in Duncan's direction, saying "Ladies and gentlemen, may I introduce you to our pastor, Father Duncan Bernardo."

A gravid silence.

Behind Niyi, a woman in a navy jacket fidgeted. Her face bore within it something close to pity. With the dizzying sensation of an out-of-body experience, Duncan understood the woman in the jacket was pitying him his humiliation. Duncan narrowed his eyes and tilted his head, silently imploring Niyi to complete the introduction, to allow some context from which Duncan could find his feet.

Niyi returned Duncan's gaze impassively, a quarter-smile playing on his lips.

Effing Olaniyi.

Just as Duncan was preparing to forge ahead with a vague sentiment of it being an honor to meet the group, Niyi spoke again, producing each word from under his moustache with some pleasure. "And these, Duncan, are the members of the board of the Church of the Earth."

The weight of these words crushed any nascent resourcefulness which Duncan had been summoning. He had entirely forgotten. The fact of his forgetting was doubly dispiriting, because Duncan self-identified as being organized and punctual—utterly paralyzed by the cognitive dissonance of not having recalled this important event. He had never met the members of the Board in person, even though it was the corporate organ which had approved his appointment to this job. Placing his hand on the navy jacketed woman's shoulder, Niyi added, with a flashy cruelty, "Whom we have been of course eagerly expecting."

These words were true. And Duncan felt a kindling hatred

of Niyi for having uttered them.

The Board's visit was an important event, critical to the future of the East African mission both in terms of funding and affiliation. Critical to Duncan's career. Names flooded back to Duncan. The chairman of the Board, with whom Duncan had corresponded via email extensively in preparation for this visit, was Mr. Leighman. The same Mr. Leighman who had insisted on the leaf-blowing machines. Machines which had been deployed on the grounds precisely to evidence how seriously Duncan took the Board's guidance in such matters.

Duncan could see, in his mind's eye, the quote at the bottom of each of Mr. Leighman's emails:

But they that wait upon the Lord shall renew their strength;
They shall mount up with wings as eagles.

Duncan supposed it was exhortative, but it also seemed to encourage a passivity, for "waiting upon" unfathomable some-things. He had admired the expression "mount up", which had sounded like it belonged in a Spaghetti Western, but beyond that had failed to make any real sense of the words. This was increasingly true of most of the scripture Duncan read, or rather forced himself to look at. It seemed watery, blurry stuff, vaguely poetic and devoid of any helpfulness. In his more cynical moments, he wondered if it was even devoid of the intention of helpfulness. But it had helped the Legishons, so maybe it was just him?

All this Duncan remembered.

But the Board's arrival he had forgotten.

It was as though his head could not simultaneously contain the parallel realities of witch doctors and corporate governance meetings. The one had entirely displaced the other. With these unhelpful thoughts buzzing in his head, Duncan stepped towards the Board. "Ah. Welcome. Karibu. Mr. Leighman?" This question Duncan lobbed at the group at large, in the hope it might elicit a conversational rope onto which Duncan could latch.

A florid man in a boxy suit stepped forward and said in exact syllables, "Mr. Bernardo." There was a certainty to the man's disapproval, as though he was accustomed to sitting in judgment over the quotidian and that each such occurrence required as a matter of course that he dispense a ruling in its regard. Altering facial expressions to convey disapproval was beneath the stature of this sort of powerful man. Accordingly, Mr. Leighman's face bore an even expression, poised between smile and sneer. The blasted capillaries of Mr. Leighman's spongy nose brought to mind the wings of red-veined dragonflies.

Although Duncan had nothing to say and had no desire to contribute to the conversation, he felt distinctly it was his turn to speak. So, he said, "Hmm, yes." In the ensuing silence, Duncan began to chew on the skin of the big knuckle on his right hand.

On Niyi's face, a smirk flitted like a film projected on a hung bed sheet at night.

Effing Niyi was openly enjoying the predicament.

This outraged Duncan. And reminded him of what was at stake. That Nice's predicament still vastly outweighed any office politics. The anger gave Duncan a measure of backbone to redress the situation.

Duncan placed a hand on Mr. Leighman's elbow, the suit material yielding expensively, and pulled him aside. In this quasi-aside, but still well within earshot of the gathered Board members, Duncan spoke in a grave, measured tone. "Thing is, Mr. Leighman, there's been something of an emergency last night. I have been in a car-jacking and am just now on my way to the police station to report the incident."

"My word, son, that is terrible. Just terrible." Mr. Leighman's face rearranged itself into an expression of concern.

With one eye fixed on Niyi, and buoyed by the intensity of Mr. Leighman's empathy, Duncan said, "Thank you, sir.

Thank you. I am truly sorry for not being able to welcome you suitably after your long journey. But I am certain that Niyi, who is as you know, my Deputy, will do a fine job of showing you our set-up."

"Certainly, my boy, certainly," Mr. Leighman reassured Duncan. Mr. Leighman relished his role as elder and was happy to play the corresponding part to that played by the earnest young cleric. Mr. Leighman also seemed relieved at having a true emotional channel in which to pour his gravitas. Maintaining that dignified equanimity seemed, in the equatorial climate, to have drained him.

With a slight bow, Duncan said, "If you will please excuse me, ladies and gentlemen." The Board issued a murmuring of assent. Eager to perform a show of power recalibration, Duncan turned to Niyi. "Niyi. A word please."

In the sun-dappled portico, Duncan stood in front of Niyi. Neither spoke. Duncan nursed his rage in silence. He was utterly unable to build any kind of rapport with Niyi. Duncan was his boss after all, not that Duncan was in the habit of thinking in that vein. Still, even if they were not friends, the term "boss", with its attendant implications, should have applied to their relationship automatically, like a law of physics. It was just, Duncan thought, so unfair.

Niyi pushed his Malcolm X spectacles up the bridge of his nose with galling insouciance. "Everything OK, boss?" Though the use of the term "boss" was common in Kenya, it sounded ironic to Duncan's ear, as though there was an unseen listener to their conversation.

But Duncan also recognized how tired and anxious he himself was. At the best of times, following these emotional eddies with Effing Niyi was a matter of picking battles. And this was not the best of times.

Duncan sighed. "I'm just tired, that's all. Look, I really need to go to the police. Are you able to manage this situation okay? I mean, the Board's schedule is already set out in great detail, so it's mainly a matter of following along." It felt good to speak authentically, about matters in his actual control, so Duncan added, "Do you need anything?"

Niyi shrugged. He seemed, as usual, oblivious to the workings of Duncan's mind. In the world, there were people who were just not drawn into complicated lines of thinking. Perhaps Niyi was one of these? Or, more likely, Niyi wanted to ensure that he could not be blamed for anything regarding the Board's visit. To draw a sharp contrast between himself and Duncan, in the eyes of the Board. The forensic attribution of blame was Niyi's defining characteristic.

A few months ago, Niyi and Duncan had taken a matatu to a church outreach group in a suburban slum. On the highway, their vehicle had struck a man on a motorcycle. The matatu passengers were disgorged onto the hot pavement (no refunds, the hawker made clear with palms upturned as though to make plain that this was *force majeure*). The boda boda man writhed in the street, his leather riding trousers stirring up the dust, his face and hair coated in it. The rider's helmet lay sectioned like a cantaloupe in fragile-looking plastic shards beside the front wheel of the mini-van. Unmoved, Niyi had gestured with his chin at the man. "But it is this man's fault-o. He should not have merged lanes like that."

In that same spirit, Niyi said, "I tried calling you." Duncan explained that he had lost his phone and that Niyi should not call that number. Duncan added that he had taken the spare phone from the safe. He instantly regretted having shared this detail, seeing in Niyi's face the turning of the cogs. In addition to Niyi's day-to-day responsibilities, he was also supposed to be Duncan's understudy, to ensure "business continuity" and the "localization of talent" (corporate phrases which Duncan used with a carefully contained revulsion). As such, Niyi had full access to the grounds, the buildings, and the safe.

There seemed nothing more to say, so Duncan turned to leave. As he was passing under the jacaranda trees, Duncan heard Niyi call out, "Good luck." Coming from Effing Olaniyi, this was a tender sentiment. Possibly a threatening one.

Duncan waved, gave a tight smile. It didn't matter. None of it did. Save for Nice.

Then he walked out of his compound, into the dusty indifference of the city beyond.

15

CADAVEROUS MARABOU STORKS held silent vigil atop the Makaneri Police Station. Despite driving by the police station almost every day, Duncan had never before noted the presence of the birds.

Was this a sign that Duncan should not have come here, as Ciru had warned him? Did the storks and Ciru have some sort of CCTV-in-the-sky arrangement? Maybe this was no more ludicrous than the Christian conception of an omniscient being, performing a passive-aggressive tally in some cosmic blockchain.

Duncan shook his head clear of these thoughts, that crazy witch had gotten to him. Still, he did not admit to himself that he averted his face from the gargoyle-like storks and hurried into the police station. Duncan's boda boda driver had refused to take him into the police station compound, saying that just being spotted by policemen with a paying customer was grounds for being shaken down.

At the reception desk, a long-necked policewoman in khaki was bent over a ledger. Her bob haircut accentuated the beauty of her nape. With her red nails and gold bracelet, she seemed like a person dressed up as a cop for a party. She took in Duncan's arrival, gave him a faint smile, like the corners of a cloth being tugged against her sharp features.

Duncan approached her, still unsure of what he intended to reveal. "Good morning."

Her half-smile faded. "Morning."

Duncan braced himself. "I would like to report a missing person."

She shut the ledger on her table. From a drawer in the desk, she pulled a second ledger, this one leather-bound. Opening it to the marked page, she said, "Please sign in."

When Duncan had done so, the policewoman stood. She asked Duncan to follow her down a hallway, jingling as she walked. At the end of the hallway was a closed door, bearing a sign: "Harambee Conference Room". The policewoman unlocked the door with a key from a bunch at her waist. She ushered Duncan into the Harambee Room.

Duncan entered the room and turned to face the policewoman. "Now, I am in a bit of a rush. Will this take long?" He had not anticipated this, with time being so tight for his meeting with Edmund, the witch's son.

"A detective will be in to see you shortly." She closed the door as she left the room. The lock turned. Duncan frowned as he understood she had locked the door. He forced himself to count till thirty, and then tried the handle of the door as noiselessly as possible. It was locked.

He tried again, this time without concern about noise.

Duncan tried to calm himself by coming up with explanations for the locked door. Standard protocol? People, men in particular, reporting missing persons tended to be easily spooked? He considered pounding the door, possibly breaking it down as he had done his own just this morning.

But he couldn't break down a door in a police station. What was he even doing here? He bit his lip and reminded himself that involving the police in Nice's retrieval was a back-up plan—one which, if correctly initiated, would run its course independently of his own, more proactive efforts with Edmund. No, better to stay collected. For all he knew, the police could be observing him right now, to get some sort of insight into his state of mind.

Duncan turned and faced the jumble of upturned chairs and blue cabling wire on the large conference table. This seemed a shame, because the face of the conference table was caramel smooth, expensive. Duncan ran his hand along the silky edge of the tabletop.

Above the table hung the standard issue portrait of the President, the red tie and manly bearing undermined by the panicky boredom in his blood-tinged eyes.

The last time Duncan had gone to the US embassy to get his passport renewed, he had noticed a similar portrait of Obama above the passport officer's desk. Was this some contemporary trend, to decorate officialdom with such ritualized portraiture? Or was this yet another way in which the world aped America? The leader of the free world, his over-eager eyes champing at the bit of his restrained costume. Brother Obama's unduly optimistic smile bespeaking his spotless conscience, as if a starry void floated between his pinstriped spacesuit and the blood-soaked past, and, inevitably, the blood-soaked future. How did these people sleep at night? What did they tell their children as they put them to bed? Fascinated and repulsed, Duncan had stepped, hands clasped at his back, closer to the portrait, as if to find some clue in the twinkling eyes. Just then, the passport officer, who had stepped out for some form or stamp, had returned. In a tone of nationalistic syrup, she had said, "Isn't he great?" Her voice gave a reverential curtsey on the last syllable. Yes, Duncan had quickly agreed, yes—seized by a panic that she might refuse to issue him a new passport if he didn't agree with her vigorously enough.

In the Harambee Room, Duncan leaned over the conference table and extracted a chair from the jumble. Duncan was about to sit, when he noticed one of its legs was missing. Without a thought, Duncan threw it, overhand, back into the pile of furniture on the table, where it landed with a satisfying crunch. Let the police observe that. This small act of vandalism felt good. Alive. Something he would not have done before Hinga had stuck a gun in his face. Something was distinctly altered within him, an appetite for violence long dormant, now stirred. Perhaps now a detective would want to check on Duncan.

No one came. Duncan selected another chair, checking first that it could bear his weight. He took the chair to the front of the room, beside the locked door. A newspaper lay in the corner, *The Daily Republic*. He bent to pick it up. As he did so, he saw an electrical outlet. Duncan took out his phone and the charger and plugged in the phone.

The Daily Republic bore today's date. This cheered Duncan as a sign of recent human presence in the Harambee Room. Shrill headlines announced fresh scandals—army uniforms, fertilizer, shipping containers, sugar. Each a rich avenue for arbitrage. How did one get into these sorts of scams?

Duncan scanned the piece about a Kenyan sugar baron sponsoring a local music festival. The sugar baron's arrival at "big man" status was like the promotion of the pawn which, having survived the bloody march across the chessboard to attain the furthest reach of enemy territory, automatically transmuted into a queen. No further questions asked about the march itself—immediately and mandatorily. The newspaper article, accordingly, did not touch at all upon the provenance of the sugar baron's fortune—he was simply a barrel-chested, red-tied industrialist emerging from a black limousine.

The lock turned.

The door swung open, obscuring Duncan from the person who entered the room. A man's voice came from behind the door. "Hello?" The even voice, and its owner, seemed prepared to accept that the room might be empty.

Duncan dropped the newspaper to his lap. "I am here." A bearded man poked his head around the door, rimless glasses flashing. Closing the door behind him, the man said, "Ah, Mr.—", and paused to consult his clipboard. Satisfied, the man continued. "Mr. Bernardo? Yes. I apologize for keeping you waiting. And for your short incarceration. I have explained to the receptionist not to be quite so proactive." He laughed, closing his eyes as he did so. "My colleague informs me she had doubts as to your character, and 'therefore detained you'.

Her words."

The bearded man's pensive laugh disarmed Duncan, who retrieved his phone and charger and stood up.

The other man extended his hand. "We are shorthanded, what with our Big Brother Obama about to arrive. I am Detective Njema."

Njema wore jeans and a white shirt with the sleeves rolled up to the elbows. He motioned at the ruin of the conference table. His every movement seemed spare, as if Njema were husbanding limited resources. Even his beard was trimmed, neat and economical.

The two men sat at the table. Njema asked, "Coffee?"

"Yes please."

Njema called at the closed door. A moment later, it opened, and the policewoman with the bob haircut appeared. Her red fingernails clicked on the door handle. She cast her eyes at Njema, then Duncan, raising her eyebrows in question. Duncan frowned at his would-be captor, but she did not notice it.

Making a "V" with the forefingers of his right hand, Njema said, "Two coffees please."

The policewoman closed the door behind her. Njema said, "So."

"So. I told your colleague. I am here to report a missing person."

"And who is this person, and how do you know them?"

"She is an old friend, visiting from out of town. She arrived a day or so ago and-"

Njema held up his pen. "A day? That hardly makes this a missing-persons matter, especially with Obama about to arrive. Did you know that three quarters of people reported missing make themselves known within thirty-six hours?"

Duncan was silent. Njema's contented smile suggested he placed great stock in such statistical conversation-enders.

The version of the story Duncan wanted to tell, to have on record so as to get the investigative ball rolling, had been hashed together on the back of the boda boda and was impressionistic at best. His story, Duncan realized, probably had many gaps like these, where facts had been extracted like teeth, leaving only a bloodied smile. Duncan contemplated just unburdening himself and telling Njema the whole thing. Or nothing perhaps, just getting up and leaving.

Njema's head was cocked sideways, as he took in Duncan's cogitations.

So, Duncan said, "Well, we were in a car accident yesterday. Along the new bypass." Duncan bit his lip, thinking of Nice crying in his car, her bony shoulders shaking under the sodium lights. "I passed out. And when I awoke, she was gone."

Njema gave a sad smile, the skin around his eyes crinkling. "Your friend, what is her name?"

Duncan told him Nice's passport name—Theresa— so unfamiliar on his tongue. Njema wrote nothing and this concerned Duncan vaguely. Duncan had, he supposed, put down the relevant particulars on his sign-in sheet.

The policeman continued. "And she was visiting from?" Seduced by the comforts of truth-telling, Duncan said,

"Mogadishu."

Njema half rose and drew back his chair. He reached for the clipboard, placed it on his lap, and wrote. Extravagant scratchings against the clipboard. He stretched his legs under the table. It looked a posture he had taken many times before. The fingernails of Njema's right hand were making slight movements on the table-top, like a lie detector inking

its observations. "Your friend is Somali?"

"Oh no, she is a Canadian, working there. You know, aid work. She comes to Nairobi for rest." Duncan put his hands out like the scales of a balance, as though to show that Canada and Somalia somehow canceled each other out. "Big city, bright lights," he stupidly added.

Njema clasped his fingers across his belly, balancing clipboard on his lap. "What date and flight number did she arrive on?"

Duncan told him.

Njema also took the license plate of Duncan's car. Njema was about to speak when the door swung open, and the receptionist walked in, trailing the steam and scent of two chipped red cups of Nescafe. She rested them on the smooth hardwood table. Duncan scanned for coasters.

Njema excused himself, taking the flight and license information with him. Duncan took up the coffee cup, milky and sweet—Niyi would have liked this, he thought. In the circumstances, even Duncan liked it.

Njema strode back into the room. His demeanor had soured. "Why the delay between your accident and this police report? Did you not have a police response to the accident itself?"

It seemed a good question, a response to which Duncan should have had at the ready. A wave of self-pity washed over him, he'd had such little time, such little rest. The more he thought, the longer he took to respond, the sadder Njema's eyes seemed to get.

Duncan bit his lower lip. "There was a policeman at the scene of the accident, so I thought perhaps he had made a report. I am a foreigner and not used to the way these things are done here. I thought his report might be in the system, and I needed to rest. Which is why I have come now, as soon as I felt up to it, to follow up."

Duncan was aware he was rambling in long, not-necessarily-responsive sentences, so he forced himself to stop speaking. He made a show of cradling the coffee cup in his hands and then took a long sip.

Njema waited until Duncan put down the coffee cup. "This policeman you mention, the responding officer. Do you recall his name, his badge number?"

Duncan forced himself to take another sip of the sweet coffee, before responding. "Hinga." He looked Njema in the eye. "Is it a common name? If not, perhaps you could contact him."

Njema broke eye contact and wrote a word on his pad.
Then underlined it noisily.

The policewoman re-entered the room without knocking.
Njema's eyes remained fixed on his legal pad. Behind Njema's
chair, she spoke into his ear, a rapid stream of Swahili. As she
stood, her eyes grew wide when they took in the word on Njema's yellow pad. Njema sensed this too, perhaps with some regret, and looked up at his colleague, his brow furrowed.

She was quick to understand she had overstepped and
excused herself. The door clicked shut behind her.

The detective trained his eyes on Duncan, who rested his
coffee cup on his knee.

Njema spoke with the same economy of his physical
vocabulary. "Hinga is not a common name." He scratched a
nostril with the nail of his thumb. "No immigration or customs
record of your friend having entered the country. What do you
make of this?"

Duncan played dumb.

Njema was a detective, so he should do some detecting.
Duncan figured he had given the man enough of a head-start.

Instead, Duncan took the role of the respectful foreigner.
"What can I make of it? I can't speculate on such things beyond
my control." Duncan tapped his fingers against the table,
gaining assurance with each truthful utterance. "What I can
assure you, Detective Njema, is that I did collect my friend from
the airport. That we did have a terrific accident. And that I am
extremely worried for her wellbeing."

Duncan was also conscious that he needed to end this
meeting if he was to make the rendezvous with Ciru's son— his
only glimmer of immediate hope, after the way this session had
gone.

Duncan said, with an attempt at finality, "You can reach me on the number I put down on the sign-in form. Is there any other information I can provide to assist in this matter?"

Njema's chin wag was barely perceptible. Duncan stood.

With his hand on the door handle, Duncan turned back and said, "Njema. That means safe, doesn't it?"

The man in the chair did not look up from his clipboard.

16

THE STORKS SMELLED OF ROTTING THINGS. Duncan stood in the portico of the police station, gathering himself, when he was startled by a screech of sheet metal from above. A stork had ripped a piece from the corrugated roof and held it in its beak. Unblinking beady eyes regarded Duncan.

What were these creatures still doing here?

Duncan felt a hand on his shoulder. He noted the red fingernails as he turned to the bobbed receptionist. Her limbs boyish in the boxy khaki uniform.

"Sorry," she said. "For what?"

"For misreading your energy. And then locking you into that conference room."

"My energy?" He laughed, and it felt good to find something humorous, to allow oneself the luxury of authenticity. "And what sort of energy is that?"

The policewoman put out her hand, gold bangle sparkling. "My name is Muthoni."

He took her hand. "I am Duncan, as you know from the forms you had me fill out." Duncan grinned. "What is my energy right now?" Her hand felt good, and he liked her haircut. There was an absurd urge to lean in and smell her hair. He was glad that he was out of his clerical uniform. What was wrong with him?

Muthoni paused. She looked away from Duncan's face, at the clamoring traffic. "You are angry. You regret your past. You are afraid you are not equipped for where you find yourself." These things she said in the tone of a doctor pronouncing the diagnosis of a lifestyle-induced disease.

Duncan's grin died.

He took his hand from hers and followed her gaze onto Mathenge Road.

Muthoni continued, "That is how I misread you. I saw darkness about you, in you. But I see now you are afloat in it. It is not something you are emitting. For now. But you must get your bearings quickly."

Still not looking at Muthoni, Duncan said with as much bitterness as he could muster, "And what is the charge for this psychic analysis?"

She did not take the bait. "I have this ability. I know it needs fine-tuning, maybe more than that. But I have it. And that is why I became a policewoman, because I can— She stumbled for the word she wanted, then continued—I get glimpses of things, of people. Anticipate them perhaps."

"Is that why you take the liberty of depriving people of their freedom in conference rooms? Because you anticipate their guilt? There's a term for that. Kidnapping."

Muthoni looked down. "Look, the officer at your accident, Hinga. I've read his energy, and his file, and . . . if there's anything I can help with. Well, you should just know that he is a dangerous man. Prepared to go to dangerous lengths."

"Was," added Duncan, turning to look at Muthoni. "Was a dangerous man." A vision of Hinga's knee cap split open, the obscenity of the pale-yellow cartilage.

"What do you mean?"

Duncan regretted his indiscretion instantly. "Nothing. Look, he hasn't even filed a report. I just need to find my friend. Can you think of anywhere I could look?"

Muthoni brought her red fingernails to her mouth. She chewed her lip. "So you think the Somalis have taken her. Makes sense, as a working theory. It sounds like you shouldn't be doing this by yourself."

"But I'm not. Which is why I came here. To let the professionals handle it. But I'm not sure how or when your assistance will come, since you have no record of my friend even having entered Kenya." Duncan thought for a moment, then asked, "Could Hinga have been able to falsify the immigration records?"

Muthoni shrugged. "I don't know. Maybe. What I do know is the fact that he is involved usually means something big is happening. His last two partners on the police force have been shot to death, in apparent encounters with gangsters. Both times he ended up reporting the incident and getting a medal."

"Was he investigated?"

The policewoman looked at her feet.

"And cleared, both times. Look, Mr. Bernardo, you may think the police are just looking out for ourselves, but you should know that there are those of us, young officers, who entered the force with the intention of making a difference." Her bangle flashed in the sunlight. "Of not letting life be so cheap. Of building a society in which dignity is not something only afforded to some people. This is the infrastructure of opportunity. This man, Hinga, he is the enemy of these ideas. Of course, he does not see himself as opposing any particular ideology, because he is on a path that was chosen by circumstances for him a long time ago. But—and let me be clear with you before you go and do whatever it is you intend to do—I am prepared to oppose such men, such people, to the very boundaries of the law."

Her throat caught, her eyes glinted. "I did not have the audacity to think I could make a difference. Forever waiting for the big man, the chief, Obama, whoever, to arrive, to save me, to save us. But what I've learned, there is no Obama. Not really, no matter how much he grins, his hands are full of blood. I am my own Obama." From the breast pocket of her oversized uniform, she took a shred of paper and handed it to Duncan, who accepted it without looking away from her face. Muthoni whispered, "Be your own Obama."

It surprised and moved Duncan to hear her speak like this. Patriotism was like religion in Kenya—practiced in public, on prescribed occasions, in prescribed rituals, following the American model. A frenzied melancholia for a vague set of ideals, which could be funneled into war lust, or in peacetime the support of a sports team.

But to hear a young person speak like this, for no audience other than himself, and with an earnestness and specificity defying his most jaundiced views, was humbling. Duncan began to realize that his faith, his religion, indeed his profession, was the horse to which he had hitched his hopes of belonging to something bigger than himself. And that horse was proving increasingly lame.

And he had begun to despise himself for having invested his spirituality, his youth, his manhood, his very being, in an off-the-shelf product. For not having had the stones to pursue Nice, or any other woman since. For not having had the courage and creativity to craft his own concept of something meaningful. To build his own infrastructure of hope. Maybe this was the reason for that pool of rage, smooth and dark as glass, hidden within him. When had it started to build?

Yet this young policewoman was so clear-eyed in her self-belief, of being an agent of change in a society riddled with inequality and despair.

Duncan said, "I admire you." He paused, unsure of how much to share. "And I think I am envious of you."

"Envious? What of?"

Duncan shook his head. "I don't know." "The answer is yes."

"What? I never—"

"You don't need to say it out loud. The answer is yes."

Duncan held up his hands, confused. "I don't know what question you think you're responding to, but…"

"Is it okay to be you? The answer is yes, Duncan."

She used his first name. Feeling a hot stinging behind his eyeballs, Duncan steeled himself against tears. "I don't know what I will do. What I am even capable of. But I must go to get my friend."

Before Muthoni could respond, a firm male voice came over her shoulder. "Is everything all right?"

It was Detective Njema, arms akimbo, leaning his shoulder against the door jamb. Duncan and Muthoni turned towards him, forming a tense triangle.

Muthoni spoke in a tone transformed by Njema's arrival, a tone containing within it a professional apology. "Yes. Yes, Detective. He was just leaving."

Duncan made his way down to Mathenge Road, where he waved down a boda boda.

Njema asked, "What were you talking about?"

Muthoni stood with her hands splayed on the balustrade of the portico, chin thrust at the parking lot. "How to be human. I think."

They watched Duncan study the piece of paper she had given him in his hand, look back up at them, at her, and then put the paper back into his pocket. Duncan put on a red helmet, mounted the boda boda on the dusty shoulder of the roadside.

The motorbike entered the stream of traffic. Muthoni tracked Duncan, until his red helmet was visible no more.

17

CIRU PUSHED HER HIPS FORWARD, hands resting on her upper buttocks.

Maybe she was getting too old for this sort of thing? This line of work.

She thought of her grandmother, who had raised her. Nyanya, the healer, that fierce matriarch whom people came to see for miles around. Even in her nineties, Nyanya had never been too old, or too scared, to help.

Once, as a child, no more than eleven or twelve, Ciru walked into Nyanya's room to show her a charcoal drawing she had made at school. There, prone on Nyanya's bed, lay a naked woman, her back covered in weeping sores. The patient was sobbing, as Nyanya, sleeves rolled up to her elbows, lanced each boil with a long needle, exquisitely careful, then covered each deflated pustule with a green poultice the consistency of porridge. The sharp odor of the poultice filled the room. Nyanya hummed as she worked, pausing only to make smiling eye contact with her granddaughter.

But Nyanya and her clinic were ultimately done in by family members. In particular, the snaggle-toothed Uncle Hizzy, who repeatedly tried to get the young Ciru to be alone with him, have her sit on his lap, stroke her hair. It was worse when he drank changaa, which he did often, from plastic bags, slurping and belching a visible miasma of sorghum-flavored alcohol. It was courage born out of exasperation that caused Ciru to tell Uncle Hizzy that what he was doing to her was wrong. To which he had smilingly replied that it could not be wrong, or else God simply would not allow it to happen. The leering logic had stumped Ciru, as she watched him peel off his sweaty shirt and hold out his arms to her.

Perhaps Uncle Hizzy had a point, wasn't this more or less what the Bible said, what the schoolteachers taught? It was, to her child's mind, like learning of a new law of physics, implacable, utterly indifferent to her. This alienation was somehow more frightening than the sight of her drunk uncle, struggling to wriggle out of his trousers. In sheer panic, she had burst out of Uncle Hizzy's hut and run up the hill to Nyanya's clinic.

Ciru had intended only to seek counsel from her grandmother, guidance on this terrifying logic, but she burst into hooting sobs at the sight of Nyanya's kindly face. Nyanya had held her, coaxed the story out of her, then made her a cup of sweet tea. Ciru still recalled a coconut shell, entirely covered in red and white beads, resting on the kitchen floor. Then, Nyanya left the clinic, bearing in her hands the pot containing just-boiled water.

As Ciru sipped the tea, contemplating her Nyanya's advice, there came a hideous howling from Uncle Hizzy's hut. And he never approached Ciru again. Indeed, he was taken to the local clinic for his burns and stayed there for some weeks.

But the victory proved short-lived.

For Hizzy had risen from his hospital bed, face like a

melted plastic bag, and then rallied the rest of the family and the local Church officials into a campaign against Nyanya's healing clinic. A ruse to take Nyanya's house and land, which he saw as just compensation for his injuries. The Church outlawed the healing practice, declaring it "barbaric" and "an abhorrence in the eyes of the Lord" in xeroxed pamphlets that were distributed in the village. And so, one day, not long after Hizzy's return from the hospital, policemen came to their home, carrying large long-handled hammers and a court order and asked Nyanya and Ciru to step outside. Nyanya held Ciru's hand, and they watched wordlessly as the policemen demolished their house, which also served as Nyanya's clinic. Ciru remembered Nyanya's hand squeezing hers when the policemen shattered the windowpanes—the deafening crash and the physical sensation becoming one.

Two weeks later, Uncle Hizzy razed a portion of the sacred forest, erected a rough shack of corrugated iron, to serve as a drinking and gambling establishment. Ciru and Nyanya were shunted into a neighbor's house, where they were tolerated in the way poor village relatives are. A few weeks after living in that jumbled way, Nyanya simply wouldn't wake up one morning when Ciru brought her tea.

She was dead.

"Her heart has been broken by the hammers," said the neighbor with whom they lived. Ciru was shuttled back and forth amongst relatives, but then decided at age fifteen that she would be better off independent, in Nairobi. Nyanya had taught her many things about how to live and the art of healing, things that she could use to make a living in the big city.

The memory soothed Ciru, made her feel rooted and strong—embodying Nyanya's spirit. Moving to America, living as a second-class person amongst impatient and ill-mannered Westerners, had made her feel unanchored, vulnerable. It was not an emotion that she had allowed herself to feel since that time with Uncle Hizzy. It was hard for Ciru, and something she had done only out of love and concern for her son, Edmund. The very thought of their time in America evoked regret. Not because she missed it. Quite the contrary, she had been happy to return to Kenya, its smiling faces, its generous climate. The familiarity of it, the ability to read nuances correctly. No, it was that life and, more particularly, the deportation, broke her relationship with her son Edmund. Edmund, to whom she had promised a new future among the funny-accented New Yorkers. Edmund, for whose sake Ciru had uprooted her own, admittedly dysfunctional, life.

To Ciru, America was a code-word encompassing the thousand disappointments in Edmund's face as they sat, elbow to elbow, on the hard bench of the immigration holding cell. Tattooed men spat and swore in Spanish. One man seemed to be asking Edmund for his new-looking basketball shoes. But her son only stared at the dirty floor in silence. In a defeat born of betrayal.

She picked up her phone. The only contact under her Favorites was Ed. She pressed the dial button, then quickly hit cancel. Edmund had told her not to call him, explaining that SMSs sufficed, except in the event of emergency. She began to thumb a text message, but stumbled on the choice of words. How could a text message begin to capture all that roiled in her heart—that she was sorry, that she would make things all right, that all she wanted was to hear his voice, cook a meal for him, be a family. That their time was slipping between their fingers. That she remembered the smell of the talcum powder from when she used to change his cloth nappies as a baby. How he used to ask her for "a story from your mouth" at bedtime. She shook her head, deleting the text. Tears welling, she dialed Edmund's number.

No response.

To distract herself, Ciru turned her thoughts to business. By the sunlight slanting in, Ciru could tell it was mid-afternoon, so it had been eight or nine hours since she'd put Duncan in that matatu. He'd seemed all right, a bit shaken to be sure, but seemed to have responded well to the imperative tone she had set for their interactions. She might get away with the money from the white man, the drugs from this Nice, and getting Hinga out of the way definitively. Not a bad day at the office.

Ciru hummed as she walked to the kitchen table. On the rough tabletop, in a patch of sunlight, lay Duncan's honey-colored leather wallet. She flipped it open. Some bank notes, business cards, no photographs. Ciru rifled through the business cards until she found the slim deck of Duncan's own cards. She took up her phone and dialed the mobile number listed.

A chirruping came from under the bed behind her, where she had left Duncan's phone.

Ciru shook her head. Maybe she was getting too soft. Perhaps this bit of business would be her last, giving her a rolling start into retirement. Into really trying to fix her relationship with her son. Perhaps she could consider taking him to Australia, or Canada. They were all the same to her—faraway, full of tall, awkward obstacles to be navigated. But she would go, with a smile on her face, if only he would speak to her, so they could plan this together.

She thumbed the keypad of her phone again, this time dialing the landline listed on Duncan's card.

It rang several times, before a sleepy male voice answered.

Ciru said, "Hello, is Father Bernardo there please?" As she spoke, she spun Duncan's driver's license between the poles of her forefinger and the table. The edges of the laminated license formed a blurry white plane.

The voice lost its sleepiness. "I'm afraid he is not in." An uncertain pause. "May I be of some assistance?"

Ciru let the driver's license fall flat against the tabletop. Duncan's faded photograph looked up at her. A younger face, but still that thin smile hinting at suggestibility. Her ears pricked up at the solicitousness of the phrase "May I be of some assistance?" No receptionist, in Ciru's experience, would use such a sentence. Rather, the person on the phone held a position of some responsibility at the mission and may consequently have some fresh information about how Duncan had spent his morning. They may well have spent the morning together.

Ciru was silent. A healer was first and foremost a professional listener. Did the voice have a foreign accent? African but not Kenyan, perhaps?

The voice came again, deep, cleared of any cobwebs of boredom or drowsiness, and seeking to establish a tone of professionalism. "Hello? Madam. Are you still there?"

Ciru said, "Yes. Yes, I am here. I am sorry I am just a little shaken. You see I was just calling to see if Father Bernardo was all right."

"Ah, you mean the accident. Did he give you his card?" Ciru jumped at this thread, "Yes, the accident. He was bleeding. The car was on fire. Oh, I just want to know that he
   is all right."

"Yes ma'am. He is fine. In fact, Pastor Bernardo is at the police station."

Ciru stopped chewing her lip. "The police station?" She placed the ball of her thumb squarely on Duncan's smiling photograph, then picked the license off the table using only the moisture of her skin.

"He's gone to make a statement."

Ciru made no reply. The plastic laminated driver's license fell from her thumb.

In her earpiece, the voice asked, "Were you a witness?

Perhaps you could also make a statement. It could help." "This is a good idea. And what is your name?"

"My name is Olaniyi. Please call me Niyi. And may I have your name please."

"Thank you, Niyi. Do you work for Father Bernardo?"

With a distinct sniff, she heard him say, "We are colleagues, yes." His earnestness cooled.

Ciru smiled. "Please tell Father Bernardo that Dr. Mikende called to wish him well. Please also tell him that I am happy to make a statement to the police. It is in times like these that we must keep our friends close to us, in safe places. Our friends are relying on us. Do tell him that for me please." Niyi asked, "And may I take your number, Dr. Mikende?

I am sure Pastor Bernardo would like to—"

Ciru cut him off. "He knows how to reach me, Niyi." Then added, with measured menace, "He knows how to reach me."

Niyi was about to say something when Ciru hung up. She stood there, holding the phone in the dusty silence of her room. The embers of fury stirred in her skull. Ciru put the phone on the table and held her hand out, its bony fingers quivering.

What had the fool gone and spoken to the police about? Was he just naïve, the way some foreigners could be in the face of peril? Or just as pathologically unable to resolve issues for himself, reared as Westerners were to be soothed at the teat of neon-jacketed authorities at every stage of their lives? Or did he truly have the stomach for a fight?

It seemed unlikely, but the line of questioning chipped away at her iron self-belief so critical to her ability to do her job. Like water seeking a means of egress, fear and doubt sought to corrode their way into her consciousness. She covered her face with her hands. If the corrosion grew too deep, she could not be in this game without posing serious risks to herself.

And to Edmund.

To gather herself, she picked up her phone. Her fingers still trembling, she redialed the mission's landline.

Niyi answered on the first ring.

Ciru said, "On second thought, young man, I fear the Father may not be able to reach me. Do you know if he still has his phone?"

"I am so glad you called back. No, Pastor Bernardo did mention he had lost his phone in the accident. Could I perhaps have your number so that I may contact you?" He paused, then added, "I mean, so that I may pass along your details to Pastor?"

Ciru took the phone away from her ear, smiling to herself. This Niyi had potential. She could sense the resentment he felt for Duncan, humming in the microwaves connecting their voices. Ciru decided to engage him in an open-ended, medium-term sort of way.

She gave Niyi her mobile number. Niyi repeated the number in slow fragments, whispering a "Yes o" once a digit was confirmed by Ciru as correctly repeated, until he felt satisfied that he had transcribed it correctly. He had to be Nigerian.

Then Ciru said, "Feel free to call me if I may be of any assistance. Our interests are aligned."

Niyi's voice was lined with exploratory overtures, "What do you mean, Dr. Mikende?"

Oh dear, thought Ciru, are we dealing with a cunning dunce? But she also knew the importance of patience in such ambiguously plotted alliances. With a solid warmth in her tone, she said, "To see Father Bernardo move past the accident."

"Oh." Palpable disappointment.

Ciru was feeling better already. These were familiar waters for her, making subcutaneous suggestions in conversations, like landmines placed and mapped, and then traffic funneled this way or that, depending on the outcome she wanted. The bile of doubt and anxiety retreated and she could scarcely believe she had been worried, dealing as she was with such rank amateurs.

For exactly moments like this, Ciru had memorized a series of quotes, which she would sprinkle strategically into conversations. Well-chosen quotes were useful as conversational set-pieces because they furthered bonding and camouflaged the true extent of her own knowledge—all without coming across as threatening or pompous. Winston Churchill was a favorite of hers, because Anglo-Saxons were generally raised to believe that Churchill was some sort of demi-god who had turned back a tide of pointy-helmeted demons by holding up one doughy hand and blowing smoke rings in their faces.

But for a man like Niyi—seething under the daily assault of perceived slights, professionally religious, for a man like that, scripture would work much better.

Neither Niyi nor Ciru had spoken for several seconds. She could imagine that either held the phone in the exact same pose, separated only by a few kilometers of concrete and forest. Ciru was as comfortable inhabiting the murky depths of a pause, as Niyi must have been twitching with nervous energy. As Ciru waited for Niyi to speak first, she felt something pass between them.

Niyi said, dry-mouthed, "Are you still there? Dr. Mikende?"

Ciru stayed silent, establishing her mastery of the pacing of the conversation. Then, worried that this oaf might actually hang up, she spoke in slow, clear syllables, "But be ye doers of the word and not hearers only, deceiving your own selves."

No response from Niyi, so Ciru added, in a low urgent voice, "Are we together?"

"We are together."

Ciru felt vital and sated. This feeling only blossomed further when Niyi asked, "Do you want his number? His new number, I mean?"

Ciru took down Duncan's new number, smiling the while.

18

"THEY CALL ME THE SURGEON." Edmund was bent over the grass-green ping-pong table, with furrowed brow, and an orange orb in the palm of his hand. In his attitude of fierce concentration, his fine features, the cable of muscle twitching in his jaw, he resembled his mother, Ciru, a great deal.

Duncan had found Edmund easily enough in the downtown bar. It being the middle of the day, there were no other patrons. Edmund cut a striking figure, lean as an adolescent boy, with oversized glasses, and an expensive- looking watch shimmering on his narrow-boned wrist. It had also made it easier for Duncan to spot him, given that Edmund had drawn a lot of attention to himself, engaged as he was in a high-volume discussion with the barman about the pub ping-pong standings and how they may have been arrived at using a less-than-arms-length methodology.

Edmund seemed to have been at the bar for some time by the time Duncan showed up.

Once they met, Edmund had been cordial and host-like. Despite this quasi-proprietorial approach, Edmund did not offer to pay for the beers which he insisted they order.

Duncan, his mind still grinding for ways to connect

the dots from this bar to rescuing Nice, and eager to establish rapport with the quirky young man, had cheerfully agreed to the beers and cheerfully paid for them. Duncan put his lips to the glass, feeling the pale cool lager before tasting it. He took a first, tentative sip, guilty at the thought of being here, then a long pull, feeling an immediate buoyancy, a sense of recusal from any responsibility for the present scene—or indeed any consequences which could arise from it. He was here to find a way to rescue Nice, to drive some sense of urgency into the witch, Ciru. With this clinical and as yet unsloppy eye, Duncan took in the sockless and hairless ankle of Edmund above the fawn suede driving moccasins, black rubber buttons studding their soles and squeaking against the barroom floor.

One beer in, Edmund said, "Let's play."

Duncan absorbed a pointed look from the barman, who seemed, while slowly polishing glasses behind his weathered mahogany counter, to survey the interactions between Duncan and Edmund with wary yet friendly eyes.

And then there was the ping-pong parlor. Behind the bar, through a set of sliding and green-tinted glass doors, the "PPP" as Edmund referred to it with a distinctly proprietary air, lay in an air-conditioned hush—no players, no piped-in music, no windows. Under bleaching tube-light, six or so ping-pong tables were lined up. Under each table was a wicker basket containing the table-tennis bats.

Edmund had been eager to play before even talking to Duncan, or finding out what had brought Duncan to Nairobi, or may have set this meeting into motion. Edmund's behavior seemed to suggest that he made same-day appointments for table tennis, for ping pong, with random people over social media all the time.

Which is how Duncan, beer sloshing in his belly, found himself crouching over his end of the table, awaiting the Surgeon's serve.

"Here comes the pain," said Edmund.

Edmund's serve was backhanded, viciously undercut. The orange missile skimmed the net, incandesced past Duncan's outstretched bat, clipped the white-lipped diagonal corner of the table at Duncan's elbow and hit Duncan in the groin soundlessly. The ball clattered to the floor at Duncan's feet.

"Honoré de ball-sac," added the Surgeon.

Duncan had hoped this ping-pong outing was to be conducted in a spirit of ironic levity. As an accompaniment to the consumption of alcohol. But the Surgeon gave no such indication—his eyes were dead earnest behind the flashing of his thick-rimmed glasses. In fact, the Surgeon had now produced from his person what appeared to be a cut-off tube sock, which he proceeded to wear around his head. This sweatband, if that was what it was intended to be, bore red snowflakes all around the base of the Surgeon's skull. Atop Edmund's thick-framed tortoiseshell glasses, the butchered tube sock gave a maniacal and mismatched impression.

To buy time, Duncan stammered, "Why do they call you the Surgeon?"

"Because," said Edmund, pursing his lips with impatience, rolling the orange orb across the knuckles of his right hand and surveying the table like a fireman would a burning building. "Because, I only operate along the lines." Edmund pointed a long forefinger at the white lines which divided Duncan's side into two rectangular halves.

"Aha."

The games were, mercifully, quite quick. Duncan made

sure to drink a lot of beer, a ready excuse in the event Edmund recriminated him the lack of meaningful opposition. But the Surgeon was evidently a gracious winner, making no mention of the lack of sport.

They sat on a backless bench, sweaty and savoring the lick and hum of the air conditioning. The barman had invisibly refreshed their beers. Duncan thought it was their third, although he had, in the fury of chasing the plastic balls across the table, lost count.

By way of addressing the elephant in the room, and in an attempt at humor, Duncan said, "Well, Surgeon, I believe the patient could not be revived."

Edmund snorted. "You stink. Why did you even want to play?"

Duncan rested his elbows on his knees and clasped his hands. He stared at the triangle thus formed by his forearms. He wanted to level with Edmund, who seemed a decent, if strange, fellow. The beer lapped at his skull.

Duncan knew that his window for taking the initiative in this interaction was limited. He felt, in trying social situations, a keen need to be likeable, and, with any luck, liked. He needed to cut to the chase and explain the situation and the stakes to Edmund. But as a Westerner, Duncan felt compelled to place conversational down payments—small talk in which he made himself marginally but demonstrably vulnerable—before addressing his true agenda or expecting a reciprocal show of cards from his interlocutor. This was not necessarily the anatomy of dialogue in Kenya, or indeed most places Duncan had traveled or lived that were not Canada or America, where perfect strangers could ask, without any intention or thought of overreaching, for instance why Duncan wasn't married. It was just a point of fact, which must have a reasonable explanation and not some sort of existential Rubik's Cube. People here tended to be confused when this line of questioning generated angst in the questionee. Duncan glanced over at Edmund, who was frowning, furiously thumbing his phone's keys.

Neither spoke. Duncan looked away, steeling himself for the required next steps.

Edmund's face soured, and he put down his phone. "Well, that settles it."

"Settles what?" Duncan felt a wooden tiredness under the effects of the alcohol and his own indecision.

"Just a debate on a chat board. Some joker is insisting that the quote from Lone Wolf & Cub is, 'Will you slay me with your slender arms?' when of course it is, in point of fact, 'Can you slay me with your slender arms? Can you execute the executioner?'"

Duncan said, "Hmm, you into Japanese cinema?"

"Not all of it. I find its sexual politics quite baffling, for instance."

Duncan back-pedaled, not wanting to offend. "Of course. Of course." Perhaps saying something true about himself was the right course of action. So Duncan added, "I practice martial arts. Hung Gaar five animal kung fu"

Edmund turned on him and growled, "Taai-ga style." "Precisely. The tiger is taught to beginners, because a tiger's engagement in battle is based on proximity. You don't need to project power beyond yourself, which is more demanding. And a tiger's way of being, the way it leaps and lands on prey, requires great physical courage. Physical courage is a building block for martial artists, because it allows you to believe you are possessed of more meaningful forms of courage." It felt good to speak of things he knew.

Edmund crossed his legs primly, his ankles winking as he did so. "Show me." Edmund held his beer stein in his lap, like a bucket of popcorn at a movie.

Duncan stood.

He recalled his first sifu, a Chinese-American postal worker, demonstrating the choreography of a Hung Gaar form in a draughty Lower East Side loft. The form was named "Subdue the Tiger Fist", and the sifu's white-socked feet danced across the faded parquet. As Duncan had himself mastered that form and the many subsequent ones, each with names of a similar rickety lyricism, he had envisioned and internalized the basic overarching structure of each, like the floorplan of a cathedral, the naves and transepts of the choreography transpiercing each other. This shorthand allowed for quick recall.

Ninety-seven seconds later—Duncan knew from long and hard practice—Duncan bowed to Edmund. At the close of the form, Duncan's left hand, straightened save for the tucked- in thumb, circled from his waist and met his right hand, which was balled into a fist. Sun and moon. Sword and pen. A time for each. A place for each. The hardwiring, so painstakingly laid, remained operational, buried though it was under quotidian detritus. The machine still ticked true. Duncan felt the serenity which comes with having accomplished something beautiful, something earned at great personal sacrifice, an endeavor in which success was not guaranteed.

Edmund clapped three times, the sound echoing in the empty bar-room. He tilted the beer glass back and drank it dry. Then he stood and, as though convinced of the quality of merchandise which Duncan was representing, said, "Let's go back to my place."

Duncan padded his pockets—the right back pocket held the wad of cash retrieved from the safe. He had peeled off a few notes and placed them in the other pocket. He withdrew these and paid the barman, conscious all the while that he was using the Ministry's emergency funds to buy beer. Edmund stood a few paces away watching the transaction with pursed lips, hands jammed into the pockets of his distressed jeans. Edmund made no attempt to pretend he had any intention of paying, or even that the interaction could in any way be conceived to bear any relation to him. Duncan found this transparent aloofness simultaneously intensely irritating (given the limited funds at his disposal) and refreshing in its brazenness. Looking at Edmund in the mirror over the barman's shoulder, Duncan thought that Edmund even seemed inconvenienced by this unpleasant business of waiting for Duncan.

As the barman handed back the change, Edmund, as if to hurry the matter to a close, said, "I live near." Duncan began to count the change, but Edmund arched his eyebrows and tilted his head, to signal impatience. Cowed by this gesture, Duncan simply thrust the limp notes into his back pocket.

Less than five minutes later, Duncan and Edmund stood in the hushed cool marble lobby of Edmund's building. The aesthetic of the building seemed, to Duncan, to ape a Manhattan apartment building. The mutely reverential top-hatted doorman, the extravagant potted hairbrush cactus (each of its pricks removed), the brass-buttoned elevator panel. In the lobby, like an indecipherable modernist structure, stood four-foot-high red lettering—ARB5. This was the name of the building (signifying, so the discrete signage informed, the property's five-acre footprint giving onto the arboretum).

Edmund opened the door of his L-shaped penthouse unit

and waved Duncan in. The foyer gave onto a sparsely furnished living room. It was pervaded with the sort of monochromatic minimalism intended to project costliness.

Past the television, large and sleek as a fighter plane, affixed to the wall in the manner of a painting, was a door which opened onto the balcony. This sliding door was open, the breeze blowing the gossamer curtain liner into the flat.

"Hypnotic, isn't it?" said Edmund.

Duncan turned and saw Edmund also looking at the dance of the gauzed material, framed as it was against the swaying treetops in the backdrop. Duncan said nothing.

"You haven't said that it's a nice place," said Edmund, stepping sideways out onto the balcony.

"Right. No, it's a beautiful place," Duncan replied quickly. He had no frame of reference for Edmund's expectations, conversational or otherwise.

Edmund gestured to one of the two wicker chairs on the balcony, and Duncan sat. Edmund then turned his back to Duncan and stood at the two-doored drinks cabinet.

As Edmund opened the doors of the cabinet, he said, over his shoulder, "No, that's fine. I mean most Westerners who come here say, nice place, with an undercurrent of surprise, as though I had pulled a fast one on the cosmos. It's another reason why I'm happy to be back in Kenya. It takes a lot to surprise a Kenyan—we make fewer assumptions."

Duncan looked back at Edmund, but Edmund was bent over the cabinet counter. Ice cubes clinked into glassware. Silence was the best course of action until he could figure out how to take this forward. Maybe the best thing to do was just to ask Edmund for help, maybe he could reason with Ciru. At least they weren't in a public place anymore, that seemed to open up potential options for the interaction. Besides, Edmund seemed perfectly at ease with pauses and nonsequiturs.

Edmund turned to face Duncan. Between the forefingers of Edmund's left hand was a prodigious joint. In his right hand, he palmed two thick-walled tumblers of what looked like a pale Coca Cola. Edmund set down the tinkling glasses, already bedewed with condensation, on the table between the two wicker chairs, but did not sit. He produced a red plastic lighter from his jeans, and, shielding its wavering flame with a cupped hand, lit the joint.

Edmund took a hit. "That is the true Guns, Germs and Steel of the West." He said this as though it were a strand of some narrative he had been weaving for some time. Again, Duncan forced himself not to respond, reminded himself that this conversation was something that was essentially happening outside him, to him, like being splashed by a passing bus on a rainy day.

Edmund blew out a bank of blue smoke which stood for a second, then dissipated into the arboretum.

He continued, "The ability to have awkward conversations, I mean. The rest of us, black and brown people, hate and fear awkward conversations. So we don't have them, as a rule. And so we generally don't fix what ails us." Edmund drew again on the joint, eyes closing in pleasure. "At the end of a meal in a restaurant, for instance, an English guy will likely delve into an analysis about who had starters, who had numer- ous cocktails and so on. With a view, of course, to divvying up the bill in an equitable way—I mean, he has no malice in this regard. The rest are left in toe-curling embarrassment. And I suppose it was the same with Africa, or the Empire. I suppose they saw Africa like some sort of uranium and diamond en- crusted pizza. The same for climate change, or human rights. No real ill-feeling for the local chaps, but just a situation in need of optimization, after a few awkward conversations. You know?"

Duncan did not know.

Edmund jabbed the glowing tip of the joint in Duncan's direction. Duncan blinked and shifted backward in his chair. Sensing that Duncan had not understood him, Edmund reached across the table and proffered the joint to Duncan. Duncan shook his head, no. A muscle in Edmund's jaw rippled. He sucked his teeth, took the joint back and drew on it.

Edmund said, "Do you know why the Israelis make all young people join the army?"

Unable to contain himself, and relieved that the business of the declined joint seemed forgotten, Duncan said, "National security?"

Eyes reddening, Edmund smiled at Duncan. Edmund's teeth looked tamed, as though he had worn braces. Edmund said, "Dirty hands."

Duncan was blank, so Edmund elaborated. "The premise being that if we all have hands which have been dirtied in the course of communal corvée, then it will take that much more backbone to call it out when the emperor bends over in his new clothes."

From behind him, Duncan heard the susurrus of the curtain liner twisting in the breeze.

"Similarly," said Edmund, again extending the joint at Duncan.

Duncan paused, then held the very tip of the joint between the tips of his thumb and forefinger, as though it were a piece of vital evidence. The sweet taste of the hash instantly activated long archived memories. An urban playground in dying sunlight, its seesaw broken in half at the fulcrum. An old friend's VW Golf, her glove compartment full of tiny coke bottle Haribo candies, water bottles littering the floor. And Nice, shivering on a pebbled beach with Duncan. Goosebumps on her arms. The desire to hold her, feel her warm skin on his. Duncan must have had a smile on his face because Edmund said, "Ayrie, my brudder," in an awful fake patois. Duncan laughed with an honesty in his throat, began to cough. He stood to overlook the balcony. His arms tingled, and he took another drag, this one pre-meditated: long and smooth. Edmund handed Duncan a glass, and Duncan sipped at its bittersweet liquid.

Edmund said, "I do like me a bit of Tangawizi when cogitating the state of the world."

The trees formed an ancient and verdant belt around the building. The same breeze which played upon Duncan's cheek also made the treetops sway. Such a beautiful place, no wonder our ancestors had chosen East Africa to emerge, mud-caked and thin-limbed, from prehistory. Here, where climate and food availability ensured the viability of survival.

Against the cloudless blue above the treeline, there wheeled a solitary bird, pterodactylid in profile and size. Was it moaning? Was it one of those hideous storks, unrecognizably ennobled by flight? Ciru. He had to act, he had to get to Nice. Duncan looked away from the airborne speck, down at the snarl of traffic, knotted far below, and his mood curdled. Humans. Humans could be relied upon, in the long term, to ruin things.

Edmund joined him, elbows on the railing of the balcony, overlooking the traffic. "Obamacare," he said.

Duncan gave him a questioning look. To which Edmund replied, "That's what we call it." He waved a hand at the diverted traffic, the crawling bulldozers, the shirtless laborers. "The beautification of our city to prepare for Obama's arrival—Obamacare. What a joke."

He turned towards Duncan, as if to clarify. "Obama, I mean. So you're black. Big deal, so am I. Yes we can?" Ice tinkled as he took a sip of his drink, "Shoot. Then perhaps you should, man. Kills me that he thinks his job is to make speeches, and he seems entirely at peace with this."

Duncan rubbed his forehead with the heel of his hand, contemplating the scurrying Obamacare.

"So how come you reached out to me?" said Edmund, extending his hand to retrieve the joint from Duncan. Duncan handed it to Edmund. Duncan sat, head swimming pleasantly. This was it, he simply had to say something, do some- thing to make this meaningful. To stop pretending that this was business as usual. Duncan licked his lips. "Your mother, Edmund." The words surfed the exhaled smoke.

Edmund looked at him, eyes red and hooded over the glow of the joint-tip. His cheek so smooth. The world now came at Duncan in technicolor pulses, and he forced himself to remain anchored in this interaction. He had already dishonored Nice, ddishonoredhimself, by whiling away the afternoon with beer and ping pong, as if he was playing truant from school. So, Duncan stepped carefully over the gathering mists of his mind and picked words, like rocks for a slingshot. Duncan leaned back, crossed his legs. "Your mother has kidnapped my girlfriend." The term "girlfriend" surprised him, a secret desire stated plainly to the world. In the emotional desolation of adulthood, he had never spoken in such a way. To this revelation, which crystallized so much of Duncan's recent experience, Edmund delivered that devastating di- alectical upper cut. With a curl of his lip, he asked, "So what?" Duncan was too stunned and stoned to formulate a sentence. Edmund sat back in his chair, the hiss and glow of the joint masking his face.

Edmund went on, "I mean, so what? Is that why you came here? To ask me, on your behalf, to reason with her. What a joke. She is as stubborn as a mule, she will do as she has always done, the only thing she is, frankly, equipped to do. No, no." Edmund shook his head, exhaling from the side of his mouth as he did so. "I am cordial with her, I permit her to be in touch with me, so long as she keeps me in the black with all this—" Edmund gestured at the trees, the curtain liner, his apartment.

He rested his elbows on his knees and asked Duncan, "Is that why you've come here? You really are a crazy bastard. I'm a little impressed actually. But you're just a rhombus."

Edmund's red-shrouded eyes twinkled. "You know—another square being leaned on?"

The hash sang in Duncan's head. His mouth was dry, too dry to inject the malice he felt when he said, "You make her do those things, live among those people, for this? For a flat screen television and designer jeans. You spoiled little—"

Edmund stabbed the joint onto the table, its wicker strands sizzling in muted protest. "I don't make her do anything. She only knows that life, you know, like the tiger trying to leave the jungle. I wanted her to leave it when we were in New York, so I could study and work. Build a different life for us, make us safe from her crazy work people. She promised me she would let me. So that I could keep her, keep us, from this insanity. But she went and got us deported because of her craziness before I could even finish my degree. She took from me my shot at life, and so she owes me."

Edmund stood. "What the hell am I even doing discussing this with you? Talk about awkward conversations."

Edmund pointed at the balcony door. "Get out."

Duncan stood. The tree-lined horizon wobbled, as though in a heat haze. Why had he come here, what was it that he even wanted Edmund to do? Edmund was just a boy, an entitled child. A confused desperation swam in Duncan's veins, as he began to realize that without this he had no plan whatsoever, only to rely on the mercy of Ciru and the people upstream from her. The cops would do nothing, Niyi would do nothing, he was utterly alone in this venture. No one was coming to save him.

Between clenched teeth, Duncan said, "By God you will help me, or I will—"

"You will what, take me to the ICC for hurting your feelings?" Edmund gave a bitter, braying laugh. "You arrogant fool."

His mother's son.

Duncan shot out his left fist, striking Edmund's chin. Edmund went boneless, as though felled by a sniper in a treetop, and collapsed, his head bouncing off the coffee table before hitting the concrete floor of the balcony.

A fire punch, thought Duncan with mechanical recall, rises quickly from hip to target.

Like fire.

19

THE SMELL OF COOKING FIRES mingled with that of the sea. Turreted clouds framed the dusk, sodden and pyrotechnic.

Toogood loped, lean and naked, his back to the darkening sea, up the slope of Brava Beach. His hip bone catching the dying light. To his clothes, neatly folded on the concrete promenade jutting like a swollen lip from the shattered face of L'Etoile de Mogadiscio, the erstwhile domicile of five-star glamour in Mogadishu. Now, bearded men squatted in post- apocalyptic fashion around wood fires built directly onto the floor of the lobby, feeding the flames the few remnants of paneling and joinery. Exotic woods imported to build the grand palace of a hotel, self-destructing in the campfires of desperate souls.

An apt Mogadishu metaphor.

This was a time of solitude, the only time of any sort of peace in Mogadishu. It was paradoxical, Toogood mused, that the peacefulness only came about because people were afraid of the transition from the relative normalcy of the day, to the utter lawlessness of the night.

This suited Toogood fine, straddling as he did those two worlds. His student life was fading though—the canceled lectures, the frightened professors, the violence circling the dusty university campus. Still, he clung to the faded ritual of his bicycle ride to the campus, to his satchel containing his only textbook, The Responsible Manager, having belonged to one Patricia McHale before him. Patricia had written, almost embossed, her name on the first page, in a girlish curlicue. Toogood often ran admiring fingers over that inscription, its methodical neatness bespeaking in his mind an entitlement of order, of a predictability that he had never known, but which now slipped further and further into abstraction, a feast of which he would never partake.

But increasingly, Toogood went to the university because that's where his clients were. Where there is despair—where there are homo sapiens, he supposed—there will be a demand for narcotic substances, for relief from intolerable selfhood. And these did Toogood supply. Specifically, tightly packaged samosas made from newspaper, containing within them a relatively high grade ("untrodden", in the poetic parlance of the wholesaler Toogood dealt with) heroin. Toogood bought low and sold higher. But more importantly, to his clientele, and therefore to his prospects, Toogood was honest, punctual and not unkind.

People liked him. And in general, Toogood liked them back. Once, he had delivered a dozen little samosas to an Indian-Kenyan UN rapporteur of something or other. Toogood had clean forgotten about the deal until he bumped into the man a few weeks later at a neighborhood vegetable stand. In front of a pyramid of dusty potatoes, the Indian had spontaneously pulled Toogood into a hug and exclaimed, without any contextualization or self-restraint, in an Indian accent undiluted by two centuries of East African residency, "Too good yaar. Toooogood!"

And this was the name with which Ibrahim was introduced to the Indian's constellation of friends and acquaintances. Friends and acquaintances who were much more cosmopolitan than the people Toogood was used to dealing with at the university. The ticket size of his average sale improved dramatically—less work for more money. These people flew in on Hercules aircrafts, wore $200 Nike desert combat boots and spoke rapid-fire English peppered with the staccato shorthand of UN abbreviations. These people had disposable time, confined as they were to air-conditioned shipping containers, which served as their quarters. Finally, and in fairness to these people, they daily saw what were, for them anyway, pretty grim aspects of the human experience.

The exchange of goods for money itself took seconds, but the clients made clear, in unspoken fashion, that they would appreciate it if Toogood would be discrete enough not to make their interaction nakedly transactional. That this was, after all, their only peer-to-peer interaction of the day—perhaps of their entire tour—with an actual Somali.

Toogood, ever keen to make the most of a situation, considered them immersive English conversation sessions and felt free to ask pointed questions about idioms. Toogood shyly repeated words and expressions he liked, trying them out in sentences of his own. This often drew the foreigners in, causing them to abandon the socio-economic embattlements they felt awkward manning in the first place.

Especially the ladies.

The flak jackets and the chatter of helicopters were portents of good business—both for the UN crowd and for Toogood. Piggy-backing the spike in turmoil and international aid, intertwined like strands of DNA, Toogood's book of business had grown, in importance and diversity.

In fact, this sunset walk on the beach was a celebration of sorts. And a self-baptism. For Toogood intended to hang up his student's satchel and turn full time to a life of self- improvement through chemical entrepreneurship.

It had been surprisingly easy to plan. Speaking with an Italian UN staffer after delivering an order of samosas, Toogood had learned he was not the only Somali dealer in the camp. So Toogood had made it his business to learn more about the competition—Nooruddin, a middle-aged man from a different tribe, with a wife and children. The man's trading name was Noor, or the Light.

Once Toogood had understood Noor's supply chain, he made a move. In the dusty shade outside the gate of the UN camp, Toogood strode up to the Light. Never one for too much artfulness, Toogood explained that his was an exclusive holding over the UN camp. The Light, from behind his heavy beard, regarded Toogood, without uttering a word of response, weighing Toogood's lithe youth, his ambition, his hunger. A wolf weighing the cost of taking up a challenge.

Then the Light held out his hand to Toogood, by way of formalizing the arrangement.

And for several weeks, Toogood had in fact held a lucrative monopoly over the camp. But then there were sightings of Noor, cross-legged, drinking tumblers of sweet tea with the blue helmeted peacekeepers, who were high- value customers. Emboldened by the fact that he held no tribal allegiance to Noor, Toogood had brought the matter up with his childhood friend Teesh. Teesh, in his stolid way, had insisted it was downright unSomali to go back on your word. "This, we cannot allow," Teesh had said. It surprised Toogood how disarming he found Teesh's use of the word "we". But no particular plan was agreed upon, and Toogood assumed the discussion was to be revisited. The issue became moot when Noor ceased to appear in the camp. Weeks later, when delivering a samosa to a Nepali peacekeeper, Toogood had asked what had become of the Light. The smooth-faced Nepali squinted, "Heard his wife was killed in a botched robbery. The Light is full-time daddy now, no time for us anymore."

When Toogood asked Teesh about the incident, he had shrugged, as if to say, "It's a bad, bad world." But the Light's investors had been more dogged in their investigations. In due course, Toogood was contacted via phone by a person who represented the Light's backers.

Would Toogood care to make them whole? The threat was implicit.

On Teesh's advice, Toogood had suggested to the man on the phone that he would act for them in the UN camp, on an exclusive basis. Toogood figured the conversation was heading that way anyway, better simply to get ahead of it.

"Foot in the door," Teesh called it.

A few mutually profitable months later, Toogood received an offer to become a minor equity partner in an East African narcotic joint venture. The opportunity would catapult Toogood several rungs up the food chain. It was a ladder that enjoyed, in the unlovely words of the "The Responsible Manager", a "mitigated risk profile".

But it would require full-time commitment. The amateur era of his drug-dealing career would have to end. The other shareholders of the joint venture had long ago transmuted themselves into Big Men, legitimate businesspersons, pillars of their various communities scattered across East Africa and beyond. They spoke, especially when discussing matters of criminal enterprise, a sanitized corporate-speak drawn from oak-paneled board rooms. When Toogood had been negotiating the terms of his equity stake, for instance, one pinstriped elder had coughed into his sleeve and said, "As a junior partner, you will take a haircut on your dividend."

Toogood brushed sand from his shins, pulled on his boxers, and sat, cross-legged and erect, to take in his last sunset as a quasi-student. The next time the sun rose, it would be upon Toogood, the clear-eyed professional. Toogood had seen enough of the industry he was entering to understand that it was impossible to avoid degradation altogether—something he currently did only by not asking Teesh too many questions— but it seemed a fair bargain. Besides, what alternative did he have for changing his circumstances? He thought of Teesh, the loud, clumsy childhood friend turned slow-burning gangster. Teesh, upon whose violent unpredictability he was growing increasingly, and paradoxically, dependent in his quest for respectability. This investment, which tied up the bulk of his money, would remove him from street-level risk.

Toogood closed his eyes, took in the sound of the surf.

A darkness curtained him. Toogood looked up at where the sun had been. An Indian woman, her back to the sea and her face shrouded in shadow, stood between him and the sinking sun. She sat beside him, and the flash of sunset echoed against Toogood's retinas.

"A melancholy time, in a melancholy place," the woman said. Her voice was throaty.

Toogood had come across this word "melancholy" with a client once, a Spanish woman also with a deep voice and sad eyes. Draped in bedsheets, and drawing on an unfiltered cigarette, the Spanish woman had explained that the term contained within it a multitude of sentiments, seething like maggots in a pawpaw, consuming yet productive.

Toogood closed his eyes once more. He smiled, cheek-bones gaunt above the patchy beard.

With his closed eyelids glowing bronze, Toogood said, "What would you say if I said I was busy?"

The woman's laughter floated like a red balloon into the crepuscular sky.

He continued, "In my culture, contemplation is considered an intimate and important act. I am at a crossroads." She said, "Big decisions, eh? Well, if it's any consolation, ninety-nine percent of what concerns us is inconsequential—I mean it simply won't matter one way or another in three, or five, or certainly ten years. So, if you're not hurting anyone, just do what you want."

Toogood's eyes opened. She too was cross-legged, leaning back on her arms, which were planted in the sand behind her. Her face was smooth, sharp-featured.

Toogood said slowly, "Oh, but that's the thing. There's a good chance people will get hurt."

"That's interesting how you phrased that. In the passive voice, removing yourself from the arena. But that's not how it works." She blinked at him, her dark halo of hair swaying. "You have it within you to define your relations with this world."

Toogood thought for a moment and was on the point of saying something when the woman stood. She shook the sand from her salwar kameez and said, as if by way of farewell, "Nothing can happen unless you want it to."

She turned to continue her walk. Back to an idling Land Cruiser VX no doubt, thought Toogood, in a cynical effort at not being impressed. The sun had fallen into the oily sea.

But he was impressed. "Wait," Toogood called after her, "what's your name?"

"Nice," she said, walking backward away from him.

20

IN THE LEAFY NAIROBI SUBURB OF WESTLANDS, in a sun-dappled beer garden, Toogood resisted the agonizing urge to re-check his phone. As he waited for Nice's call, Toogood waved away the obsequious bow-tied waiter. The last thing he wanted was to cloud his thinking with another beer. A lot rested on this delivery. Perhaps he should not have used Nice as the mule, given her baby.

His baby. Boy or girl? He hadn't thought to ask.

Hands trembling, Toogood withdrew a blue pill from a plastic box. He swallowed the drug, chased it with the dregs of the beer, and scanned the garden for that bloody waiter. He imagined the chemicals streaming into his blood, like commuters late for work.

The funny part of how he had met Nice, thought Toogood, was that Nice had had no recollection of that Brava Beach conversation when he had brought it up, months later, at a house party in Mog. Over the deafening music chosen by bullet-headed Marines, they poured rum into red plastic Solo cups (brought in at great US tax-payer expense) of Pepsi, stirring the syrupy cocktails with their forefingers.

Toogood, newly powerful and wealthy in a city awash with

hangers-on and hyenas, a local celebrity on the UN secured compound, had found Nice an invaluable anchor. It had helped that Nice, without judging him or rendering herself willfully blind to his profession, remained thoroughly unimpressed with Toogood's newly-minted status as a Big Man. She neither asked nor received any material favors from him, nor did she keep tabs or ask him to do, or not do, anything. Toogood mmarveledat Nice's elastic code for life-living, a sort of filter through which any sort of decision or situation could be elutriated—to separate those parts that "Kept it real", from those that did not. Things that fell into the latter category were to be frowned upon, or at least viewed with extreme circumspection. It was the first time Toogood had heard of this business of "keeping it real". His life had, thus far, been a long and tedious exercise in removing himself from his reality.

Their friendship and Toogood's career had blossomed in concert. He found himself drawn to her, seeking her out, following her—just the way he had when they had first met on the beach. She was, he realized, a watermark of his morality—a "before and after" of sorts. Except, he had not expected his "after" to come quite so soon.

So much so that, eighteen or so months later, Toogood had bought himself a Kenyan passport and created an auxiliary base of operations out of Nairobi. To further remove himself from the "risk nexus"—Toogood used these terms from his textbook to get a laugh out of Nice. They spoke openly of each other's work, the frustrations, the opportunities. Nice joked that Toogood should pay her consulting fees, advising him as she did him on things foreigners liked, such that he could brand himself the "expat-friendly" dealer.

Having discussed the matter with Teesh, Toogood had

convinced the principals of the joint venture to conduct a feasibility study into concocting a bespoke narcotic intended to straddle the local and expat markets, to be cheap, reliable and locally sourced—used by frantic housewives carrying fifteen kilos of firewood on their heads, and Bangladeshi UN peacekeepers alike. An East African meth—the opiate of the honest everyman—that had been Toogood's elevator pitch (another concept thrust upon him by Nice).

The shareholders hemmed and hawed, but did agree to allow a limited budget for the work, provided that Toogood would be personally responsible.

The field tests were successful, with relatively few unpleasant side-effects. Certainly, there were some overdoses and psychopathic episodes with the early adopters (mainly retired child soldiers suffering from post-traumatic stress), but Toogood and Teesh worked with the chemists, a trio of nervous young Kenyan PhDs, to ensure that feedback was incorporated into the new recipe. There was inevitable unpleasantness and convincing – cost of doing business but Teesh had taken the laboring oar on this. Still, something turned in Toogood, something beyond daily reckoning and not marked by a discrete moment—an internal climate change. The pressures of managing the investors, his partners, and the ever-shifting equation of sourcing and distribution chains across blurry borders—these were making him jumpy, which was making him ingest more of his own supply to keep his head on straight. And there was an incident during which he had actually asked Teesh to step aside, and himself thrashed a stubborn child soldier with a hockey stick. The boy, drugged and wide-eyed, regarded his broken forearm as though it was a dry branch snapped in two. Outside of his own body.

It had surprised Toogood. That he had done it, that he had

enjoyed it, and that no remorse had followed.

Still, the drug itself held promise. And he knew he had to get it into the right wholesaling channels for him to scale the venture up.

So when Nice had needed to get to Nairobi, it seemed apt. A relatively low risk way to get a high volume of his starter pack into the country, and then to his shareholders, so they could run their own tests. "Trust but verify" had been the words of one bearded elder with a thousand-acre estate in Nakuru, shrouded in mist and dotted with wild zebra.

But now she was not picking up her phone.

Her flight had landed in Nairobi almost thirty-six hours ago. The anxiety was unbearable. The peacefulness of his surroundings only made things worse. Amongst the bejeweled cappuccino drinkers and the pork-pie hat wearing young men, Toogood felt intensely alone. The light kaleidoscoped off a woman's ring—his drugs were quality. Buoyed by this spot check, he summoned the waiter.

"Another Tusker."

He reached into his wallet and pulled out a scrap of paper, onto which were scrawled, in a blurry pencil, ten digits. This was the telephone number of the Kenyan policeman whom Toogood had hired to ensure the safe passage of Nice through the airport. Toogood did not tell Nice of this precaution. Given the importance of the cargo, Toogood made the expensive arrangement with this policeman, by way of an insurance policy. After all, someone with Nice's profile and credentials would need no help clearing customs. And Nice would never even know there had been an overwatch, it was an invisible precaution—trust but verify. The Kenyan's references had checked out; he was a policeman who had worked for years with the usual suspects of this corridor. He had good contacts at the airport with Immigrations and Customs. Though, one reference had damned the man with faint praise, his body of work ultimately won the day. The policeman's name was easy to remember: Hinga.

Hinga had instructed Toogood not to call the number, except in the event of an emergency. Told him not to save the number on his phone. Toogood had thought him melodramatic, but had agreed. 36 hours of radio silence, Toogood reasoned, met that standard.

The waiter set the sweating beer on Toogood's table.

Toogood plugged earphones into his phone and dialed the number. It rang four times, sounding distant. Toogood hung up. He took a long pull of his beer. The physical sensation of his anxiety was like a column of safari ants marching up his arms, over his shoulders, disappearing into the forest of his scalp. He dialed again.

On the second ring, a woman's voice came through Toogood's headset.

"Hello?" the woman said, as though surprised the phone in her possession had rung.

Toogood, trying to shake his light-headedness and adopting the posture of a complaining client, replied, "I am trying to reach Mr. Hinga, please."

The woman drew the silence out. Toogood watched a teardrop of condensation roll down his pilsner glass and melt into the wooden tabletop.

"He is not around."

Toogood felt a tingling of his scalp. This was, he knew, a precursor to a full-blown electrical storm of anger, and he bit down on it. Anger was opera, he had learned, to be deployed like a theatrical device, and only when one was in full mastery of it. Besides, losing his cool now would not be conducive to information gathering.

Toogood exhaled through his nose. "And he has, aah, entrusted you with this number?"

"Yes, yes, we are partners," came her quick reply.

Partner? Now this was a word rich with corporate significance, and Toogood seized upon it as an invitation to discuss business.

Toogood said, "Can you discuss business matters—as his partner?"

"I can."

She seemed sure of herself. He alone seemed to be suffering. At a table behind Toogood, a blonde woman released a laugh that cascaded like a peahen's call.

Screw it, Toogood simply could not take another moment of not knowing.

"I am awaiting delivery of a, ahh, shipment. From the airport?" His voice had risen on the last syllable, and Toogood knew he sounded young and green when he spoke like that. He forced himself to control the pace.

"Yes?" the woman said. She was a pro.

The invisible ants trickled through the columns of his dreadlocks.

"It hasn't arrived." Toogood allowed a tone of petulance.

She met the looming disagreement head on, without hesitation, with the self-assurance of a clerk in a post office. "Please describe the package." Her petulance matched his perfectly.

Toogood removed his headphones, in sheer frustration, to look back at the laughing woman. What was that blonde woman finding so bloody funny?

He put the headphones back in. "Yes. The courier was an Indian female, mid-30s, date of arrival would have been a day or so ago."

Silence.

Afraid they may have been disconnected, Toogood looked at his handset, "Hello? Are you still there?"

The woman said nothing still. Perspiration stood on Toogood's forehead.

Finally, she said, "Umm, yes, I am just checking the records."

Toogood gulped back his beer and signaled to the waiter for another.

She continued, "Now, we do have a record of such a package. What were the delivery particulars please?"

Between gritted teeth, Toogood replied, "As soon as possible, I—"

But the brazen woman cut him off, saying "That is not helpful. It is in the nature of this business."

Toogood was about to remonstrate when the woman's voice came again. "I can feel your anxiety. Look, I can have the package delivered tonight, at a location of your choosing within the Nairobi city limits?"

Toogood allowed himself to breathe, to relax. It was OK, Nice had made it across, she was fine, just delayed. It surprised him how much the knowledge of Nice's safety relieved him. Maybe it was the baby. But the thought of the investors, who would not be quite so relaxed about the deadline, focused his mind.

Toogood pushed his luck. "I need it sooner. I have a sub-delivery to make before then."

Silence.

Toogood took a pull of the fresh beer. His throat was parched. "Are you still there?"

The woman's voice came again, "Just checking the manifest. Not possible. Tonight is the best I can do."

Toogood forced himself to master his anxiety. He laughed into the phone and said, "Okay, thanks for checking. Please could we meet at the coffee bar in Baringo Plaza tonight, say 9?" Then, he added, "Look, I'm sorry. Just a lot is riding on this."

She was not prepared to accept his apology, simply saying, "A little manners goes a long way."

Toogood was about to ring off, when it struck him to ask, "Wait, wait, how will I know you?"

"You'll know me," came her reply. She rang off.

At the other end of the line, Ciru felt the heat from Hinga's phone radiating in her palm. What sort of deal had Hinga struck with this Somali fellow, Toogood? She felt an enormous relief that he was gone. Dead, she reminded herself, dead.

From their conversation, it was unclear whether Toogood was after the girl, the drugs or both. Perhaps she should not have let Nice leave. It was an uncharacteristic risk for her to have taken. But the girl was pregnant and could perhaps use the second chance. A second chance the sort of which had never been granted Ciru. Or Nyanya. She shuddered to consider the future of baby Pendo if Nice did not turn herself around. No, Ciru knew, from experience, that when the drugs themselves were delivered to Toogood, any half-baked concerns he might have about his girlfriend would fall away.

But she still needed to deal with Duncan. Whom she was to meet in a couple of hours.

She picked up her own phone. Best to rattle Duncan's cage now, to remind him of the pecking order.

21

DUNCAN FELT A MILD AROUSAL from the violence. It had, undeniably, been pleasurable to hit Edmund. Not just hit, but strike, without the mental noise of premeditation, and with a liquid efficiency. It was the pleasure of discovering a skill that had useful applications in the real world.

Once, while at university, Nice had asked, holding up Duncan's sweaty helmet like a soiled diaper, whether he could "beat someone up". Duncan laughed off the question, both because of its childish phrasing and because he felt he would be performing a parlor trick by answering. But Nice, in her dogged way, insisted on an answer. To end the conversation, Duncan said, "The truth is I just don't know. So much rests on that particular day." Nice, who knew nothing of martial arts, pronounced the response unsatisfactory.

Perhaps, Duncan replied, but it was a truth. And, as such, a rare and vulnerable thing.

On Edmund's balcony, Duncan looked at his left hand. He did not remember slipping it into his pocket, but that is where it nested, like a holstered pistol. This too pleased Duncan, the automaticity of his arsenal.

Then he remembered he was stoned.

And, having just assaulted his host, he was now a trespasser in this white-hued spaceship of an apartment. Duncan's pleasure turned to dust. His mouth bone-dry. Duncan tilted back Edmund's glass of Tangawizi, his lips tingling against the ice cubes.

Edmund had not moved a muscle. Duncan, having become aware of his own chemically altered state, began to feel a revulsion against Edmund. This wastrel, a blackmailer of his own mother, loyal only to the shifting edicts of his ego. But— and the thought made him need to sit—was Duncan himself so different from the young man who lay drooling onto the grey slate floor of the balcony?

Duncan licked his lips, which felt chapped and tried to find a reasonable route away from this question, which threatened his hash-induced harmony. A familiar and low- grade self-pity rose, beginning to curdle into viciousness. He spat drily against the expensive flooring, and wiped his mouth with the back of his wrist.

The treeline still swayed.

For the first time, he recognized that he had entered his profession precisely in order to be solaced by its formal codification of how to behave—down to the very details of how to dress, when to kneel, when to stand. He remembered reading of a pope who did not watch television, having made a solemn promise to the Virgin to this effect.

Duncan's life prior to entering the Church had been a period of bafflement as to how his peers were consistently able to decipher how to act—how to pick a major at college, how to bereave a loved one, how to describe a piece of art seen at a museum, how to introduce oneself at a party with that precise alchemy of artful humility. They all seemed to know this stuff. But how? Duncan had, after all, read the same books, listened to the same teachers, lived in the same context, but there lay a chasm between him and this easy appropriation of social mores. Watching the world parade by on television, the screaming adverts, the lurid flashing of brands, Duncan felt an alienation bordering on anthropological.

And the anxiety of these things, more precisely the inability to grasp at them, had hardened, in Duncan, into a quietly sneering claustrophobia. Duncan willed himself into first believing, then broadcasting, that he was an outsider, with the highest setting of his emotional engagement dial set at bemusement. This belief, and his aloofness, served only to increase the distance between him and others around him. Duncan did not think himself an introvert, but he joined and dropped clubs at university and had few friends. The sudden move from New England had not helped. Only Nice. And, even with her, he had the distinct feeling sometimes, that his consciousness was a rodent-sized version of himself, peering out at the world from the cockpit of this strange meat spaceship.

The Church had come to Duncan in a hash-addled haze, a bitter February evening in Montreal, three months before he was to graduate, as he made his unsteady way between banks of heaped snow on campus. An earnest voice had called out to Duncan from the promontory of the student union building. It startled Duncan, who was utterly consumed with navigating a safe passage, measured in mincing steps, across the ice sheets of Peel Street. An apple-faced man in a parka waved at him, as if they knew one another.

Curious, Duncan approached him.

Without much preamble, the parka-man issued a grave-faced offer, to join the grandly named Church of the Earth. The offer was as out-of-the-blue as it was synchronous with Duncan's life. By signing one document (which, the parka-man generously insisted, Duncan should consider at his leisure and in consultation with family and friends) Duncan would be removed from all this—the howl of the February wind scything the bleak skyscrapers, Duncan's constant money worries, his inability to overcome his unrequited feelings towards Nice, his wildly impotent desire to stop spending his days in a cannabinoid cloud, the sheer lack of moorings in his life.

Instead, the Church's shiny brochure (so smooth it felt lacquered) promised, via the obligatory images of dark- skinned children with hard potbellies, a life of purpose, of vigor, and, most alluringly, of an outsider-hood anointed with a bulletproof legitimacy. And some vague possibility of a resumption of relations with his parents.

Duncan signed on the spot, the felt-tipped marker trembling between his fingers, placing a full stop after his surname. This dot blotted on the page. Duncan's rapid, seemingly unconscious decision caused the parka-man some consternation, suggesting as it did that Duncan was an unsuitable, perhaps unstable, candidate. The parka-man urged Duncan to take the form home, that there was no rush, that the form was mainly an information gathering tool anyway and did not, in and of itself, signify anything.

But to Duncan it did. It was an end to, or at least a relief from, the fug of impotence. A decision. A cosmic lifeline from an invisible vessel, onto which he would clamber, red-faced and spluttering. Not so much to embrace the vessel which had come to his assistance, but to get out of the waters in which he found himself floundering.

The February air had knifed Duncan as he exited the student union building, but he did not wince.

Duncan smiled as he recalled that moment and the weeks which followed. The cinematic flourish of the meeting in the student union building had been followed by tedious piles of paperwork, correspondence, and medical exams. But they vindicated Duncan's decision because they set out a much looser set of canonical guidelines than had his New England seminary, the one from which he had been expelled. The Church of the Earth seemed a religion-without-borders sort of international development agency, and that suited Duncan just fine. The recruiter had certainly been right about that initial document not being binding. Duncan had signed the final forms in a considerably less ceremonious fashion, his breath pluming as he draped himself over a red postal box, before sliding the documents in.

When the Church decided, in its unilateral wisdom, to send Duncan to Nairobi, he had been pleased. Not overjoyed, but certainly pleased. What Nairobi lacked in war-zone exotica, it more than made up for in martial arts studios, coffee bars and general continuity with the life Duncan knew. There was first to be a month of training in India, just north of Delhi, where the Church was also in the business of saving souls.

So that, once finally airborne, a strangely solemn farewell dinner with Nice behind him, Duncan saw the mast of the Olympic stadium falling away like a discarded twig. He knew, in that moment, not precisely happiness, but a lightness. His sense of claustrophobia at the meanness of his peers' concerns filled him with both envy and revulsion. He had even been happy to part ways with Nice over dinner at a Thai place, happy to push away uneaten the under-ripe mango and sticky rice dessert, happy at the formal way in which she studied the bill, before insisting that she pay. She had seemed impressed at his decisiveness, but wary of this rash embrace of religiosity. Her lips caught the tealight in the dark restaurant, and the cloying plum wine rushed to Duncan's head.

She had made a toast, lifting the chipped porcelain cup, "To our many-pathed future, where we shall meet to shelter from life, into which it must rain."

Duncan watched as her lips met the cup, the words themselves beyond his reckoning. Bereft of the benumbing quality of hash, Duncan felt over-stimulated, anxious to be out in the cold street.

It would be good to have relief from her.

Duncan recalled little of the Delhi-based training sessions, which easily blurred the lines between theological and corporate. Each trainee was required, after all, to minister both to the spiritual needs of their congregants and the more mundane operational realities of their respective missions. What Duncan did remember experiencing vividly, in the novelty of his new role as religious ambassador, was a sense of superiority of his own monotheism over the chaotic parallactic constellation of Indian deities. The anarchic traffic was, alone, enough to make clear that a society arranged according to the whims of impish demi-gods was less orderly than one in which there was a single coherent set of rules.

Duncan said nothing of this to his fellow trainees.

Once he settled into his routine in Nairobi, once he had become relatively accustomed to navigating the ambiguity with which expatriate living is freighted, Duncan found himself uncovering his own emotional center. In order to obtain anything resembling the outcome he sought, he had first to articulate to himself the desired outcome, and then to be adamant about the details of the transaction meant to give it effect. Something as mundane as a taxi showing up on time required Duncan to follow up via text and phone, all the while having a contingency plan at the ready.

From this sort of imposition of his micro-desires upon the world emerged a pointillist portrait of Duncan, for the first time visible to himself.

Enjoying a newfound anonymity and clear-headedness, Duncan also consciously emulated Nice's self-possession and felt no compulsions to incubate friendships in his new city. The work kept him busy and in near constant contact with colleagues, both in Nairobi and further afield, so he was grateful for some privacy when he closed the door of his little flat.

A small smile, one of which Duncan was himself unaware, bloomed on his lips as he recalled his arrival in Nairobi. A happy time.

Then Duncan shivered as he looked over the railing of the balcony.

Here, on Edmund's balcony, Duncan was not warmed by the reflected fire of recent memory. The vague thoughts Duncan had of trying to rekindle a romantic relationship with Nice seemed ludicrous. Not least because she had been taken by this young boy's mother. And he was back to pining passively for her. No. What Duncan had taken as permanent emotional growth had proved to be merely the distraction of novelty, and, as it receded, it laid bare the unmoved and rotting abscesses of his own lack of connection to the world. And the increasingly unbearable incoherencies of his Church.

The hash misted his mind.

The Church of the Earth. A child of fear. And how fear too was the parent of all cruelty. With its improbable fiction and

God-as-CCTV-in-the-sky fairy tales. No wonder Duncan had thought the same of the marabou storks when he saw them at the police station. Even the real work which Duncan oversaw, the concrete-slabbed toilets or the hissing hand pumps, bore an abandoned and Ozymandias-like quality when he visited them on monitoring field visits. In Kenya, it was difficult to tell whether things were getting better, or worse. This uncertainty was, of itself, a gloomy realization.

The placebo effect of his own association with this august corporation seemed to be waning. In the vacuum of its absence, Duncan's old anxieties at being incomplete, and a newish one, the questioning of his religious faith and the merit of having invested so heavily in it as a pillar of identity, unfurled. Duncan recalled the revolver the cop had brandished, a fin on the end of the barrel surprisingly unmoving.

Edmund groaned.

Duncan was wrenched from his reverie. A dried rivulet of blood ran from Edmund's nose, Duncan hadn't noticed that before. Seeing Edmund lying there, Duncan was pierced by a shame at not having helped him earlier. This was just a boy playing at the real world after all, the wayward child of an insane mother, the product of a wildly dysfunctional childhood.

As Duncan contemplated how he would apologize, his phone buzzed in his pocket.

New text message:

"Hi Father! Hope all well. Please don't be late for our meeting, which is in 1 hour. ☺ Please save my number to your contacts. Ciru."

The world swam.

Duncan fell into the chair. How had she gotten his new number? Was she watching him somehow? Duncan scanned the sky for birds. Did she know Duncan had harmed Edmund? The chirpily intrusive tone of Ciru's text suggested not. The sensation of disorientation which the text had brought upon Duncan gave way to exhaustion. And thirst.

Duncan stepped over Edmund, back into the flat. He had to clear his head.

The drawing room gave onto a short corridor, at the end of which lay the bedroom. Duncan crossed the monumental television, walked into the bedroom and found the bathroom. It too was starkly white. Duncan washed his face with cold water. He placed some toothpaste, a cheerful trio of red, white and blue, on his forefinger and brushed his teeth. In the mirror, his eyes were bloodshot.

The phone buzzed again. Another message from the witch. "Pick one option: (A) BETTER HAVE MY MONEY, or . . ."

Duncan ran his tongue over his molars, then spat into the sink. He did not wash away the toothpaste-laced sputum.

There resurged within him a viciousness and vague realization that only action, any action, would console his unease at the impotence he felt. The impotence of having a revolver in your face. The impotence upon which Ciru was playing.

The hand towel felt expensive. When Duncan had dried his face, the towel was streaked with the dust he did not even know had accreted in his pores.

Again, the buzz of the phone.

Ciru's telegram in two parts continued. "(B) i WILL pull your skirt up. See you soon ;)"

Duncan began thumbing a profane response, but realized there could be no surer way to broadcast his utter powerlessness.

He left the bathroom and sat at the foot of Edmund's bed.

Above the desk on the far wall was a framed LP cover. Duncan walked over to it. Six black-hoodied men, their faces obscured by the sheen of stocking masks, knelt before a darkened altar.

Across the photo of the men was scrawled in red Sharpie, "To Ed—represent from Shaolin to Africa".

Duncan's phone buzzed again. He reached for his pocket, then paused, willing himself not to check the phone.

Instead, he took the framed LP and smashed the glass against the corner of the desk. Then Duncan withdrew the LP cover, withdrew and tossed the LP onto the bed. He folded the cardboard cover in half, and again in half. He stuck this into the back pocket of his jeans, next to the comforting wad of US dollars.

Duncan opened the drawers of the desk and withdrew from it, as though he had known it would be there, a roll of silver duct tape. With this in hand, Duncan strode through the gauzed balcony door. He bent over Edmund and took in Edmund's citrusy expensive smell.

If this crazy witch wanted to do a deal, then Duncan would bring a bargaining chip.

Above the treeline of swaying yellow-barks, a wheeling marabou issued its primeval clamor.

Duncan grunted as he tore another strip of duct tape with his teeth. By the time Edmund was bound and gagged, Duncan felt less high. Just thirsty.

And repulsed by himself.

Edmund remained senseless, bearing the impression of a man manhandled mid-nap. Duncan hoped the tape-job was secure but would not result in any unintended consequences, such as asphyxiation. He had never done anything like this before. To be safe, he loosened the gag in Edmund's mouth.

Then Duncan dragged Edmund out of the balcony and into the bedroom. He tried, and failed, to lift Edmund onto the bed. Duncan grabbed a pillow and blanket and placed Edmund in their embrace, on the floor where he lay. A paranoid second-guessing seized him, and he bent to feel Edmund's wrist and throat for a pulse. Satisfied, Duncan stood and held his head sideways to scrutinize his handiwork.

No sense in the man being uncomfortable.

In the bathroom, Duncan laved water over his face and neck. He knew he had to stop putting his departure off—his meeting with Ciru was in half an hour. Out on the balcony, the abrupt equatorial sunset was already bruising the sky. Taking one last look at the apartment over his shoulder, Duncan pulled shut the front door.

Exiting the cool hush of the lobby, Duncan hailed a boda boda. The figure—Duncan could not tell the gender of the operator because of the full body yellow leather jumpsuit—came to a screaming halt. Duncan got on the bike, which began to rocket into the traffic almost before his feet were off the ground. After a moment, Duncan shouted his destination into the back of the driver's helmet. By way of wordless acknowledgment, the driver's left hand reassuringly patted Duncan's kneecap.

In the swinging lurch of the traffic, in the smearing sodium streetlights, Duncan recognized that Edmund stocked high-grade hashish.

22

THE TIME HAD COME. Of this Ciru was convinced. The time to walk away. For a while at least. Hinga's death meant those he owed money—and these were a lot of people— would make inquiries. And letting that girl Nice go; this was the sort of flashy generosity which got one killed. No, for Edmund's sake and her own, it was time to go upcountry. Lay low, regroup, and perhaps plan to take Edmund to another Anglo- Saxon country.

Ciru sighed, touched the dial of the hulking lockbox. The burnished steel of the safe still leaked the heat of the receding sun. Low clicking of the dial, as the safe swung open. She regarded the contents, neatly stacked thousand-shilling notes, several phones, each with their charging equipment, and a ccream-colored shoebox containing the memories she had to have when it came time to flee. Atop the shoebox, a clear plastic sandwich bag in which lay a matte black pistol. She withdrew the gun and placed it, still in its sandwich bag holster, into her Hello Kitty backpack.

Then she opened the shoebox. Edmund's library card from the Brooklyn Library, with which he borrowed strange, futuristic-sounding music albums, big books of art photos. His face young, open to the future.

Ciru had mixed feelings about having a son who had so easily become American. She was, on the one hand, hugely relieved that Edmund was enjoying himself, and it was true maternal pleasure to see him grow in span and confidence— his cartoonish basketball shoes and strange idioms, confusing and amusing in equal parts. On the other, Edmund had simply shed his Kenyan-ness like a dull weight. Ciru rationalized that young people needed to assimilate quickly, but a part of her knew it was also Edmund's way of trying to close an unhappy chapter in his young life and step more fully into that new and bright-hued world. It felt a little like a rejection of the life she had made for them in Kenya.

She had nearly broken herself trying to provide a secure childhood for him—navigating the sharks on a daily basis to pay for the speech therapy to correct the boy's stuttering, the stupendous expense of his braces, his collection of comic books in their clear plastic envelopes.

Edmund was, in fact, her second child, her second son. The first had simply stilled his heart at the tender age of thirty-eight weeks, pulling irrevocably in the ventricle, like a shutter to keep out the clamoring world. At the public clinic the attending doctor, a horse-faced English woman with a barely comprehensible accent, had matter-of-factly informed Ciru that the Doppler revealed total silence in the womb—that the doctor was sorry but the only thing to do was to deliver the baby to find out.

Ciru recalled the precise moment she was given this information in that darkened room, the doctor's grave face underlit by the beeping machines. Then there was the clockless pain of the labor, the exquisite agony of extruding the already deceased infant. The dead boy, smiling mysteriously, slick as a river stone, was handed to Ciru. She held him and held him.

No tears came.

After a time, the doctor sheepishly held out her own arms, with which she would remove the boy, who was after all a corpse, and place it upon a steel tray which she would cover with a white sheet not much bigger than a napkin. As Ciru handed back her first-born child, the doctor had declared its birth idiopathic. This too had stayed with Ciru.

Idiopathic. That her idiopathic boy would have been Edmund's elder brother, and Edmund was, in a sense, cheated of having had a brother to look out for him. It made her clutch unreachably for Edmund.

The duality of her life, the petty criminality by night, and the dutiful housewife routine by day, placed impossible demands upon her. Demands which had begun in earnest when her husband Josephat, a small-time conman, had gone in with Hinga. What Josephat had lacked in education and conventional ambition, he made up for in the department of family loyalty. The rent, the school fees, and the utilities were paid, and the family ate goat meat at least once a week on the red-white checkered tablecloth.

This tranquil, if dysfunctional, family life was disrupted when Josephat, about his business of relieving country bumpkins of their big-city earnings while they waited to board up-country coaches at the Machakos bus depot, was arrested by Hinga. Josephat was a grifter—his true expertise was in weaving long narratives of deferred contentment for dusty rubes. In the midst of one such investment pitch, Hinga found Josephat, wanted on a number of open warrants, and wordlessly walked him out into the sun-stunned chaos of the bus stand.

But instead of feeding Josephat into the maw of the Kenyan criminal justice system, Hinga had pressed Josephat into service as a confidential informant and general errand boy.

Some weeks later, Hinga insisted Josephat participate in a robbery in the leafy suburb of Runda. "Routine break-in, keep an eye on the boys," Hinga said.

Hinga's intelligence had been faulty; the routine break-and-entry turned quickly into a full-blown home invasion. The owner of the house, a recently retired UNICEF official and keen outdoorsman, was supposed to have been out of the country. But when Josephat and his colleagues arrived, their scalps tingling under ski masks, they quickly understood that the homeowner was upstairs. Worse, it transpired the homeowner had barricaded himself behind a steel safe-haven door. Hinga had made no mention of the steel door, or the safe haven.

Josephat, a man who feared violence, knelt to bargain, his cheek against the door's cool smoothness, with the owner of the house to open the steel door in return for a guarantee of safety. On the other side, separated by two inches of Israeli- steel, the owner had placed the mouth of a waterfowl shotgun. Hours later, first responders found Josephat's head hanging between shoulder blades from a strip of tendon, a look of astonishment upon his sightless face. The incident report noted that the steel door had been riven from its hinges, and the safe haven ransacked.

Not that Hinga shared any of these details with Ciru at Josephat's closed casket burial in a sleepy upcountry village. The country pastor droned on about Josephat's "promotion to glory," to Ciru's enormous disgust.

While toothless women sobbed into colorful kangas, Hinga, with due delicacy, explained to Ciru that she was now responsible for her husband's debt. Hinga offered for Ciru to work off the debt over time, by collaborating with Hinga on various schemes. Failing which, Hinga's eyebrows and upturned palms had risen in concert, indicating the dark unpredictability of the consequences Edmund's upbringing would doubtless suffer. Ciru remembered this moment with a technicolor clarity—Edmund, a toddler, crawling about on the clay floor of the church-house at the time the threat was uttered.

The very first job irrevocably removed Ciru from her previous life. At the time, Ciru was working as a housekeeper for an Australian couple, living on Riverside Drive. When their daughter, Mathilde, was born, Ciru became her nanny. Mathilde, then four, had known Ciru all her short life and called her Cha-lo, having adopted the Kikuyu struggle with "r" and "l" sounds as her own. After months of pressure, and knowing that the family were scheduled to leave the country for another posting, Ciru agreed to allow Hinga's men into the house, on the promise that no one would be harmed. Only electronics, cash and jewelry would be stolen.

The plan was sound, and the parents, scared witless, were soon bound and gagged. Ciru wore a Spiderman mask as spontaneous camouflage from Mathilde's toy chest. Inhaling the plastic smell of the mask, Ciru was utterly unmoved by the spectacle of Mathilde's mother, a supercilious and racist woman, sobbing. But at the sight of little Mathilde being tied up, Ciru could not contain herself. Hinga, wearing a Stormtrooper mask, swore at her to be quiet.

But Mathilde had recognized Ciru's voice.

Looking up at Spiderman, Mathilde enquired in her toddler falsetto, "Cha-lo?"

Ciru had fled the room, just as the Stormtrooper approached the child, duct tape in hand.

Keen to move past this bitter memory, Ciru took up a piece of lined paper from the shoebox. The handwritten note trembled in her fingers. Notes had been for so many years Ciru's primary means of communicating with her latch-key son. "Your dinner is in the oven," Ciru would write, in the slatted light of the kitchen counter, after Edmund had left for school but before she began her own day.

And when Ciru would come home, utterly spent from a day of justifying her work to herself, she would find her own note embellished with Edmund's careful angular handwriting, "Thank you. The ugali was delicious. Goodnight." He would have washed his solitary bowl, spoon and water glass. They stood mutely on the dish rack, bearing damning witness to her maternal absence.

Tears. Tears at the hand she had been dealt. Tears at the way in which she had played it.

But also an iron resolve that the time had come. But first, that money from the hapless pastor. Money which would give her the ability to bounce back from this, stronger than ever. She locked the safe and stood, patting the reassuring bulk of the gun in the Hello Kitty bag.

Ciru was shown a table at joe-va house café. A table at the rear of the outdoor terrace, giving onto the play area, which had a climbing structure resembling a double-helix. A few children clambered on this, shrieking and chasing each other. These noisy exertions were soothing to Ciru, because they were normalizing. Despite the ravenous jostling of the world, it still contained little people whose greatest concern was to climb, repeatedly, this bizarre wood and plastic strand of DNA and, from its top, scream their victory.

She ordered a tea, black with honey and lemon, waved off the waitress and put the Hello Kitty backpack on the chair nearest her.

This was a good place to have this meeting. Hopefully showing up on time had not been a tactical error. Nor had allowing the woman to leave. Ciru ran knuckles across her mouth, pondering the uncharacteristic decision, the sort she had seen undo others, her very own husband. Perhaps it would have been better to keep the good pastor waiting a little bit, for him to better understand that she was his only lifeline. It had rattled her when the Nigerian told her about Duncan's decision to go to the police. That would introduce variables which would take this transaction beyond her control. She wanted to close this whole thing out quickly. That was essential to her plan to leave the country, lay low for a while in anticipation of the heat which was even now gathering, just beyond the horizon.

The tea arrived and Ciru sipped at it. Over the edge of her menu, Ciru studied the patrons of the café. Be-talcumed UN types sat around tall glasses of beer. Sunbirds appeared and vanished like dreams. And there was the mzungu pastor, red-eyed and tired. He had not yet noticed her, seemed to be fiddling with his phone. He had not responded to her taunting messages. What could be so urgent? Could he be in contact with the cops? She scanned the café once more, no policemen appeared visible, and it was unrealistic that they would be in plainclothes on such short notice.

23

DUNCAN WALKED INTO THE Café, listing a little from his time on the motorbike.

He checked his phone once more. The third buzz from Edmund's place had been another message, the pixelated image of an unopened envelope doing a jig as if it needed to use the toilet.

Expecting another vicious message from Ciru, Duncan stopped short.

"Last calls from and to Hinga's phone are to an Eastleigh-based Somali operator. Ibrahim, doing business as Toogood. 0730005504. Delete this message. Do not contact me again. Muthoni"

A fat pink man in a safari outfit walked into Duncan, who stood stock-still at the entrance of the café.

"*Entschuldigung!*" More accusation than apology.

Duncan blinked, and apologized. When the fat man had gone, Duncan stood to the side and read once more the message from Muthoni.

A wolf whistle cleaved the restaurant. Looking from the phone and over the crowd, Duncan spotted her. The witch sat at the far end of the dining section, beside the play area. Just like her to pick a table like that, when neither of them had any children. Well, of playground age anyway, Duncan thought with a twinge of guilt. She waved at him, then rummaged through her backpack, seemingly lost in inventorying its contents.

Duncan dodged his way through the cedar wood table-tops on the terrace, the green sun umbrellas open in vain supplication. Ciru looked up at him from across her table. He smiled instinctively, then felt ashamed for having done so, and raised instead an upturned palm in more neutral salutation.

When he reached her table, Ciru took her backpack from the chair and placed it on the tiled floor. Between her fingers she held a slip of paper and, with it, gestured at the free chair.

Duncan sat. It seemed like months had passed since they had seen each other, like the events of the last forty-eight hours were a palimpsest over which had been inscribed normal, everyday events.

Ciru knew how to be silent. Duncan fidgeted his buttocks, which rested on his pocketed plunder from various treasures, and tried not to be the first to speak.

"Would you like a coffee or tea?" asked Duncan.

Ciru pursed her lips and shook her head no. As if to explicate, she took up her teacup, raised it at Duncan slightly and drank a long swallow, regarding Duncan the while over the rim. Duncan watched her larynx convulse.

The waitress arrived, her hair corn-rowed and beaded in the red, green and black of the national flag, pencil in hand. Duncan ordered a coffee.

As he watched the waitress retreat into the restaurant, Duncan felt the façade of the quotidian crumble. This was not the first time that Ciru had made him feel as though time was no particular issue, or that what had passed between them, what continued to pass between them, did not change everything. That Nice was not in mortal danger. He waited until she had taken another sip, steeling himself against her unblinking eyes.

"So here we are," said Duncan, as though beginning some sort of negotiation.

Ciru sawed the jointed knuckle of her thumb back and forth under her nose, the cartilage bending audibly.

"How is Nice?" added Duncan.

Ciru's eyes narrowed, and she placed her hand over her teacup. "Fine. She is Fine."

"I have the money," said Duncan, quietly, "here, now."

Ciru cocked back her head and with her chin pointed at the bare tabletop between them. Duncan palmed the wad of dollars from his back pocket and showed it to her under the table, like a pornographic image in a schoolhouse. She raised her eyebrows for an instant.

"Unless those are thousand-dollar bills, you're short." Ciru took a sip of tea. "Very short."

"Right." Duncan replaced the money into his pocket, anxious not to irritate Ciru. "This is all I could come up with on such short notice, but I can have the rest in a day or so. I thought this might—"

"You thought?" Ciru said, as if to a child who had been cautioned several times already. "I told you before, the time for you to think is over. The time now is for consequences. Consequences."

She put her fingertips together as if in prayer, then began again in a more composed tone. "I know, this is confusing to you Westerners who think that life is supposed to be fair." Ciru unclasped her hands and pointed at Duncan. "And that if something unfair happens then you can claim some form of compensation. Like an airline paying you for losing your bags? Is that not what the Bible says?"

The volume of Ciru's voice rose with every word, almost at par with the shrieking children atop the playground behind their table. She seemed to grow conscious of this, gathered herself and crossed her arms. She shook her head as though much disappointed, "But this is not how it works here. You will learn this."

The waitress materialized, open-mouthed and bearing a silver pot of coffee, muted terror in her dark brown eyes. Ciru wordlessly gestured at her to put down the coffee and be gone.

Ciru held her hand out across the table. It took a moment for Duncan to understand that she wanted the money. At the touch of the banknotes, Ciru's demeanor seemed to soften. She gave a conciliatory smile. "Where were you on the day of Westgate?"

Duncan, taken aback by this change in conversational tack, thought for a moment. "At home. At home, I watched it on TV. But we could hear the gunshots from the garden wall."

Ciru sipped her tea. "I was there, in the mall. I went to meet a client and found myself hiding in the supermarket. In the appliance section." She gestured to the steaming coffee pot. "Drink, before it gets cold."

Duncan poured, keeping a cautious eye on the witch. He took from his back pocket the folded LP and placed it on his lap, a weapon at the ready.

She continued, "So I'm sitting there, behind a row of refrigerators, and I can hear the shouting, the shooting. And these long silences. No pattern to when the silences occur, or for how long. I'm not sure what to do. As I think this through, someone taps me on the shoulder. I almost jump out of my skin."

A child seemed to have fallen from the play structure behind them and was rolling about the rubberized floor. Ciru looked back over her shoulder at the wounded child and gave a good-natured shrug.

She turned back to Duncan. "It was an elderly Indian couple, also in hiding. They sat cross-legged, quite serene. We mimed our communications mainly, expressing our fear, our indecision as to what to do. The woman, I remember she had this wonderful smile, and that smooth skin Indian women of a certain age have, she offered me her packet of toffees. Looking at the toffees, I realized my own tongue had swollen in my mouth, from the stress I suppose, so I shook my head no. The woman shrugged, then started rummaging through the packet to get at the sweets. The noise of it, the rustling of the plastic, the un-wrapping of each individual toffee, was so loud. I was sure we would be found. And shot."

Duncan wanted to interrupt, but Ciru's eyes bore a dreamy look, as she replayed the scene.

"But the couple each took a toffee, placing the gold foil wrappers carefully in the breast pocket of the man's shirt and began to suck noisily on the toffees."

What bearing had the story on the present situation?

Over Ciru's shoulder, the injured child's guardian was carrying her off the playground, lengthwise in his arms, like a whimpering child-bride. Under the table, with the palm of his hand, Duncan ironed the creases of the LP cover on his knee.

What was he waiting for?

"I wanted desperately to tell them to please keep it down. But they were simply not aware, like old people watching television, of the noise they were making. So I said nothing. Being polite, even in the face of a very real death." Ciru laughed.

"Later, when it was all over, and we were being escorted out of the mall by the police, the woman took my arm in the street. She looked at me, and I realized, from the way her mouth moved, from how close she stood, that she was a deaf-mute. So was her husband."

Ciru shook her head over her cup of tea. "I'm not sure why I'm telling you this story. There is a moral there somewhere, but I've forgotten it."

Duncan took the LP cover and placed it on the tabletop next to his coffee cup. The child's crying was heard no more.

"Maybe the moral of the story is that there is a time for everything," said Duncan, his head down, his voice firm. He ran his forefinger along the ridge of the LP cover's fold. "And now is the time not to pretend that we are friends telling stories, but to face up to the harsh realities in which Nice finds herself."

Ciru gave a bemused tilt of her head. An errant forelock fell over an eye, giving her an impish look.

Duncan pushed the LP cover across to Ciru. She moved aside her empty teacup and brought the cardboard square before her, the better to study it. Ciru then rummaged in her backpack and put on half-moon reading spectacles.

"What is this? Some sort of film advertisement?" asked Ciru, over the rim of the glasses. Her glasses, and her loosened hair, made her look vaguely elderly, in a way that Duncan had not noticed before.

Duncan began to explain in the knowing and patient way of the missionary. "No, that is an album cover. The packaging in which music is sold in a shop."

Ciru turned over the LP cover, as if to examine it from another angle might reveal clues as to its relevance. She looked up and removed her glasses.

214

"So, what of it? Why do you show this to me?"

"Well," said Duncan, his throat bone dry. "I think it is of interest because this particular album cover belongs to Edmund."

"Edmund who?"

"Edmund your son." His voice was sharper than he had intended. Duncan wasn't sure how much the woman actually did not understand, or was being intentionally obtuse. He recalled Hinga's astonished face as he was lynched and reminded himself of just how ruthless she could be.

Ciru made a show of putting her glasses back into her purse. She fixed her naked eyes on Duncan and leaned on the table between them, resting her forearms over the faces of masked men on the album cover. She made as though to speak, but then stopped herself.

She sat back. "You know my son?" "Yes."

Ciru shook her head and narrowed her eyes. "So, you are saying what, exactly?"

Duncan drank the bitter dregs of the coffee and ran his tongue over his teeth. "Your son is not in a good place right now." He rested his elbows on his knees and bit his lower lip. He had to press on, to pressure the witch. "No, let me be plainer still. Edmund needs your help to get out of danger."

"Danger in which you placed him?"

Duncan restrained himself from responding, even from blinking. This woman, her sort of people, had done too much already. Let her reach her own conclusions. Let her feel some of these consequences she kept banging on about.

Ciru slapped the tabletop with an open hand, the silverware jumping. "Danger in which you placed him? In order to have put pressure on me? To release your friend?" Duncan could see in this pause, gears moving behind her eyes. Had she misjudged him, she seemed to be thinking. "If Edmund has been   " Ciru stopped.

Duncan pursed his lips and tilted his chin sideways. It felt good to see her squirm, to realize she was just a human. Just a con artist with a series of tricks at her disposal.

She took a deep breath. "So you think," said Ciru, her face contorting into a sneer, "you have leverage over me? That you have some sort of cards to play here?" Her voice rose with each word.

Duncan raised his eyebrows and splayed his upraised fingers before him, as though to form a protective shield.

"Let me guess," Ciru said, mastering the volume of her voice once more, "you don't have children, do you?" She did not pause for an answer. "And because you don't, you think you don't have vulnerabilities. And yet . . ." She stabbed a finger at Duncan. "Yet, you fail to understand that my very vulnerability is the source of all my strength. That is the nature of children, because that is the nature of love. You can't understand this, just like a fish cannot understand how lungs work. You haven't evolved to that point yet." Ciru's words came with a mist of spit.

The waitress came by to top off their cups, and both Duncan and Ciru waved her away without looking up.

Ciru fished out her glasses from the pink backpack and took another look at the LP cover. She issued a deep humming from the base of her throat as she did so.

She put down the LP cover and regarded Duncan evenly from behind her reading glasses, as if she had found new information upon this second examination. The animalistic anger had leached from her eyes, replaced by an eerie calm.

Was she unstable, or under serious medication?

Ciru spoke, her voice soft. "Where we lived in Brooklyn,

Edmund and I, it was a so-so neighborhood." She made a waffling gesture with her hand. "And unlike most new immigrants, I found the reality of my America—the sweaty nights, the thin-walled housing, the nightly gun shots—all this I found reassuring more than off-putting. Similar to home, but with the possibility of improvement. Like it was a place which held in it many Americas, of which I could in time select mine, like a pawpaw at the market."

She ran her fingertips over the LP cover. "Anyway, outside the salon where I braided hair, you could always see a gang of young boys loafing about, up to no good. African Americans." She stretched the word out, the hyphen a pause of disdain. "Everyone knew they dealt drugs, wore guns tucked into their waistbands, didn't go to school. As Africans, we had nothing to do with these people, so it didn't concern me personally. And I knew Edmund was too smart, too busy at school, to get involved with such nonsense."

She made a swiping motion, dismissing such an outlandish scenario. "So on a long summer night, when we kept the salon doors open, and that African-American music blast- ed through the humid air, one of these boys was shot, right in front of the salon. I'll never forget it, the blood seeping through his white undershirt as he lay on the sticky pavement. But what amazed me, what made me laugh out loud, and the other ladies thought I was crazy, was how surprised the boy was, how big and wet his eyes were, like someone had smashed his Lego castle. And then of course his friends wanted the po- lice to come, like a teacher at a playground."

Ciru laughed at the memory easily, sweeping her hair back.

"Doesn't sound funny to me," Duncan said. "Senseless death of a young man."

"That's not what I found funny. Just that they could not believe that this was bound to happen, the inevitability of it was right there," she turned her palms upwards, "yet completely beyond their grasp. They were astounded that there could be consequences, like the well-fed American children they were, playing at life. Just like your fat-calved soldiers, coming home from flattening villages, tracking headaches and nightmares like muddy footprints into their sleeping children's bedrooms. Just like lyrics in a rap song, going from swagger to self-pity in a single stanza." She glared at Duncan. "Just like you fail to grasp that this isn't amateur hour. There will be consequences now."

She turned away from Duncan and toward the backpack, rustling about in it. Duncan began to wish he had told her about Edmund outside the café, in a more private setting. There was no knowing what she was thinking, just how angry she might be.

With her back to Duncan, Ciru muttered, "You think love is weakness, when it is in fact the source of all strength. Where is Edmund now?"

Duncan hesitated. His plan seemed, in the light of day, to have been poorly conceived. What had he expected Ciru to do, just release Nice? Still, he had to be firm. Nice's life depended on it. This was the only plan he had.

Duncan sat back in his chair. "It's simple. Give me Nice, and you'll get Edmund back. I'll throw in the money for free."

Ciru stood. "We're leaving." "You'll take me to Nice?"

She shook her head. "You're taking me to Edmund's place. And you'd better pray to your Caucasian God that no harm has come to him."

"Taking you?" Duncan paused. "Have you never been there before?"

Ciru's face grew small, and Duncan understood how wounded she was. And, Duncan understood, how helpless she was. That little prick Edmund had never even had his own mother over, to the flat that she paid for.

But her features hardened once more. She spoke in the flat tones of unwavering resolve, dipping a hand into her Hello Kitty bag. "You will take me to Edmund or I will kill you." The matte black of the gun stark against the cartoon branding.

Images of Hinga's egg-white patella hanging from his torn trousers.

Ciru looked past Duncan, motioning over the waitress. "The bill please."

Then, turning to Duncan, "Give me your new phone."

24

NICE STUMBLED, caught herself against a chain link fence. Each breath shallow, visible in the chill air. Goosebumps on her arms, as she rubbed her belly reflexively. It'll be OK, Pendo. In the surprise that she had been set free, in her urgency to get away from Ciru, the acknowledgement that the madwoman may well change her mind at any time, Nice had simply shuffled in quiet desperation from one alley to another in the slum. Only hoping that she would not make a full circle and meet her erstwhile kidnapper. Or that Ciru had already regretted her decision and was seeking her out.

Nice kept to shadows. As it was late, there were few people about, but she did not delude herself that this amounted to safety.

As she leaned against the fence, she grew aware of the smell of roasting goat meat. A nyama choma restaurant nearby. It awakened within her a profound hunger, a hollowness, a sense that she was operating on diminished capacity. Pendo sending a beacon to her mother. And so Nice righted herself and began to walk in the general direction of the aroma, now tinged with rosemary. Nice clenched her fist, knowing a hunger such as she had never before, a primal desire to strip flesh from bone, to feel the juices dribble down her chin.

Nice came upon the nyama choma joint from the alley behind it. It was a good location for a restaurant, giving, as it did, onto the larger thoroughfare at the edge of the slum. A white Toyota drove slowly past.

From the corner, Nice turned her attention back to the grill which abutted the alley. A canvas safari tarp covered the kitchen, which consisted of a charcoal-laden oil barrel, sawn in half, lying horizontally upon a rack. An obese man in a bloody apron minded the leg of lamb, which sizzled upon the grill. He tore sprigs of rosemary, releasing its flavor, and sprinkled them with care. Behind him, on meat hooks, hung another leg, still with wool and hooves attached. A black transistor relayed the urgent commentary of a football match. Two customers sat on plastic chairs, bottles of beer at their feet. One of them, his long legs spilling into the alley, reached into a pocket and fished out a crumpled packet of Sportsman cigarettes. He placed the pack on a low plastic table, next to a plate of food and a phone.

Nice took in the sight of the meat. Closed her eyes to draw in the smell. Beneath the crackling of the radio, the grilling meat hissed. The three men with their backs to her, oblivious to her need. She ran a hand over her tummy, an unspoken promise to Pendo that soon they would be fed. Soon, they would be well. The primal insistence of her desire astonished her, bringing unbidden to mind that pyramid of human needs she had read about once. The hunger narrowed the aperture of her senses, of her very being.

She went down on all fours and began to crawl towards the seated men in the dark corners created by the tarp. The men did not notice her, as she came behind the low plastic table. The meat glistened. She reached out, fingers trembling in concentration.

The tall man guffawed at something his friend had said. His hand, long and brown, with pink, almond-shaped fingernails, reached for the table.

Nice froze in her crouch.

The man plucked a red plastic lighter from the table and turned back around towards his friend. He inclined his head, flicked the lighter, lit the cigarette stabbed into the corner of his mouth. Without turning back, he replaced the lighter on the table, next to the plate.

Nice extended once more her hand to the plate and grabbed as much of the meat as she dared. It burned in her palm, but she made a fist. She began to shuffle backwards when she noticed the phone. An old Nokia. This too she palmed in her other hand and began an inching retreat on all fours, her knees bleeding.

When she was clear of the shack, safely in the alleyway, she stood upright. Fighting the urge to cram the fistful of meat into her mouth, she walked, as fast as her body would permit, towards the larger road. The one on which she had seen the car drive by.

Shuttered shopfronts lined the road. A chill drizzle began to veil the sodium light. A street boy, no taller than her hip bone, staggered towards Nice. The child's head was over- large for his frame, which protruded under his potato sack shirt, like a wire hanger within a garbage bag. On the boy's sternum, from a bicycle chain, dangled an open plastic bottle, from which he took deep huffs of its oily contents. He said nothing, rocking slightly on his heels, eyes growing oyster- sized as the drugs entered his bloodstream.

Nice crossed sides to be away from him. The road was

broad and better lit than the warren from which she had emerged. Nice walked as far as she dared along the road. Towards the hulking towers of the CBD, away from the nyama choma restaurant. Ducking into the cover of a padlocked doorway, Nice shoveled the meat into her mouth. Her blackened palm slick with fat. She shivered, closed her eyes, chewed noisily, imagined the sustenance radiating to her unborn child, to herself.

Sated, Nice wiped her hands on the tattered remains of her kurta. She peeked into the road from her slim hiding spot. No one came. She allowed herself to study the stolen phone, catching sight of her reflection in the glass. Her eyes desperate hollows, tear-lines bisecting soot-stained cheeks. Who had she become? She wiped her face as best she could on her sleeves, gathered herself. For Pendo. But also for Duncan. Duncan, who was out there somewhere looking for her. She had thought it old-fashioned, bordering on sexist, when Duncan had insisted she memorize his number. Good old Duncan. She had been wrong about a lot of things it seemed. About him, about her feelings for him. And, if she was honest with herself, about his potential as a life partner. She had wasted a lot of time, a lot of opportunities. But no longer.

It was a good thing the phone was an older model; the newer ones would have had a password. Fingers trembling, she punched in the digits of Duncan's number. It rang for what seemed a long while. She had just brought the phone down from her ear, to look at the screen to ensure that it was in fact ringing, when the call was answered.

"Dee, is that you?" Silence.

Nice added, "Dee? Can you hear me—" "I thought I told you to leave the city."

A wave of panic washed over Nice. It was the witch, Ciru,

it was as if she had been expecting this call.

Ciru spoke again. "I am watching you. Think of your baby, baby Pendo—"

It had been a mistake to tell Ciru Pendo's name. Nice leaned forward, peeked into the road. A group of drunks lurched away from her at the far end, jeering and laughing. A smudge of dark movement at the edge of her vision, descending from the flood-lit sky, to rest upon a sodium streetlight. A marabou stork landed awkwardly, its talons screeching on the metal. Its head motionless, eyes hooded in dark. The streetlight swayed under its bulk, arousing in Nice a sense of seasickness.

She was still holding the phone to her ear, in mute terror. "I—Please." Nothing more would come.

The voice whispered. "We are watching you."

Nice hung up. A gagging possessed her, shook her. The food she had eaten seemed ill-judged, toxic. Hands on knees, she threw up, eyes watering, her belly in angry spasms. Spent, she leaned against the dank doorway when a waft of something rotten came over her, bringing forth the bile once more.

It was the stork, waddling prehistorically over to her. Its eyes dense pinpoints of night, its face a scrofulous mask. An ancient thing, as tall as her shoulder. Closer it came, its claws click-clicking against the asphalt. It regarded her face evenly, as if posing an unspoken question. Then it tracked her neck, her arm and rested its ravaged gaze on her hand, in which was still clutched the phone.

Nice threw it on the ground, into the puddle of vomit. The stork bent its long neck, began to lap at the puddle.

Nice forced herself to move, to step slowly around the massive creature. She had to get to the Mission, and then she had to get out of the city.

On the road, she allowed herself to look back at the bird. As if sensing her gaze, it looked up from its slurping. In its ivory-colored beak, it held the phone. Tilting back its ancient skull, the creature crushed the phone with a neat cracking sound.

Then swallowed it.

Nice turned and fled, into the waiting city.

25

UNDER HER HIJAB, the woman's form was sleek. Veiled eyes twinkling, she *tss-tss*'ed at Toogood as he walked by her, along the stream of brake-lights in the traffic-choked Eastleigh lane. Toogood, lost in thoughts about Nice and her radio silence, snapped from this anxious reverie at the hissing. She placed her left hand on the swell of her hip, her right hand against a door frame, never taking her eyes from him.

In the chill of the early evening, the smell of open air nyama choma and wood smoke rose into the dark.

Teesh, walking beside Toogood, was a head taller than him. He bent towards Toogood and said in a rumbling voice, "What is it with these women? That's the third time we've been approached like this by a sister."

Toogood laughed his easy laugh, running his fingers along the smooth panel of a stuck car as he walked past it.

"Third time *I've* been approached," said Toogood. He snorted. "I think they're scared of you, Teesh. They don't know how harmless you are."

The large man, Teesh, shook his head and followed Toogood. The hijabed siren gave one last *tss* in their direction, then fell into a pouty silence. Neither man turned to look at her.

Teesh said, above the sounds of the slow-moving traffic, "I know this is the big city, but these ladies are very friendly? I've never seen anything like it."

"That's because you're a bushman. This is Eastleigh, my man. Don't worry, I will guide you." Toogood slapped Teesh's thickly muscled shoulder blade. "They are professionals. Working girls. The hijabs are so they can charge more to the pious brothers who come here. Who says Islam has a capitalism problem?"

Teesh was about to say something when Toogood's phone rang. The urgent trilling transformed Toogood's demeanor. The phone's bore of white light framed Toogood's gaunt face in the otherwise darkened street.

Private number.

Without looking away from his phone, Toogood held up the index finger of his left hand to Teesh. Obeying this instruction, Teesh bent his head so his skull touched Toogood's. Together they listened.

"Speak," said Toogood.

"Are we in a material breach scenario?" This voice was digitally altered for anonymity, such that it sounded as though it came from the throat of a tweed-jacketed robot. "I trust we are not in a material breach scenario."

Underlit by the phone, a cable of muscle twitched in Toogood's jaw. "Not yet. Not yet. We still have five hours or so to deliver." Toogood swallowed, then added with a firmness in his voice, "We will deliver." A firmness he did not feel.

"You must. Timely. We did stipulate that time was of the essence, did we not?"

"We did." *You did.*

A matatu blaring reggae music blocked the intersection and incensed motorists began to lean on their horns. Toogood jammed his finger into his ear, the better to listen to the lawyerly automaton.

"I knew we could count on you." A crackly silence, long enough that Toogood thought the robot may have rung off.

The metallic voice added, "Oh, and Toogood, should you need something with which to focus your mind to the task at hand, a project you brought to us, and which undertaking you have invited the elders to invest in "

Through the handset pressed to Toogood's ear came what sounded like the whimpering of a hungry puppy. This was not digitally modified.

The robot came back on the phone. "Your sister goes to a fancy boarding school, wears blazers to meals. I understand she is fifteen." A pause. "But looks much younger. In this business, *our* business, I might add, it is a nice differentiator. Did you know she has a trigonometry test next week?"

Toogood's throat tightened, but he knew that losing his temper or making threats would not help. He had been on the other end of phone calls like this one.

The robot spoke further. "That you are surprised only reveals how much you have to learn. We trust the inner circle, but we always verify."

Teesh grabbed the back of Toogood's head with one huge hand and yanked it so that the two men were looking into each other's eyes. Teesh put his index finger, long and crooked, to his lips and nodded at the phone. The words were unspoken: *Be cool.*

Toogood replied, his voice straining for evenness, "She is a good student. She will do well on her test."

The robot seemed unmoved by this assurance. "Let's hope you are right, Toogood. Please ring my associates in a couple of hours, such that we may be updated on your progress."

The line bleeped, then was dead.

Toogood's body sagged from the knowledge, buried deep within himself, that there were simply no rules for the business he was in. This newly acknowledged sense of vulnerability shook his basic sense of the world, of the assumptions he had made of it, of the decisions he had made premised on those delusions. He looked at Teesh with narrowed eyes. Inner circle.

Perhaps sensing the kernel of doubt, Teesh held Toogood for a moment and then shook him by the shoulders.

"Look at me, Toogood."

Toogood's chin sank onto his chest, his vacant eyes not taking in the plastic bag shuffling its way between sandaled feet.

Teesh slapped him backhanded, knuckles connecting drily across cheekbone. A woman and a child walking ahead of the two men turned back at this cracking. When the woman saw Teesh's hulking profile grasping Toogood's slender one, she took her child's hand and hurried into the crowd.

"I told you a long time ago. You should have ended it with that girl. You should have ended her." He spat, as if disgusted. "But now, you need to pull yourself together now. This is the path we have chosen."

Toogood regarded his friend, as if for the first time.

How had that voice known so much about Aisha?

In a softer voice, Teesh added, "Come on Toogood, for all we know, they don't even have Aisha. These are just scare tactics. How many times have we pulled this same stunt? Let's call the school." Teesh's voice was even. He exhaled slowly through his nose, then added, "And even if they do, it doesn't change the plan—get the merchandise, as soon as possible, so we can call the investors and close the deal."

Toogood nodded limply.

Teesh took the phone from Toogood, began scrolling through the contacts. He selected a number, dialed and handed the phone back. "Speak to the school. Let's check that Aisha's OK." Toogood gave a blank grin, to buy time if nothing else. Teesh added, "It's a pretty standard bluff."

Toogood was roiled by nausea. The ringing seemed so far away. It sickened him to think that so much could depend on the outcome of a telephone conversation. That his choices may have put his sister in harm's way.

A British-accented receptionist answered the call, sounding as if she'd been interrupted in the middle of something important. "He-llow?"

The school, and its administration, drove Toogood nuts. Snooty and aloof, as if they were doing him a favor by taking his money. But, in fairness, that was what drove the elite Kenyans to the establishment. Its old-school tweedy Britishness. It was what the school was selling, a caricature of colonialism. And it was what the parents were buying with their multi-comma'ed tuition cheques. The brand of the school was well represented by its inscrutable and tweed- jacketed headmaster, Mr. Roberts, who looked alternately bored with and pained by every interaction with the parents. Until he came to describing the croquet lawn, or the cricket nets. Toogood had half a mind to pull Aisha out of the place, into a normal school, but it was too late now. She had been assimilated by the place.

Toogood explained why he was calling, that he was Aisha's guardian. After many would-you-repeat-thats and I'm-sorry-I-couldn't-follows, the receptionist asked him to hold. Toogood looked over the phone at Teesh, who gave a lukewarm smile of encouragement.

Then the woman was back. "I'm sorry, sir, but Ms. Aisha's class is on safari in Samburu until the day after tomorrow. It appears that you signed the consent forms at the start of the term."

Toogood remembered Aisha excitedly asking him to sign the papers. It seemed a lifetime ago.

The woman continued, "As you know, we forbid our pupils mobile phones, and we are proactive in our communications with their guardians. Nothing has been reported, sir."

Teesh began to mime something.

The woman's voice came again, "Sir, is something the matter—"

Toogood thanked the woman and rang off. No news was good news. It was highly unlikely that the school would be in on anything. Too many moving parts, too many assumptions required of the theory.

Toogood said, "All clear. Aisha is away on safari and only back day after."

Teesh nodded. "Those sneaky bastards must have known that we would be unable to call their bluff." He looked down, rubbing his chin. "But this changes nothing for us. We need to deliver to the investors. We solve that problem, and the rest is fixed."

At the intersection a man on a boda boda was shouting at a woman driving an ice-white Mercedes Benz. She rolled up her smoked windows and leaned on her horn.

Over this blaring, Teesh took Toogood by the shoulders and shouted, "Where is Hinga's partner, the witch? When did she say she would bring the goods to us?"

"Tonight."

"We need it sooner. We need to meet that deadline." A short pause. Then Teesh added, "Did you explain that delivering Nice is optional, that we care only for the parcel."

Toogood shrugged, paralyzed by his inability to tell whether the threat to Aisha was real or not.

Teesh jabbed Toogood in the chest with a long finger. "I told you that girl was trouble. Now we need leverage over that policeman. Over the witch. What do you know of them?" Toogood watched the gears working in his friend's eyes. Toogood knew that Teesh considered his sentimentality unseemly, if not downright dangerous.

"I'll call around. Find a pressure point." Teesh spat. "Don't call Hinga's number again until I tell you."

26

THE POLICE MADE NIYI NERVOUS.

His Nigerian reflexes perked up, cops were inherently unpredictable, requiring a premeditated precaution. Consequently, he especially didn't like places where they congregated, like police stations. So, this decision to report Duncan to the police was not taken lightly.

Still, Mr. Leighman and the Board had been riding him hard, asking all sorts of difficult questions about Duncan and his fitness for the role of pastor. Niyi had responded with calculatedly faint praise, up to the point when Mr. Leighman had asked Niyi to go to the police to report the matter. Mr. Leighman had been visibly relieved when Niyi had waved off the offer to accompany him. Better to handle this in person, until he figured out what was going on with that strange woman who had seemingly hypnotized him over the phone. She had claimed to have witnessed Duncan's crash, perhaps even to have been an acquaintance.

Shaking his head as he stepped over the slumbering askari, Niyi paused outside the gate to light his cigarette. As he stood observing the jacaranda-lined street, two men seemed to be half-carrying a slight figure towards him. Niyi pushed open the metal gate, made to retreat into the security of the compound, when one of the men doing the carrying called out.

"Wewe! Are you with the Church?"

Niyi drew on his cigarette, annoyed at this intrusion of what was to have been the only quiet moment of a very busy day. But he nodded all the same. As the trio lurched towards him, Niyi understood that the person being half-carried was a woman.

"This woman needs help."

Niyi held up his hands. "No trouble here. Please, go to the police."

The woman looked up, her amber eyes making contact with Niyi's. Her face bore a strange ferocity. "I am a friend of Duncan's. I—We had an accident and—"

Niyi stamped out his cigarette, stepped forward and took her by the elbow. Her bones birdlike. Was that blood on her tunic?

She allowed herself to be helped. "My name is Nice."

"I am Niyi. I work with Duncan." Questions swirled in Niyi's head. Duncan had made no mention of a friend in the accident. Let alone a young woman. Was this why Duncan had disappeared so suddenly with the Church's emergency funds? He thanked the men, stepped inside the compound with Nice.

He released her arm. "He's not here. Duncan."

Nice's face crumpled. "Where is he? When did you last see him?"

Niyi pushed his glasses up the bridge of his nose, taking a moment to size her up. "Duncan was here earlier, but he left in a hurry, to the police station."

She brightened at this, wiped her nose with the back of her hand. "Take me there. Please."

"You look— Do you want a cup of tea, a shower?"

She paused, then nodded her soot-stained face, her jaw tightening as if she was stifling a tear. "Quickly, please."

Thirty minutes later, Nice emerged from Duncan's room, wearing an over-large t-shirt bearing the logo of the Church of the Earth, over a pair of coarse canvas overalls. Niyi took in her slight frame, her sharp features; the bruises about her forearms were of varying vintage, some scabbed with underlying yellowing, others purple and angry.

There was something about the way she carried herself, something feral, something to be admired, possibly feared. Maybe that was why Niyi had chosen to smuggle her into Duncan's room, past the splintered door jamb.

Niyi held out the cup of steaming tea, and watched as she held it in both hands, then gulped it down, as if to heat up her very bones. "Let's go."

Niyi looked back at the main building of the Church of the Earth, within which Mr. Leighman was no doubt studying scripture or budgets. He sighed as he opened the gate once more.

They walked in a shuffling silence to the Makaneri Police Station, which was just around the corner. Upon the eavestroughs of the station squatted a couple of marabou storks, each facing the entrance with unblinking, red-rimmed eyes, like lurid totems.

Nice grabbed Niyi's forearm. He turned to look at her, but she said nothing. Niyi guided Nice up the stairs, both of them avoiding the severe regard of the birds.

The receptionist was a swan-necked beauty in a boxy uniform which made her look young. She was writing in a long-paged ledger, her features a sketch of concentration. Glancing at Niyi and Nice over the ledger, she did not smile.

"Evening. I'm here to report a crime. An incident." He was conscious that he would be accusing Duncan in front of Nice. A gravid silence hung between them. Niyi thought for a second, then added, "I think?"

The young policewoman raised a delicate eyebrow. "You think?"

She snapped shut the ledger. Crow's feet appeared at the edge of her eyes, as she looked past Niyi to Nice. "And your friend?"

Niyi rested his palms on the edge of the desk, willing himself to stay calm. "Well, I know that something is not where it should be. But—"

"This is not clear." Her lacquered fingernails were bright against the frayed cloth spine of the leather-bound ledger. "Are you here to report a crime, or not?"

Niyi stood straighter, both to gather himself up, and to impress upon this young civil servant that he was not to be spoken to in this way. "Yes. A large sum of money has gone missing. And given that it was carefully kept, I can only suspect foul play."

The woman reached into a drawer, flipped open a different ledger, and clicked a ballpoint pen. She spoke to Nice, "And you? Anything to add?"

Nice stammered, "Ma'am, I think you may have met my friend Duncan, the pastor of the Church of the Earth I mean. He came earlier because we were in a terrible accident and—"

The policewoman held up her hand, red fingernails flashing. "This Duncan, a white man?"

Nice nodded.

The policewoman turned to Niyi. "And you? You are reporting an unrelated matter."

Niyi began to speak, then stopped himself. How could he be expected to know? He shrugged, shifting his weight from foot to foot, like a shackled circus bear.

"Take a seat." The policewoman stood and asked Nice to follow her into a room.

So Niyi stepped back and looked about the waiting room stupidly. Nice nodded at Niyi, as she stepped into the conference room. He looked awkward and foolish, sat uncomfortably on the sill of the open window. Outside, the mysterious cooings and scratchings of the guardian storks. The occasional siren rose above the traffic.

Once the policewoman shut the door, her demeanor instantly transformed from cold-blooded professional to concerned friend. "I am Muthoni. Your friend Duncan was here. He reported you missing. Something about the Somalis, and that he was going to get you himself—"

Nice brought a hand up to her mouth. "There's a woman, Ciru, a witch doctor. He must have gone to see her. She was keeping me, but then let me go. He must think she still has me." She stood. "We need to call her, tell her."

Muthoni crossed her arms. "Why would we call this Ciru to warn her? She kidnapped you and probably works with that cop Hinga."

"No, no. She helped me." Nice reconsidered. "She saved me. She has Duncan's phone. We just need to explain to her. Please, I have the number."

Muthoni punched the numbers into her phone, enabled the speaker, and sat the device on the table.

Ciru answered on the first ring, but said nothing. Muthoni edged closer to the phone, but Nice stayed her.

Nice spoke into the phone, "Ciru, this is Nice. I wanted to—" If Ciru was surprised to hear from Nice on this number, she did not betray it. "I told you not to call me. I'm dealing with—"

"Have you seen Duncan?" Nice licked her lips, she was suddenly so thirsty. "Please, let me speak to him."

Silence. Was the witch with him now?

Ciru coughed. "Is this a private conversation?" Muthoni nodded urgently at Nice, who responded,

"Yes, yes."

"Your friend the pastor was to deliver something to me. But he has invoked a higher order." What did she mean?

Ciru spoke more softly, such that Nice and Muthoni had to bend low to the phone. "He has involved my son in this matter." She coughed, then screamed into the phone, "And this was not our agreement!"

What was she talking about? Her son? Nice knew she had to calm Ciru down. "Listen. Listen to me. All Toogood wants is the package. He wants me and his baby out of his life, out of the country. So, all you need to do is give him the package."

More silence. As if Ciru was weighing the variables.

Nice pressed her advantage. "Reach out to Toogood, explain that I have escaped because of your cop friend, but you managed to save the drugs. He will be pleased, relieved. He will give you whatever you want. Believe me, I—"

"But my boy. He is a civilian, not to be involved in these matters, and this Duncan has . . ." Ciru's voice trailed off from the phone, as she turned her anger to Duncan.

Nice understood that Duncan was right there, standing right next to Ciru. "Please Ciru, let me speak with him."

A pause. Then a male voice came on, unsure, as though

unbriefed on who was on the other end of the phone. "Hello?" Nice took up the phone, turned off the speaker. She whispered, urgent now. "Dee. Dee, oh I'm so happy you're

OK! I'm sorry I—"

"Nice. Is that you? Where are you? Ciru told me she had you. That you were carrying some sort of—"

Nice interrupted him, "Shh, Dee, listen very carefully to me. I'm fine, I'm with your colleague, Niyi. Ciru, that witch doctor, she let me go. She only wanted the parcel I was carrying, for a dangerous man. He must have those, then we will all be free." A tear sprang at the very notion of it, the absurd waste of all that time.

Duncan seemed to be overwhelmed. "But, I went to her son's house, tied him up. Edmund, he's just a child."

The understanding flooded Nice, the understanding that Duncan had captured Ciru's son, in a desperate attempt to get her back, to save her. It was, she realized, the purest act of love she ever recalled receiving. She recalled Duncan's familiar half-smile at the airport, even as she ensnared him unwittingly into her own web of poor decisions. She did not deserve a friend like this, did not deserve this kind of love. What she had conceived of as worldly aloofness was merely a coping mechanism become cancerous: she was not to be trusted with precious things. But Pendo, her baby, that was a sure second chance to do better — to be better. "It's okay, Dee. Just let him go, like Ciru did me. She's a single mum. I'm sorry, Dee, I love you, just please—"

"Are you okay? Oh, Nice, I was desperate to get you back. I would have done anything, would still do anything. I need to see you, Nice."

"I know Dee, just come back. Please—"

Ciru's voice came back on. She spoke with determined

economy. "Now you listen to me. First, I get my son. Then, I will reach out to this Toogood of yours. But the pastor comes with me, as insurance. And if any harm should come to my boy," a low whistling, "I will take my time with all of you, Somali or not." A chilling finality to the words.

Nice wiped away her tears. "I understand Ciru. Just give him what he wants. He will not—"

"And another thing. I have that note you wrote, to the police, confessing to everything. I will show that to your Toogood, so he understands what you are."

"No, Ciru, there's no need to—" Click.

Nice blinked at the phone. She dialed again but Duncan's phone had been switched off.

Muthoni put an arm around Nice. "All he has to do is give the boy back. Then he'll be back. And you can do what you should have done a long time ago."

Nice tried to stop the tears. But failed.

27

DUNCAN KEPT HIS EYES ON CIRU'S BACK as they walked through the alleys, towards the bypass from where they would catch a boda to Edmund's place.

It astonished Duncan how little shame he felt about having brought Edmund into this mess. About holding that situation over the witch. It just seemed natural, to use violence and threats to engineer a better outcome f a difficult situation. Those were the means at hand. He evidently already had within him the wherewithal for it. Maybe he had just never been in desperate enough straits to think along these lines. Never had a love worth fighting for, like this.

All he felt, shuffling along the narrow laneways between the corrugated iron shacks, was a giddiness. Something had shifted between Nice and him, she had never before said that she loved him. All he had to do was get the witch her son back, then he would be born again. Into the warm sun of a life with Nice, away from the cloistering religiosities, the insistent hypocrisies of his day-to-day. This time, he would not waste a second. Would not be afraid to give love, and get love.

But first, Edmund.

As they walked, in the cool still air, he could see through the cracks and corners of the shacks, as their walls and doors were imperfectly joined. Behind the tin wall of the shack to Duncan's right, a round-cheeked boy sat with an open notebook at an overturned avocado crate, the end of his red- and-black striped pencil in his mouth, looking up at the ceiling of his shack as if the answer to his assignment lay inscribed on it. The flickering light of an unseen kerosene lantern threw intermittent shadows on the boy's face.

The two made evanescent eye contact through the cracked joinery between the corrugated iron wall and the plywood door. The boy's sad eyes followed Duncan.

Duncan passed on, leaving the grave-faced child to his labors.

He contemplated Ciru's smooth gait. He could encircle her bicep between his thumb and forefinger. How consoling might it be to just wring her neck, to slake his growing thirst for satisfaction? Why had he been restraining himself all these years? Why had he not had the courage to admit his own urges, however basic? How easy it would be to crack her skull against the concrete wall, fling her into one of these festering sewers, watch the black water claim her, and walk away. Then there would be no need for this errand. Edmund would untie himself in due course. No one in this city cared.

But what of Nice? Ciru had released Nice. All she wanted was money, to look after that Edmund. Seized by a panicky determination, Duncan quickened his pace to get closer to her.

Ciru's nape looked fragile. Duncan imagined the marrow, pulsing like molasses within her slim bones.

He grew aware of a white-hot hatred for Ciru, as if it had always lived within him, demanding only to be quenched, searing away any thoughts of Nice, indeed, all other thoughts.

This insouciant witch, she was emblematic of this situation, of Nairobi. A city uncaring of its people, a people uncaring of each other. Only a white-hot capitalism, searing away all that was non-transactional.

A tendril of Duncan's thought extended itself towards the satiety which the violence would bring. Its elegant definitiveness.

He caught up to Ciru.

She did not hear him approach, lost in thoughts of her own. Duncan drew back his upper lip to reveal pale teeth in the half-light from yet another undistinguishable tin shack. She stood level with his shoulder. Without a sound, Duncan placed the web of his left hand on Ciru's nape. His hand, white-pink against her caramel skin, tightened without conscious impulse around the bones—just as birdlike as he had imagined as he'd watched her walk. The muscle memory sending his thumb seeking, and finding, the carotid, which throbbed against the pressure, pounding out its unfathomable code.

She stopped dead in her tracks.

She looked up at Duncan, eyes brimming with bemuse-ment at what she saw as an undue familiarity. But the bemuse-ment melted when she beheld Duncan's unblinking eyes, and she jerked her chin towards him, straining her head against his hold, which only tightened against this counter- pressure. Her own eyes grew hard as she absorbed the electricity of his grip, the seriousness of his resolve. And she drew herself up against these things as though she had been insulted, not actually threatened by this physical contact.

She did not make to remove his hand. Instead, she held his gaze. "Yes?"

He had not expected to hear her voice and, for a second,

it froze him, the surf of blood pounding his temples. What was becoming of him, his own sense of self, to be manhandling an elderly woman like this?

The narrow column of dim air between their faces was rent with a buzzing, and Duncan drew back sharply as an unseen missile brushed his cheek.

Ciru shrieked with delight. "A flower chafer! A beauty!" There, between her collarbone and her breast, had landed a bronze beetle, the size of a pack of cigarettes. It sat there, impossibly massive and motionless, as if it had always been there. With her forearm, Ciru removed Duncan's now limp hand from her neck, and picked up the insect between her thumb and forefinger. It looked enormous in her small

hand, and gave an angry buzz.

Duncan said, "Maybe you shouldn't do that." He took one wary step away from the witch, the blood lust he had felt only a moment ago melting away, leaving him unsure of himself. And frightened of what he was capable of.

Ciru got on all fours, in the filth-strewn street, and placed the insect on the concrete, like a wind-up toy. "Just look at this creature." With childish glee, she pried apart the wings, revealing black and robotic looking articulations.

Duncan said, "Stop that, you'll hurt it."

"That's the problem with your Western religions," Ciru spoke without looking away from the insect. "All reverence, no wonder. This beetle is a cosmic force, and it frightens you because you find the words 'I don't know' so threatening." She looked up at him, the beetle buzz-sawing between her fingers. "Just say it with me, 'I don't know, and that's okay. I lied about the whole heaven thing—I don't know.' You don't have to pretend you have all the answers. It makes you ridiculous."

She leaned her face in close, parted her lips slightly, and licked the carapace lengthwise from tip to tip. The creature buzzed once more, low and urgent. Ciru whispered, her tongue flickering against the golden armature, "I have no idea what you signify. But I thank you."

It struck Duncan just how astute she was. She had named, in passing, one of his own major misgivings about the Church, about monotheistic religion generally, and his role as its emissary in particular. It was exhausting, and childish, to pretend to know it all. The Church did not, and he certainly did not, and he was tired of following this script.

If he was honest with himself, it is what he should have told the Legishons, about the loss of their son. If he had been honest with himself, he would have pursued Nice with sincerity. But there was simply no sanctioned way of saying that one did not know. Moved by this insight, and in a vague awe of the earnestness of Ciru's happiness, he too knelt to better regard the beetle, which remonstrated with purring vibrations. Then he would do the right thing, get Edmund and his crazy mother reunited.

They knelt in the street, like children playing marbles.

Ciru removed her fingers from the sides of the insect. It raised its bronze-flecked wings like sails. The buzzing ceased. Duncan took in the furred forelegs, the fine venation of the under-wings.

From above came the thwap-thwap of a helicopter, the bore of its searchlight probing the indistinguishable laneways of the slum.

Duncan visored his eyes with his hand, and mouthed the words US AIR FORCE. Obama's visit to Nairobi was kicking into high gear, maybe the man himself was up there, beaming down his blessings.

The helicopter passed on, leaving them in a sudden dark silence.

And when they looked back down, the beetle was gone. In an impressionistic blur of gold and black, where there had once been a beetle, now there wasn't. A tear rolled down Duncan's cheek, a tear he could not explain.

He felt a hand on his shoulder. Ciru said nothing.

Still kneeling, Duncan looked up at Ciru, like a choir boy. "I'm sorry Ciru. Sorry about your boy. He is safe, I promise."

Ciru nodded, and held out her hand. Duncan took it, and stood. Together they walked on.

When they emerged onto the street, Ciru summoned a boda with a one-note wolf whistle.

Straddling the bike, Ciru turned to Duncan. Are you sure Edmund's all right?"

Duncan nodded, ashamed.

Ciru handed him the helmet. "Take me to him." Duncan sat behind her on the motorbike.

Ciru added, "And pray to your white God that no harm has come to my son."

28

THROUGH THE DUST-STREAKED plate glass window, Toogood could see them, as though through a one-way mirror. The shopping-bag-laden mother, the lead-footed toddler tugging at her hand. The mother seemed to mime the act of reasoning with a child. But the child's face melted into a sneer. From his stool, Toogood could almost hear the child's whine through the barroom window, over the torpid reggae music.

He took a long pull at his beer, peering over the bottle to see what the mother would do next.

The woman's face was taut under the makeup. She set down her plastic bags with care, one by one, in a column, such that only the bottom one was touching the pavement. Then she turned, bent to the child, and gave it a hard slap.

Toogood smiled as the little boy helped his mother collect the plastic bags.

Toogood had always had low tolerance for whining. As far back as he could remember, he had been conscious, like a tadpole somehow aware of the water in which it is birthed, of how adults whined about the state of the world. And the district of Yaqshid, north of Mogadishu, where Toogood had spent his dusty childhood, had provided many things to whine about.

As a boy he had been repelled by his father's excuses about his bakery being shuttered, the endless protection money which served to buy no protection, the shabby corrugated iron shack in which they lived, Toogood and his three siblings having to go to school on alternate days. Toogood knew intuitively that whining was an infirmity, a white flag fluttering before the gathered armies of entropy.

And it disgusted him.

The arrival of his baby sister Aisha, when Toogood had been nine, was the final step in his commitment to utter self-reliance, to never whining.

His earliest recollection of this promise to himself was watching baby Aisha crying in her cot of soggy plywood. She had had a curious way of crying, never emitting so much as a whimper, even as fat tears rolled down her cheeks. There seemed, to Toogood's mind, a muted defiance to this baby, and he loved her intensely for it.

Once he had become a part of the criminal community, it had astonished Toogood that the people he dealt with professionally were, almost to a man, unethical and unwilling to assume ownership for their mistakes. Teesh had agreed, shrugging his big shoulders, and commenting that their colleagues were, after all, career criminals, so there was a degree of self-selection at play. Not in so many words, for Teesh was a man of few words, but a vast equanimity. But neither Toogood nor Teesh considered himself, or the other, unethical—it was a paradoxical point of pride which had drawn them further together, even as the slums of their childhood receded.

Just months into the Toogood-Teesh partnership, right when Toogood and Nice had started seeing each other with some regularity, Teesh had grumbled about the lack of focus that a new girlfriend created. A foreign girlfriend to boot. Toogood had laughed it off, he just liked how Nice didn't have any regard for social structures. He knew that he would not be in the market for a proper girlfriend for a good while. This was expansion mode. And it was with this feeling of openness and confidence that Toogood approached another young foreigner in a restaurant. A boy really, the son of the French ambassador who, while based in Nairobi, was also accredited to Somalia. Frederic was a lank-haired youth with a penchant for flashy belt buckles and pointy-toed suede boots. He accompanied his father on missions to Mogadishu, and had grown enamored of the gleaming bulletproof limousines, the lantern-jawed plainclothesmen. And, at night, while his bookish, near-retirement father worked on his memoirs, young Frederic, the self-styled Marquis de Mogadishu, snuck out to the seaside watering holes where young men like Toogood conducted office hours.

On one such outing, Frederic had offered to bring a considerable shipment of Toogood's narcotics in the diplomatic pouch to Nairobi, where the street value was considerably higher. The Frenchman had even offered to move the product in Nairobi, but Toogood demurred, suggested that delivering the goods to the local Somali contact was enough. All this was pleasantly agreed to over glinting flutes of champagne, framed against the glowering sun. Frederic wore a signet ring on his little finger, and it too caught the dying light. Toogood had hoped the informality of the arrangement would lead to the diplomatic pouch becoming a regular (and proprietary) channel.

Then Frederic vanished with the product. News received in Mogadishu of Frederic's lavish lifestyle in the *VIIe* arrondissement.

Teeth were vainly gnashed in Mogadishu.

Worse than the death threats which Toogood had received, was the disdain of his colleagues, of his dented reputation among the partners in his firm. His had been an amateurish move, and Toogood knew it well.

But, true to his self-promise, Toogood had neither whined nor tried to wriggle his way out of the problem. Summoned before the board of directors, he took sole responsibility (and a considerable financial hit), and asked only for a chance to redeem himself. This was granted, with a severely worded caution and the ever-unspoken promise of violence in the event that the caution went unheeded. Toogood was only glad the nascent nickname, Frenchkiss, had not stuck to him like a bad odor.

By way of consolatory commentary, Teesh—that ghetto philosopher—had explained, "Any problem you can resolve just with money, is no problem at all." And Teesh had never once mentioned the matter again. For this discretion Toogood was eternally, if mutedly, grateful and loyal.

Months later, without warning or context, Teesh staggered into Toogood's apartment with Frederic in a headlock. The Frenchman's whining was repellent, his hair a sweaty, matted helmet. Released from Teesh's grasp, Frederic began a litany of slick excuses. These were soon replaced with begging, which was in turn replaced with sobbing gibberish.

Granted, by this stage Toogood had removed six of Frederic's fingernails (beginning with the little finger bearing the signet ring) with the white-hot tip of a wire hanger heated on the stovetop. Teesh claimed to have invented the technique, which he called "unstitching". It was demanding work, what with the boy's shrieking and wriggling about, yet satisfying. And Toogood had stuck to it with the grim concentration of a man applying himself to an unpleasant but inevitable task. One that, once completed, would bring a warm sense of a duty performed—like completing a tax form.

Frederic's suede boots grew bespattered with blood and vomit. But there was nothing for it, the boy had spent all the money. And even if he had the money, right there in his Hermes wallet, Frederic had, using Teesh's definition, a true problem on his nail-less hands—the mere restitution of the money could not bleach the stain on Toogood's honor, or the nickname Frenchkiss.

Later that night, leaning against the cab of Toogood's pickup truck and wearing crisply starched Somali army uniforms bought from a nearby open-air market, Toogood and Teesh watched Frederic's body burn in an oil drum. The unwilling, then dense, flames rose and fell without pattern against the bejeweled night. Teesh had simply folded Frederic's corpse in half, like a penknife (explaining in a grunt, as he performed this feat, that this could only be done very shortly after time of death), before jamming it into the barrel so the long-maned head was pressed against the soiled desert boots in a final plyometric salute.

Toogood had said, more aloud than to Teesh, "I suppose this place will be crawling with French police soon."

Teesh did not remove his eyes from the guttering flames. "Meh, they're a long way from Louis Vuitton. Plus, I hear his father is retired, no longer with the embassy. And, if this little punk did this to us, you can be sure he did it to others." He put a meaty hand on Toogood's shoulder. "Just lay low, and hope for the best."

After a pause, Teesh added with a snort, "Hopefully, they decide this was a terrorism thing. When all you've got are Special Forces, everything looks like 9/11."

They laughed, and it was agreed, implicitly, that the

violence had been necessary, and cleansing. Toogood had been touched that Teesh had said that Frederic had conned "us." But he had also winced at Teesh's reptilian cold-bloodedness, at the popping of the Frenchman's hipbones in the fire, at the vague acceptance that this was a point from which there was no return, on some level.

Teesh's words proved sage advice, for they heard nothing further of the matter—the passing weeks swallowing the incident as a pond does a pebble. Neither Toogood nor Teesh had been fool enough to try to use the incident to even the score in public. That Frederic had been disposed of in no way changed that Toogood needed to up his game, and that blemish on his record would be the ever-flashing neon- reminder of this.

Toogood tilted the bottle, draining his beer, disgusted with himself for doing so. He had begun drinking more, taking more of the ever-available pills, to cope with the strange mix of anxiety and boredom which this job entailed. He stood, and pulled out his phone to see if Teesh had called.

Teesh had not.

Low growling rattled the barroom window. Toogood looked up from his phone, past the greasy window.

A low-slung matte black Sedan, exotically expen- sive-look-ing, had materialized. It did not belong in this neighborhood. Knots of pedestrians dispersed before it. Toogood, eyes fixed on this mechanical apparition, splayed his fingers against the countertop, as though preparing to vault over it and through the window.

Wing-tipped feet emerged from the dark interior of the car, followed by a man in white shirt, open-necked against a dark suit. He stood, stretched as though he had been driven a great distance, then bent back into the car to have a word with the driver. When the man straightened himself, he held tucked under his arm a brown paper bag.

Toogood wished he had not drunk the last few beers, or swallowed that handful of pills earlier. He felt sodden and fuzzy. Reaching under his jacket, Toogood caressed the reassuring bulk of his revolver, where it lay strapped under his left armpit, its grip towards his thundering heart.

Where was Teesh?

With his thumb on the ridged hammer of his gun, Toogood reminded himself that when dealing with his shareholders, and their emissaries, he could not afford to commit the first act of violence—it would be nothing less than a declaration of war.

Basking in the security of this same information, the suited messenger sauntered into the bar.

"I didn't know it was still acceptable to meet here for business." The messenger spoke fast and clear, gesturing expansively with the paper bag at the decrepitude of the barroom, the sawdust on the floor, the obese and mute barman.

Toogood pushed back his stool and stood, his shoulders square to those of his interlocutor.

The man threw back his head and laughed, an ugly laugh, short and sneering. "Stand down, Frenchkiss." A tendon stood in his neck as he spoke. Toogood imagined unstitching it. The man responded to the look on Toogood's face, saying, "I'm just here to give you something. The directors feel you need a short-term incentive, help you focus."

He held the crumpled bag at shoulder height. Then he brought it to his waist, and tossed it, underhanded, across the room in a high arc.

Toogood followed the bag with his eyes, understanding vaguely he might be shot as he did so, that this could be the intention behind the thrown object. Still did the slowly rotating missile hold him in its thrall as it crossed the room. Time grew torpid. The thrown bag cleaved a path through the swirling dust motes. He thought further that he had never been shot before, but guessed it would be painful.

He caught the paper bag in both hands. It was not heavy. When he looked up, the suited man had gone. Outside, through the barroom window, the lethal-looking car had also vanished, leaving only the wake of its growling engine.

Toogood sat back at the counter, hands trembling, throat parched. He pushed away the empty beer bottle. He inhaled, held the breath, and over-turned the paper bag.

A cloth-bound notebook tumbled out. On its front, in a curlicued handwriting, were the words "Aisha Musse, Trigonometry, Winter Term."

He took in his little sister's notebook, turning its graph-papered pages, crawling with incomprehensible hieroglyphs. It staggered him that Aisha's notebook, an artifact from a parallel life, could have made its way here, to the bar counter. That there must be some sort of dossier on him sitting in a country manse in Nakuru, perhaps flagged with colored post-it notes. This was beyond reckoning, that the stakes could even be so high without him having expressly consented to them. Toogood's heart hammered, and he realized he had been holding his breath. Exhaling slowly, he reached for his phone. Dialing Aisha's school, Toogood got the same receptionist, sounding again as though she had been rudely interrupted. She reiterated in her posh accent that there was still nothing to report from the thoroughly uneventful safari that Aisha seemed to be on, implying that Toogood was being hysterical.

The woman said, "Are you quite all right, Sir? Is there

perhaps some emergency on your end?"

Toogood said there was not, and he was sorry for the intrusion. The woman sighed theatrically and hung up. He supposed they could have stolen a notebook easily enough; Aisha was careless with her belongings. And the test Aisha was supposed to be having could be a plain old lie. But the term "inner circle" in that robotic intonation, it had rattled him. Something—someone—had to be connecting the dots between his investors and his little sister. The fact that the game ran this deep still astonished him. Just when he had started thinking that he had a handle on it. He sat in a trance, unsure of what to do.

The phone vibrated in his hand, startling him. New text message.

From Teesh. "Good news. The witch has a child. Am on it."

Toogood ran a finger across Aisha's girly handwriting, over the baffling equations. This was a warring act. He would not let this pass.

A rage washed over him, and he welcomed the feeling. The anger grounded him, made him less jangled. The flimsy pages of the notebook rustled. He pushed away his half-drunk beer. Having realized that his own sister was in play, Toogood grew more clear-eyed, even more ruthless. That witch would bring him what was his, by God. And once he had made the delivery of the drugs, he would turn to the witch, her family, that policeman, Nice, anyone who had played a hand in this—all of them.

One by one, he would unstitch their happiness.

29

CIRU GAZED UP AT EDMUND'S GLITTERING HIGHRISE, and gave a grunt of appreciation. "Here? My boy lives here?" Doubt lingered in her eyes, but it was being replaced by an appreciation for just how far she had managed to remove her son from the slums.

Duncan was eager to get up, release Edmund, and get back to the Church, to see Nice. He gestured at the building. "Shall we?"

But Ciru seemed jittery, nervous about the prospect of seeing her own son. She looked at her feet and said, "He's never asked me to visit him here, and maybe he will be upset." Duncan's voice came out louder than he had intended. "Ciru, you are here to rescue him. We need to go up to see him." Ciru's mooning over her spoilt man-child was more than Duncan could bear. Even now, she seemed afraid of her own son.

Duncan, unsure of what to say to change her mind, said nothing. He watched her walk through the smoked glass doors, and vanish from sight. He sighed. It was good to be away from her though, to be able to think clearly without having to manage Ciru. He imagined what Nice must be experiencing. A flicker of resentment that she had put herself, and him, into this situation. The foolishness, the recklessness. He shook his head clear of these thoughts. These were precisely the qualities he also loved about Nice, her spontaneity, her lust for life. No, he needed to get back to her, to keep the momentum going between them.

Ciru took Duncan's elbow and steered him towards the lobby of Edmund's building. "Come on. The streets are watching."

They rode the lift in silence. The door to Edmund's flat was ajar. Ciru padded reverentially up to it, her footsteps muffled by the thick carpeting of the corridor. She seemed prepared to believe that this was perhaps normal, in places like this—posh high-rises removed from the fray of cheek by jowl living. What need was there to lock a door in a marble palace like this? She looked over her shoulder at Duncan, as if to seek his confirmation.

Duncan held a forefinger to his lips, and motioned for her to step back. He distinctly remembered the finality of the door clicking shut behind him when he had left Edmund's place.

Duncan stepped past Ciru, into Edmund's flat. Ciru seemed to acknowledge her role as a follower in this new and strange place. The white curtain liner along the balcony door was trapped in the sliding glass door, which had been shut. This was somehow more worrying to Duncan than the fact that the sleek black TV had been ripped from its mounting on the wall. The TV itself nowhere to be seen.

Following her maternal instinct, Ciru had gone straight to the little kitchen off the living room and opened the fridge, examining its contents to see just how poorly her son was eating.

"He seems to eat a lot of pizza. Not a single vegetable in here." She glanced over the fridge door at Duncan, and took in the seriousness of his features.

Having confirmed that something was amiss, Ciru pushed past Duncan and stood in the middle of the room, stock-still, as if sniffing the air. She turned and stood before the destroyed TV mounting, taking in the violence, weighing its gravity. She gave Duncan a look, half question-half threat, and then slid open the balcony door.

No one there. The wicker chairs stood just as Duncan remembered them. The treeline of the arboretum beyond the balcony now swallowed by the dark.

Ciru leaned over the railing of the balcony, standing on tiptoe to get a sense of the height. Without turning to look at Duncan, she said in a flat, unreadable voice, "So where is he?"

"I left him in the bedroom."

"Left him?" She turned to face Duncan, a frown on her face.

"It's just over here." Duncan stepped through the door, back into the flat. Ciru followed him into the bedroom, pausing only briefly to examine the ruined TV mount again.

Duncan wanted this done with. He walked quickly into Edmund's bedroom, saying, "He's just over—"

But Edmund wasn't there. On the floor where Duncan had left Edmund, remained only the nest of blanket and pillows. One pillow bore a streak of blood.

Ciru, not having understood, said with impatience in her voice, "Where? Where is Edmund?" She walked over to the bedside table, on which was a bronze statue of a leopard, and a framed photograph. Edmund, aged three, on a pony, his entire face alight with joy. A young, beautiful Ciru holding the boy's pudgy hand, looking askance at the horse. She took up the frame, ran a thumb over the sepia-hued faces. What had become of those people?

She had to see Edmund, to make things right, whatever it took. "Where is Edmund?"

As he watched her holding the picture, Duncan's mind reeled, as he sought to come up with a rational explanation. They stood looking at the room. On the foot of the bed lay a canvas duffel bag. Duncan had no recollection of it, and walked over to it.

Unzipping it, Duncan removed a shoe-box sized parcel, wrapped in butcher paper. The duffel bag contained nothing else. For its size, the parcel felt heavy, bearing the heft of something sodden. Duncan made to unwrap it, and Ciru said, "Wait. Is that Edmund's?"

Duncan did not meet her eyes, began to tear at the tape. The parting butcher paper released the scent of rosemary. Ciru smelled it too, and she came to stand beside Duncan.

Within the butcher paper was another layer of wrapping, this one clear crinkly plastic. Within it were several cuts of refrigerated meat, marbled with fat and beautifully presented. Between each chop lay a sprig of rosemary.

"Are those lamb chops?" Ciru asked.

Duncan did not reply. The chops were still cold to the touch. These had been left here recently. But why? And by whom?

"Where is Edmund?" Ciru's voice hardened, almost cracking.

"I don't know. I left him here. He was secured." Duncan stared about the room, his mind racing.

"Secured? What does that mean?"

An insistent trilling. Ciru pulled out her phone. "Hello?" The animation leached from her face, as she took in the caller's words. She nodded, grim-faced. "Yes, I will do it now."

She peered into the phone, as though trying to find something. After a few seconds, she looked up at Duncan. "Put it on speaker."

Duncan took the phone from her and did so. A crackling came from the handset, and Duncan placed it on the bed. The lamb chops glistened in the unnatural light of the handset.

Ciru seemed stunned, incapable of speech. Understanding that no context was to be forthcoming from Ciru, Duncan said, "Hello? You are on speaker now."

A metallic voice came from the phone. "Greetings, mzungu friend."

Duncan blinked, looking at Ciru for some sort of explanation.

The voice from the phone said, "You have received my gift, yes?" When Duncan made no response, the caller spoke again. "I too am Nice's friend. Toogood."

Duncan's eyes goggled, and he took a step towards Ciru, as though to explain. Her face remained smooth, but her dark eyes tracked Duncan.

From the phone came Toogood's laughter. "Don't try and act like you didn't want this to happen. Didn't plan this all along. You tricky whites, that's how you conquered us so easily. You do one thing, and then act another. Tell the poor woman the truth. About her boy. About what you've done."

Duncan kept his eyes on Ciru, and took one more step towards her over the sheepskin rug. She stepped away from him.

Toogood's voice was hypnotic in its insistence. "Take the witch's hands. Tell her what you've done."

When Duncan did not move, Toogood's spoke again. "Take her hands. I have a camera in the room, I have eyes on you."

Duncan looked around the room to assess the plausibility of this claim, to try and find the camera. Pursing his lips, he moved in to take Ciru's free hand. In her other, she still held the photograph of baby Edmund.

The phone came alive with Toogood's voice again. "Good. Now tell her, how you bound and packaged Edmund, and gave him to me."

Duncan, looking at Ciru's hand, said, "I did tie Edmund up, but I thought you and I would—"

Toogood's voice thundered from the phone, "You gave me a piece of meat, bound and packaged." After a brief silence, Toogood spoke again. "And I, I have returned your gift, with a similar package of meat, bound and packaged. In my culture, we do not like to be indebted."

Duncan appealed to Ciru, taking her by the shoulders. "Honestly Ciru, I was just desperate and—"

Toogood interjected again. "You have invoked forces beyond your control."

Ciru dropped the picture frame she had been holding. The glass cracked. She began to cry, looking both girlish and old. She looked past Duncan to the phone, knelt before it at the bed, as if in prayer to it. "Is my boy okay? Please. Please, I will give anything, do anything to have him back."

Toogood's voice was impassive. "Much rests on you. Have you got my goods, and how soon can you deliver them?"

"Yes, yes, I have them. Here, on me."

"Good. My associate will bring you to me now."

As if on cue, a bald man in a camouflage jacket, a head taller than Duncan, walked into the room from the toilet.

Toogood spoke again, "This is Teesh. He will stir the drink."

Teesh gave a slight nod to a cast bronze statue of a leopard on the bed stand, as though to greet Toogood via the hidden camera. He gestured at Ciru's bag, and she handed it over. Teesh took the bag, tossed it into the open bathroom door. Then he took Duncan's elbow without a word.

Ciru stood, and began to follow them out of the room. "Wait," came Toogood's voice. "Put the lamb chops in the fridge. We could use that grill on the balcony." Teesh's rumbling laugh echoed in the hallway.

30

TEESH'S MASSIVE FRAME, HUNCHED OVER THE PICKUP'S STEERING WHEEL, took up most of the space in the cab. Beside him, Ciru and Duncan sat silently, shoulder to shoulder.

He drove fast. They lurched through the central business district, deserted and glistening under a drizzle. Like most young cities, Nairobi's conurbation gave up the fight quite suddenly, and soon they were on the Eastern Bypass which formed a thin ribbon of tarmac across the darkened landscape. Duncan smelled the Nairobi sewage treatment plant before they saw its sodium lights. The pickup plunged on into the night, then Duncan was without landmarks.

Teesh took an exit abruptly, the tarmac yielding to a rutted road of murram. On either side lay expanses of bush. In the bouncing headlights, Duncan could make out dense knots of trees, and the sparser acacias. The profile of a giraffe appeared briefly, distinct and improbable as a dream, before being swallowed by the dark. Duncan wanted to ask if anyone else had seen it.

Teesh hummed as he drove.

Following a metallic rattling in the well beside the glove compartment, Duncan noticed three silver bullets, each as long as his forefinger, bouncing along. Teesh followed Duncan's regard and met his eyes with a smile.

Over the growling diesel engine, Teesh said, ".357s. For elephants." He laughed, downshifting to take a hill, and added, "I'm joking. They're for people."

Ciru had not spoken a word since they got into the pickup. She held the handle above the passenger door with both hands, shawl wrapped about her, staring out into the night.

Teesh checked his watch, then turned the dial on the radio, tuning into the unmistakable sound of a politician seducing an audience.

Obama's honeyed rhetoric began to fill the cab of the pickup, transporting them despite themselves from the reality of what faced them.

"But we have chosen. I said we have chosen, not to be defined by violence." Obama's voice swelled, and the crowd roared to match it.

Utterly without warning, Teesh swung the truck square into a thicket, gunning the engine. In the cab, it was as if the bush was trying to throttle the truck, resenting its noisy intrusion. Duncan looked over at Teesh, who only stared ahead at the branches crowding his windscreen, seemingly oblivious to the clamor.

They emerged into a clearing. In the glow of the headlamps, a man sat, elbows on knees, looking at them, as if he had been expecting the apparition of the truck.

Teesh cut the engine, leaned across Duncan to open Ciru's door. "Out."

After the clatter of the engine cleaving its way through the thicket, the night air was still and cool. The man who watched them stood. As Duncan's eyes adjusted, he grew aware of the flicker of a fire behind the man's chair. And that he had slung across his chest a short-barreled automatic rifle, like a guitarist liable to burst into a violent ballad.

The man raised a hand and walked towards them. Teesh left Duncan and Ciru standing at the truck and strode towards the man.

Duncan turned to Ciru. "Don't worry, I'm sure Edmund is fine."

"Don't. I'll deal with you later." She would not look at him.

Teesh beckoned them over to the fire.

As Duncan walked past the chair on which the man had been sitting, he noticed a large matte TV leaned against it, a spaceship's artefact transposed to the bronze age. Edmund's TV, still trailing red and green wires from the mounting.

The man, baby-faced and dressed in all black, stood with Teesh by the fire, which cast monstrous shadows against the dense canopy of the trees above the clearing.

Behind them, painted a cheerful yellow, and looking as though it had just fallen out of an aircraft, a hulking shipping container bearing the words "Lucky 7 Shipping" in black block letters. The relentless forest had begun to reclaim the container—its sidewall already covered in tendrils.

Teesh's companion walked in slow circles around Ciru and Duncan, snuffling pig-like.

"You—white man." He poked Duncan between the shoulder blades. "You came here to take our lands? This is mau mau land. My grandfather killed many British here. Hung them by their feet, hairy pink calves swinging like hams." This could not be Toogood. Toogood did not sound like this on phone. Was

Somalian, not Kenyan.

Teesh said nothing, only the trace of a smile on his face, as though allowing a child to show off its crayon drawings.

Duncan coughed, to clear up the question of his potential Britishness. "I'm American. Obama?"

At this the man gave a clap and ran back to his chair. He returned with a matte black transistor radio and held it aloft like a trophy. Turning up the volume dial, the man said, "Obama's speech." He grinned at them, recent anxieties about Duncan's provenance and motives forgotten.

Duncan had never felt more patriotic, as Obama's voice filled the clearing: *We are at a crossroads—a moment filled with peril, but also enormous promise.* Obama paused, knowing full well the crowd would fill this void with applause.

Above the sound of the crowd cheering, the yellow door of the shipping container creaked open. The smile on Teesh's face died. The guard clicked off the radio, set it down.

A lean figure dressed in khaki fatigues took weary steps down to the forest floor. In the firelight, Toogood's dreadlocks resembled a crown. With his hands clasped at the small of this back, he walked to the very edge of the fire, looking into its center. He made no sound, just stood there with the dancing fire between them like a veil.

When he looked up, Duncan could see the man was young, his sclera a vivid red. There was a jangled energy to him, like a puppet that could come alive at any moment.

Toogood cleared his throat, as though preparing to rebut Obama's showmanship.

"One fire is all fire. I like that." Toogood's voice was deep, as if he had been sleeping, or perhaps had not slept in a long while. "Macharia," Toogood nodded at the baby- faced man beside Teesh, "our Kenyan brother, Mau Mau extraordinaire, tells me there are many ghosts in these woods. Ghosts of white people, howling and confused as children at having fallen asleep in one place, and woken up in another. But I see nothing."

Toogood's figure shook its head. "Thing is, I lack imagination. Even in Somalia, where we would watch the stars on the beach as children, I could never see Orion's belt, or the giant bear, or any other constellations. Just stars beyond meaning. At first, I pretended. I would ooh and aah with the others, just to fit in." The silhouette spat into the fire. "And then I stopped. Why pretend to be something I'm not. I'm a practical man, which is why I like fire—I can see it, I can touch it, I can smell it." He rubbed his chin with the back of his hand. "I can use it."

Teesh jammed his hands in his pockets, as though he had heard this before.

Toogood toed the edge of a thick acacia branch from the edge of the fire into its glowing center. The branch collapsed the existing structure of half-burned wood, sending up a spire of sparks.

"And as a practical man, I ask you: have you brought what is mine?"

Ciru spoke quickly, "Yes, Toogood, I have brought it."

She reached into her shawl. Ciru walked with her hand outstretched towards the fire holding a Ziploc bag, as if she was going to walk into it, through it. The red pills caught the firelight.

But Toogood's voice thundered through the fire. "And where is the woman? The courier?"

Ciru stopped. "She has betrayed you. I tried to stop her, but she escaped." Holding the Ziploc bag to the fire, and buoyed by its heft, she added brightly, "But your investment is intact. And I am true to my word. Where is my boy?"

Toogood was wracked with a coughing fit. He bent over, hands on knees. There was a clinking as Macharia, the Mau Mau guard, took his gun from his shoulder, unsure as to what was expected of him. The coughing shook Toogood.

Taking a step towards the firelight, Ciru asked, "Are you all right?" She still held up the Ziploc bag, an unsteady offering to a fiery god.

Toogood leaped across the firepit, erupting from the flames, red eyes flashing, nostrils flaring. He seemed possessed, by emotion or chemicals. Satisfied that the drugs were here, he turned to give vent to his thirst for revenge. Ciru's offering fell to the forest floor, and she stepped back.

Before she could say a word, he was upon her, her throat in the vice of his hand. Ciru gave a soupy gurgling. Duncan, standing in the gloom away from the fire, felt a tingling in his scrotum.

The spellbinding Toogood and Ciru seemed to break, and he threw her to the floor. "This was never the arrangement. The policeman is not here, and you are late. Dangerously late." Toogood hissed, standing over Ciru.

Ciru held her throat with both hands, shaking her head. No words would come. She got on hands and knees, and vomited, profiled against the flames. But her voice was even when she gathered herself, looking up at Toogood. "I tried to stop her. She wanted to go to the police, the real police, not Hinga."

"Nice would never—"

"She carried a note of confession, to save her baby." Ciru gagged and made as if to vomit again. "I could not stop her from escaping."

Duncan stood stock still. Nice was pregnant? It explained much. His head swam, and without even realizing what he was doing, Duncan said, "Ciru lies."

Toogood spun to look in the direction of Duncan's voice. From behind the firelight came the distinct click of Macharia's rifle. "Oh, the good pastor. Nice said you had a crush on her." Toogood laughed, low and hard.

Duncan felt his cheeks grow hot, and for a moment he was silent. While it was cruel of Nice to have laughed at him with Toogood, the sentiment was not untrue. Besides, that was before. Now, he intended to honor the truth of it. "I suppose a man like you would find it funny. We are all pawns in your game."

Toogood kicked Ciru to the ground. With his boot on her sternum, he turned to Duncan, "You're next, white man." Holding Toogood's ankle in one hand, Ciru said, "Nice betrayed you. She did have a note, would have given it to the police, but I stopped her. I saved your—"

The vision of Hinga's broken body carried by the lynch mob came to Duncan. Ciru was ruthless and strong-willed enough to spoil this entire transaction, a simple enough trade— the drugs for the boy. "Shut up, Ciru."

Teesh moved quick for a big man. Before Duncan knew it, he was face down in the grass, breathing shallow, Teesh's knee against the base of his skull.

Ciru held out the trembling notepaper to Toogood, who took it and began to read. Teesh yanked Duncan up by his hair. He dragged him towards the fire and threw him down again, where Toogood still stood with his boot at Ciru's throat. Toogood finished reading, handed the note to Teesh.

After a moment, Teesh hmm'ed, and said, "She has endangered us all, endangered Aisha. I told you not to allow this."

Duncan would replay what happened next for the rest of his life. Teesh handed back the note, stepped back from Toogood. Teesh's boot, massive and heavy against the side of his head, causing Duncan to turn his face. Ciru was staring directly at him, supine, a half-smile on her face, side-lit by the fire, Toogood standing above her.

Duncan saw it, saw what she was doing, the misdirection. As Toogood was folding the note, there came from beneath him the flash and crackle of an electrical storm. For one illumined moment, Toogood's crotch was impaled on Ciru's cattle prodder.

Then the light was gone.

And the darkness echoed against Duncan's eyes. Reality taking on a kaleidoscopic quality, of jerky movements, of time being twisted. Here was the agonized shriek of Toogood pitching backward, tumbling into the fire. He rolled once, then lay for a moment on the bed of flames, one hand at his crotch, the other still holding the note away from his body as though to protect it from burning. He groaned, scrambled to all fours, attempting to crawl from the fire.

Duncan felt the pressure remove itself from his chest, as Teesh took his foot off. Duncan's vision pinwheeled, flashing in and out. He made out Teesh lumbering towards the fire, toward Toogood.

Toogood held out a hand, his long arm distinct against the curtain of flames. But Teesh was just standing there, over his friend. "You're no gangster. Who do you think gave them Aisha?"

Toogood seemed to gurgle, whether with surprise or rage. "You?' I will end you. Your family, you will—"

"No. You know I do not like too much talking." Teesh stepped forward, kicked Toogood.

Duncan blinked at the sharp clink of steel toe boot against jaw. And here was Toogood crumpled in the fire like a trampled spider. The flames lapping greedily at his dreadlocks. The utter soundlessness worse, somehow, than screams.

The stink of charring flesh rising thick.

Duncan looked away, at Ciru, and followed her averted gaze. She eyed Teesh from the ground, eyes unblinking with ferocity, like a cornered animal, holding outstretched the cattle prodder.

Teesh looked at Ciru, then at the figure of Toogood, already crackling in the flames, as if weighing something important. "He was too sentimental for this line of work."

Teesh picked up the Ziploc, which lay like a milky jewel in the tufty grass. As he stood, he held out his hand to Ciru. "Let's go and see your son."

She stood eagerly. Teesh took the prodder from her, and threw it underhanded, far into the darkness. It vanished soundlessly. He turned to Macharia. "Bring the boy."

Macharia took one look at Toogood's smoldering body, then scurried up into the shipping container.

A moment later, Edmund emerged, hands bound in twine and shirt torn at the collar. As Edmund's eyes adjusted to the firelight, he sized up the scene: Toogood aflame, the bitter smell of burning flesh, the ghost-like face of that crazy mzungu who had tied him up in his own flat.

And his mother, tiny and defiant next to the giant who had taken him.

Her lip bloodied, looking up at him with shining eyes. Edmund felt pierced by the ferocity of her love. She had come here to rescue him. And Edmund had known she would, with a certainty which nothing else in his life had. A certainty that now seemed a precarious luxury, of which he had not availed himself out of sheer spite.

"Mummy." Edmund held out his shackled hands.

She smiled. He had not called her that for many years.

31

CIRU CLOSED HER EYES, the better to savor her boy's embrace. She realized he was sobbing into her neck.

Teesh coughed. Ciru separated from Edmund, who seemed to have snapped to the realization that this was, in fact, a very public moment. He dried his face on his shirt sleeve.

Ciru regarded Teesh evenly, never letting go of Edmund's hand. "What is your name?"

The giant crossed his arms. "Teesh, aunty."

"Teesh? What kind of name is that? What does it mean?" "It's short for tee-shirt."

"What? Why?"

"Because I bear arms. It sounded better when—"

Ciru held up her hands. "Teesh. Fair enough. Do you have children, Teesh?"

"No, aunty."

"Ah, it is a blessing. They make you better, better than you think yourself capable of being."

"That's not saying very much, in my case. I've got a head full of evil thoughts." Teesh uncrossed his arms, spat into the fire where Toogood lay ablaze.

"Now I'm sure that you would be—"

Teesh cut her off. "Do you know what "xeer" is?"

Ciru, shaking her head, stepped in front of Edmund, placing herself between him and Teesh. Something had shifted in the conversation, and Ciru wanted to be ready for it, to shield Edmund from it. Whatever it was.

"It is our way, the code of my clan. It means that your family is liable for your actions." Teesh pointed with his chin at Toogood's body, now a blackening log in the fire. "You have brought much trouble to us. There is a debt to be repaid." He said it in a matter-of-fact way, as though she had borrowed a cup of sugar from him.

"Can this debt be repaid in another currency?"

Teesh shook his head with a slow reasonableness. "Suffering's the only form of payment accepted."

She dropped her son's hand and stood erect. "Fine. Then I am ready to pay. But leave my boy out of this."

With a quick step, Teesh closed the gap between them, bowling Ciru aside with a sweep of his forearm. She went down into the darkness. Watching from the half-lit perimeter of the firelight, Duncan shouted in rage at the giant, at Edmund for not standing up for his own mother.

"That's not the way suffering works." Teesh stepped towards Edmund. "I thought you would have been initiated by now."

Edmund held his hands up. "No, please."

"I don't waste bullets on women and children." Teesh bent before the fire and stood holding a large piece of obsidian. He tilted his head, and regarded Edmund. Teesh passed the rock from hand to hand, its smooth planes gleaming.

Edmund took a step back, his eyes enlarged with terror, glittering in the firelight. Without a word, Teesh held out the rock at Edmund, slicing from cheekbone to chin with an audible snick. Edmund fell in a heap. Then Teesh crouched over Edmund, the obsidian outlined against the firelight.

Sated, Teesh stood and turned to the fire. Blood flecked his face.

From the darkness in which she lay, Ciru began to ululate.

Teesh turned towards the sound. "Don't worry. There is still interest on the debt."

Duncan ran. The night, the sounds, these had taken on a dream-like quality. He could neither feel nor hear his footsteps, just the treeline swaying in the periphery of his vision.

The guard, Macharia, called out, "Stop."

When Duncan stopped and turned to face him, Macharia had already begun to run at him. Rifle bouncing on his chest.

Time slowed. Macharia ran, adjusting the rifle so it was at his back, and brought up his fist, swinging high and round at Duncan's face.

In that same timeless flow, Duncan intercepted the punch with the bony part of his own left forearm, reached behind Macharia's upper arm, and yanked it upwards, almost clear from its socket. Duncan smashed his right elbow into Macharia's mouth.

Macharia cried out, his mouth a pulpy mess. The sound snapping the spell.

Duncan tightened the shoulder lock, and Macharia began to cry. Teesh's voice came from the fire. "Macharia?" He seemed to be trying to find them in the darkness of the long grass.

Duncan motioned for Macharia to be silent. Eyes big as saucers, Macharia nodded his acknowledgment. Slowly, Duncan removed his hand from Macharia's mouth. His front teeth were bloodied and askew, all bluster drained from his face.

Duncan peered above the swaying grass line. He could just make out the hulking silhouette of Teesh who appeared to be bent over, the rocking movement of his torso barely perceptible in the gloom. What was he doing to Edmund?

As he looked back down at Macharia, the boy reached out to slap Duncan. Duncan turned his face, and Macharia's open palm caught his ear square. The world tilted, a piercing pressure rending his ear, his head. The very night. Duncan dropped his knees onto Macharia's chest, grabbed the boy's hair and punched him once. Was about to again, when he saw that Macharia was crying once more.

There was, Duncan understood, no point in further terrorizing or harming this boy. He brought a hand up to his ear, and it came away wet with blood. A high-pitched whining filled his skull, like a buzz saw. Duncan removed the rifle from the strap on Macharia's chest. He took a fist of Macharia's hair. "I let you go, you run away. Yes?" He could not hear his own voice.

Macharia nodded abjectly. Duncan loosened his fist, and Macharia rolled onto his belly. He began to slither away from Duncan, away from the fire.

Cradling the heft of the gun as he lay on his back, Duncan stared at the stars, nausea rising.

Duncan stood, a wave of dizziness crashing over him. But he held the rifle against his hip and walked towards Teesh's outline, hulked against the fire. The stench of Toogood's burning body had become appalling, so dense it was almost a taste.

The ringing from his ear, the dizziness, made it hard to hear, even to speak. Duncan forced the words. "Let her go. That's enough now." Duncan had to get closer, to make the gun an effective threat.

Teesh gave a hard laugh, and his outline bent to the dark of the forest floor. When he came up, he was holding Ciru aloft by the throat. Her feet dangled, as if dancing on the firelight.

Duncan stepped closer to the fire. "Just take the drugs, and give her Edmund, her boy, back."

Teesh looked bemused. "You don't have the heart to—"

Duncan closed his eyes, pulled the trigger. His skull singing with the pain and the pressure.

But the trigger would not budge. He tried again, and once more.

"Safety. Safety." Teesh spoke slowly, still holding Ciru by the throat. He threw her down and turned to face Duncan, as if he was tired by the interruption. "White man, you helped me with the boy. This is my thanks. But leave now. Or you will have my full attention."

Ciru's crazed ululation cracked the night. She must have found her boy.

Duncan ran a hand along the smooth stock of the rifle. The stench, the crashing pain, the firelight. The ululation. He hesitated, then threw the weapon down in the grass. When he stood straight, Ciru's slim form was visible, still as a phantom, strangely short, as if on her knees. Her eyes flickering firelight, watching him, taking in his cold-blooded decision-making. From somewhere in the dark undergrowth, Edmund groaned one long constant note of pain.

Slowly, and never removing his eyes from Ciru, Duncan walked backwards away from the fire. Teesh snorted once, then picked up Ciru once more.

Duncan turned, began to jog, clapping a hand over his bleeding ear. Above the grass line, between him and the truck, a semi-circle of marabou storks were stalking towards him, eyes glittering firelight.

Duncan swallowed and walked in their direction. In the direction of the truck. Away from the fire, away from Teesh and Ciru and Edmund, and the final act of their violent rituals. The birds blocked his path, their heads bobbing as though disembodied by the long grass. He took in their carrion smell, could reach out and touch their ruined faces.

The stork closest to Duncan opened its mouth, issued a low moan. Death wafted from it.

Duncan willed himself to look the bird in its unblinking borehole of an eye. "I'm sorry."

The creature tilted its massive yellow beak towards him. Duncan recoiled, but the creature had plucked the chain from his neck. The crucifix dangled from the creature's mouth. It blinked once, then swallowed the crucifix.

Then, in unison, the marabous tramped past him, to their mistress.

Duncan did not turn back, forcing himself to take step after step, eyes fixed on the goal of the pickup. Terror took root, scrambling his senses. He thought he heard Ciru singing, the marabous moaning, then the buzzing of the radio, but he did not dare turn back to look. Over the radio came Obama's parting pitch, clear and sinister in the chill dark. *"The future of Africa is up to Africans. You can realize your dreams right here, right now."*

A dusty audience exploded with applause.

Edmund's shrieks rose, then died—the last note swallowed by the indifferent forest.

EPILOGUE

DUNCAN NOTICED THAT THE FLIGHT ATTEN-
DANT WAS VERY ATTENTIVE TO NICE. She would
cock her head and coo at Nice. The way women do at
other visibly-pregnant women. And Nice seemed pleased with
the attention, the specialness afforded her.

And there sat his meal. The congealed mass of what was
allegedly an omelet. Besides the egg glistening mushrooms lay
shriveled against the plastic plate. The sight repulsed Duncan, so
he raised a hand and asked for a glass of red wine.

It was a giddying, dangerous sensation—that queasiness.
Because it brought back so much of what had happened, there,
before that bonfire in the forest. So difficult to make sense of, to
even recall correctly. What he did recall, distinctly, the decision
to abandon Ciru—that decision corroded his vision of himself.
He rubbed the hollow above his sternum, where his crucifix had
hung for so many years.

He had deflected Nice's questions about the reunion
between Ciru and her son. How Nice had glowed about Ciru, as
a good person doing bad things for good reasons— impossible
decisions foisted upon her. That it was thanks to Ciru that her

baby would get a chance at life. As a mother. Perhaps that had been their connection.

And Nice seemed to be experiencing only relief, relief at having escaped from her self-made circumstances with no consequences. Yes, there had been a visit from that police detective to the hospital bed where Duncan's ruptured eardrum was being monitored. He had been accompanied by that beautiful policewoman, her name Duncan recalled— Muthoni. Some difficult questions about how much he had known about Nice. But Nice had cried, made a scene, and ultimately won the policewoman, Muthoni, over. Even promised that she would name the baby Muthoni. Nice had been different, a lot tougher, with the detective, stating categorically that there was no evidence whatsoever to tie her to any wrongdoing. That she was on a UN laissez-passer, that he should think long and hard before pressing charges against a pregnant UN official who had been the victim of a violent crime in which no police assistance had been rendered.

Nice seemed to know what to say to people, to get her way, like a lawyer before a jury. She had never mentioned changing the baby's name since, always referring to it as Pendo. Duncan ran a finger along the rim of the plastic wine glass. There was something about Nice. Had always been perhaps, but distilled and laid bare by recent circumstances.

A certain self-serving rapacity. And there she sat, rubbing her tummy, smiling absent-mindedly.

We need to think of ourselves as good. As definitively as we need water.

It composes us.

He could not change those things that night, only the words used to recall them. And he had tried to believe those words before he told Nice about that night. It was not so difficult given his religious training. Not so different, after all, than the meeting with the Legishons. Our reality is but a hot- house version of events.

His jaw clicked at the kaleidoscopic recollections of that night.

The notion of a single Truth seemed, in the recollection of the palate-scorching stench of the body turning in muted agony amidst the flames, to be outmoded, arrogant— dangerous even. And then there were the horrors which visited him before his shallow sleep. Of the glimmering sliver of obsidian. Of a skull-smashed boy (whose name Duncan had ceased to use, even in his thoughts). Those things had extinguished Truth.

No, there had been no reason to tell of the death of the boy—he himself was unsure of what he had witnessed, or not witnessed. Of the witch's haunting ululation rising like woodsmoke. Of the slinking retreat between the column of storks, their deathly breath hot on his cheek. The empty place below his throat where the bird had stripped him of the crucifix.

It was a lot. Too much. Too much for a pregnant woman trying to do the right thing. She wouldn't understand. Wouldn't want to understand.

Too much, perhaps, for their little tendril of love.

He shivered in the fierce air-conditioning. Brought the syrupy wine to his lips, and drank deeply. He found this helped.

Nice absent-mindedly placed a proprietary hand on his knee. Duncan drained the plastic tumbler, then wiped his mouth with his knuckle. This was a closely-bargained happiness. The airplane wine burning its way to his belly, his pregnant girlfriend at his side. A one-way ticket to Canada, where they would try again, differently, to be together.

0

The conversation with Mr. Leighman had been brief, but all parties had agreed that it was best that Duncan leave. Duncan was relieved that Mr. Leighman had not tried to force him to stay. Or, frankly, press some sort of charges. And when Mr. Leighman had asked about Niyi, Duncan had replied that Niyi was a man of faith, a man of loyalty, and would be well suited to driving the leadership at the Church of the Earth.

Outside, backlit turrets of clouds passed on. All these things were far below. Duncan sighed, pushed away the tray.

"You gonna eat that?" Nice asked.

Duncan shook his head sadly and gestured to show he was offering it up to her.

"You OK, Dee?"

Duncan gestured at the flight attendant. *Another wine please.*

Nice reached over, speared the limp omelet with her plastic fork and ate it whole.

ABOUT THE AUTHOR

A lawyer and co-founder of a successful fintech startup, Akbar Hussain lived in Nairobi for 7 years and currently resides in New York. His work has been published in Type/Cast Literary Journal and the Johannesburg Review of Books.

Truth is a Flightless Bird is his first novel and has been optioned for an eight-part television miniseries with the UK-based Chudor House Productions.